THE CHILDREN OF TOMORROW

THIS ALIEN EARTH BOOK THREE

PAUL ANTONY JONES
ROBERT GREENBERGER

AETHON
BOOKS

THE CHILDREN OF TOMORROW

©2020 AETHON BOOKS

ALSO BY PAUL ANTONY JONES

Published by 47 North

Extinction Point

Extinction Point: Exodus

Extinction Point: Revelations

Extinction Point: Genesis

Toward Yesterday

Published by Good Dog Publishing

Extinction Point: Kings

The Darkening

Ancient Enemies (Dachau Sunset - short story)

ONE

WHY COULDN'T I SLEEP? I was exhausted, beyond exhausted, if that was even possible.

The zephyr-like *Brimstone* was fleeing the ruins of the collector, which had been overwhelmed by Abernathy and his... things. I still didn't have a name for them, but they were a growing army and a threat to the survival of nearly two billion humans scattered around the Earth. We fought bravely, but then, just when it seemed like we were going to get away scot-free, Freuchen sacrificed himself so the rest of us could be safe.

That big bear of man who tempered his strength with good humor, who readily accepted the amazing circumstances of our situation, and upon whom who I had come to rely on as a brother...gone. Weston Chou and Albert Glanville survived and we shared grief and anger as Amelia Earhart asked where to. I had no clear idea at first, but as it became clear, we needed to regroup. I told her to aim for New Manhattan and hoped it was still there. It was not like we had a map of where everyone wound up. Nothing looked familiar, so I felt constantly disoriented. And eternally tired.

Slumped against the cockpit's glass wall, I just stared at the blue sky, the emotions roiling within me. I wanted to cry for Peter Freuchen; I wanted to scream in rage at having to take my first life, and I was angry at the Adversary for making this all so damn hard. Another part of my mind was still reeling with questions, starting with, who is this grown adult, Michael, who says he's my son from a different timeline? Truth to tell, when I was given a choice between suicide or a second chance, I was so low that I wasn't fit to even consider parenthood let alone actually have a child. But there he was, easily seventy if not older, balding with that narrow face and keen, studious eyes.

My son.

My son, who was more than twice as old as I was and also Candidate 1, first of nearly two billion souls brought from across the multiverse to reseed Earth and give humanity its own second chance.

No wonder I couldn't sleep. It was all so staggering to comprehend. I had just been expelled from law school after getting hooked on opioids, which I needed to deal with the pain from the car accident that ultimately killed my closest friend, Oscar Kemple. I just received word his parents disconnected his life support, and he was gone. They had taken away the one person who got me, the one person who shared the exact same geeky stuff. We were soulmates without the romance and then he was gone, leaving me alone to spiral around the drain. The water underneath the Bay Bridge looked so calm, so inviting, that taking the final step seemed so easy.

Until the voice interrupted, telling me there was another path. All I had to do was accept the offer. Just when I thought the options were gone for good, here came one that sounded too fantastic to be true. But it sparked something in me and I realized I wanted to live, so I said yes.

As it turned out, I wound up in the water anyway, among the hundreds who suddenly materialized in the salt water somewhere else. Not everyone made it to shore, but those of us that did were helping one another, and realized several things over the first few days. Our newfound friends came from across time. There was 12-year-old Albert who said he was trapped in a burning boarding school in 1910 England, while Philip Youman was the author of the bestselling *Last Stand at the Maple Leaf Lodge*, a 1980s book and film I had never heard of. And then there was Chou, the six-foot-tall beauty who claimed she was aboard the *Shining Light*, a starship from the year 2374.

We were all so disoriented that it took a few days for us all to figure it out, but it became clear: each one of us was plucked from a pivotal point in our lives, when we could have died while alone, our bodies undiscovered. This voice, which we named the Architect, apparently had scoured the multiverse seeking out people to bring forward in time and settle on Earth. At first, we thought it was an alien world, but it became clear that despite the reddening, larger sun, we were actually on Earth – just an Earth half a billion years in our future. Give or take a day.

While it was nice to know Earth survived all the deadly shit we were doing to it dating back to the Industrial Revolution, where had all the people gone? That was just one of countless questions I had, that we all had.

Some of the answers had been provided by Silas, a gold-skinned giant of a robot who had been damaged and became our guide, protector, and friend as he also got repaired bit by bit. Even so, he lacked answers, including the ultimate plan for the two billion of us.

What had been clear, from the second day and ever since, was that the Architect's plan had been interrupted. Another being, thing, entity – I'm still not sure what to call it – had interfered and was trying to kill us. Me in particular. He sent ancient warriors then Nazis – yes, good old-fashioned jackbooted Nazis – after me. No one we captured and questioned could tell us why, but they had all been implanted with an image of me. Well, an older me.

A me who had just been elected President of the United States of America.

This thing we finally decided to call the Adversary wanted me and wanted Candidate 1, my adult son Michael. Why? I don't know. He's on third and I don't give a darn...Wow, my mind kept drifting, calling up bits of pieces of my childhood, and yet, it wouldn't let me slip away to sleep.

I glanced across the gondola to see Chou doing a far better job of resting than me. Albert was in the back with Bartholomew, who accompanied us from New Manhattan; Miko and Vihaan, who we rescued with Michael at the collector; and Silas. What an odd collection of people we had become, each with distinct and separate memories of lives and histories, some identical and others diametrically opposed. Yet, we somehow all banded together to stop the Adversary, save mankind, and possibly the Earth itself. And then there was the field.

When I first found Silas, he said to me, *"Candidate 13, humanity is in peril. The plan has been compromised by an external entity. This interference has introduced multiple patterns of disorder; the effects on the outcome have moved beyond predictability. Agents of chaos will be unleashed in an attempt to stop what I require of you. You must travel to the collector immediately and locate Candidate 1. They must know that the field is collapsing, and the void follows behind."*

There was a field collapsing somewhere in space, and if it reached us before we did whatever it was the Architect needed us to do, the Adversary would get its wish.

When Chou, Albert, and I found the first settlement, we discovered that I possessed the singular ability to be a walking, talking universal translator. I could speak and be heard in the native tongue of all those around me, and they could understand one another within a thirty-foot or so radius. This went a long way to helping Edward James Hubbard, World War I soldier and 20th Century poet, get his community, dubbed Avalon, well underway.

But that newfound ability may also explain why I was wanted. So, rather than endanger the others, we left and headed out in search of answers. Of course, we found, instead, a megalodon. Silas told us, *"Predators were to be strictly limited to very specific sizes to ensure balanced bio-diversity. I am sure that something of this size was not a part of that plan."* This merely confirmed for us that the Adversary not only sent Nazis after us, but vicious predators to hinder everyone. Soon after came the *Brimstone*, captained by Thomas "Tommy Two-Thumbs" Abernathy, who was detestable before being transformed by nanobots. He intended to bring me to the Adversary, but instead, we got away and he got punished, being turned into an oily-looking semi-humanoid. The nanobots transformed him and everyone else he touched into things. Deadly, vicious, nearly unstoppable things.

We got away, but it cost us dearly.

So yeah, maybe I knew why I couldn't sleep, although I must have dozed off at some point, because as I looked out the window, I saw the moon. That poor, shattered satellite, bits of itself hanging in suspension, a still image that constantly reminded us all we were far from home. We had no idea what happened, neither Silas, nor Blue Alpha, the giant mechanical robot that aided us in the collector before it too succumbed to Abernathy's icky army, had the details in their memory banks.

Bartholomew handed me a mug of soup, the steam rising in curly-cues. "Drink it," he coaxed in his friendly voice.

"Thanks," I said. I took a sip, hoping for chicken but got noodles instead. "Where are we?"

"On course for New Manhattan, about a day out," Amelia told me. I was still marveling that the famed aviatrix, who in my timeline vanished somewhere in the Pacific, was actually flying the *Brimstone*. She had taken to the unfamiliar controls and was in her glory, avoiding getting her hands dirty but still providing an invaluable service. We hadn't spoken much; there never seemed to be enough time just to speak with people I met.

"You okay?" Bartholomew Mwangi, a former resident of Kenya circa 1985, asked.

"I can't sleep," I said.

"You were doing a good impression then," he said and his face lit up in delight. It amazed me how this tall, broad man, his skin the color of umber, could look fiercely imposing one moment and then light up the room with just his smile.

"Really? I haven't slept well in what feels like weeks."

"Well, you've been a bit busy," Amelia shot from the pilot's seat. She stifled a yawn herself. Fortunately, she had taught Bartholomew the basics to maintain the high-tech dirigible so she could rest herself and we could stay in the air, furthering the distance between Abernathy and us. The plan, such as it was, was to get us to New Manhattan and regroup. I needed time to think and examine our options.

I sipped the soup and brooded rather than planned. When we left the collector and Abernathy's oily-looking army, I was determined to get proactive. Now it felt like I had no plan and the four-day trip back to New Manhattan had been a waste with the exception of putting distance between us and Abernathy. Not much of a plan, but it was a start.

It felt like that was my condition all the way over the mountains and forests, the terrain we had previously crossed. I did enjoy watching the sun rise, its golden rays reassuringly welcoming the new day, a promise that we still had a chance of saving everyone, of saving the planet.

of the free world, presuming that title still applied in his reality.

Sure enough, I had dozed off and it's a wonder I didn't sink. Until I woke with a start, the water now barely tepid, and realized a nine-foot guardian angel was in the bath cabin with me, a towel in its oddly-constructed arms. They were constructed in a way so that the arms were a series of flat, oblong segments, hinged in a way that gave it far more flexibility than your average human. Someone had polished him a bit, removing dirt and blood from his black triangular grill that served as a torso.

"Thanks for not letting me drown," I said, rising, not worried about his gaze being anything other than analytical. As I toweled off, I examined my body, noticing the lack of bruises but the beginning of actual muscles in my calves and arms. That came from all the strenuous running, climbing, and fighting. I might find myself as buff as Miko before too much longer.

"My pleasure," Silas said. *"The meal will be in approximately forty-seven minutes."*

My stomach rumbled before I could reply. I got dressed, wishing there was an REI or someplace to get fresh clothes better suited to the environment. While the Architect somehow arranged for some supplies to be brought along with people – otherwise, the communities couldn't be built – it didn't occur to it to bring a mall. At some point, growing cotton and other materials to make clothing would have to be on the agenda.

But first, there was a world to save. And Abernathy to stop.

Our dinner party, in a long, thatched building, was a reunion of sorts. I took a seat to Emily's left, and Chou, in her ever-present white outfit, which amazingly never retained dirt, was next to me; then there were Bartholomew and Amelia. Across were Albert and Miko, then Vihaan, and finally Michael, farthest from me. A woman also entered, with long, lustrous black hair, tied back with a ribbon, who wore very worn clothing but didn't mask her ramrod-straight posture. She looked to be in her forties, with crow's feet around her blue eyes. Emily introduced her as Carolyn Nguyen. Looming over us all, even from standing against the back wall, was Silas. At the furthest end was a man I didn't recognize, but Miko took one look and her jaw dropped. The man didn't seem unique, with his high forehead, shock of swept-back dark hair, and friendly eyes. Even at rest, his mouth seemed to be curling into a smile, making him appear approachable.

Emily tapped her knife against a wooden cup, freshly carved by the look of it, making a hollow knock. Once all eyes turned to her, she began, "Good evening and welcome. I want to start by making it clear that where I came from and in my time, we kept too many secrets. Not here. While we meet tonight, whatever we learn from one another and whatever we decide, it will be shared with all."

I felt myself nodding in agreement. This fit right in with the Architect's desire to eschew violence and try the peaceful approach. Inwardly, I winced at already betraying that the first month in this new world, but it wasn't like I had much of a choice.

Emily went on, making a round of introductions when she got to the newcomer. "Werner Heisenberg..."

"I knew it!" Miko exclaimed, no longer able to contain herself.

I recognized the name and knew he had something to do with physics, but after that, I was drawing a complete blank. The ever-observant Silas filled in with, *"Candidate 28141, Werner Heisenberg, winner of the 1932 Nobel Prize in Physics for his work defining quantum mechanics."*

"Thankfully, we had a German translator on hand, but with you here," Emily said to me, "tonight should be easy on all of us. When he and the latest arrivals staggered in, he was

TWO

"IT'S CALLED VACUUM DECAY," Chou said, making sure everyone was paying attention. Given the backgrounds of everyone around the table, she, Heisenberg, and Miko had the training to really understand what was being explained. I'd heard it a few times and it was finally starting to sink in.

"We should understand that everything in the universe has an energy level. The higher the level, the more energy. So a stick of wood has a high energy level that can be burned for fuel and the charred remains would have a far lower level of energy."

Okay, that was simple enough. Everyone nodded.

"Now, energy tries to find its lowest state."

"A body at rest tends to stay at rest," said Bartholomew.

"Something like that," Chou said, getting confirming nods from Heisenberg and Miko.

"Something unstable, like snow capping a mountain, has the potential energy to come to the bottom. Given the right push, the snow comes down the mountain in an avalanche, releasing destructive energy until it all settles on the ground in a stable state."

More nods.

"The more energy an object has, the more it wants to expend its energy and achieve its ground state. Now the universe operates under these principles and the quantum fields..."

"What's that?" Amelia interjected.

Chou looked at Heisenberg. He paused, hand on chin for a moment, then said, "Consider them the rules of the universe."

"Okay."

"The universe follows the rules and wants to be in the lowest possible state, which has been called the vacuum state."

"Has it?" Heisenberg asked.

"The name was settled sometime after your...career ended," Chou said kindly. "Your work was taken up by others, including Richard Feynman, Shin'ichirō Tomonaga, and Julian Schwinger.

"It was later theorized that there might be one quantum field that was not stable, named after a man named Higgs. His theory was that this one field was something else, something unstable that was called a false vacuum."

"What is this Higgs field?" the scientist wanted to know.

Chou paused, weighing the value of the distraction. With a breath, she said, "The Higgs field is unique because it gives all objects in the universe their own mass. Think about the snow that fell. We think it's at the lowest state, but it's not. There's more to do, more energy to expend as the sun warms the snow and it melts into the ground, releasing more energy. Those rays of sun could arrive at any moment, reaching just the right temperature to start the warming process. It arrives without warning. Once you start this process, once you warm the snow and it melts, there is no turning back. The snow becomes water, seeps into the ground or runs off, possibly the avalanche helps form a flood.

"Now, think about it in cosmic terms. If something ignites

the Higgs field and it releases more energy, it crashes into all the other fields in space, releasing their energy. It cascades without stop."

"Like tipping over dominoes," Albert suggested.

"Exactly, my boy," Heisenberg said, quickly picking up Chou's explanation. "Unlike the dominoes, though, which go in one direction, this new Higgs field would expand in all directions, a rain drop hitting a puddle, making circles."

"Just amazing," Vihaan said softly, earning him a look from Heisenberg. I sensed some hero worship going on here and our German friend wasn't thrilled about it.

Everyone was nodding in comprehension with more than a little fear in their eyes.

"So what happens?" I asked before Vihaan said something silly.

"If the field collapses, then the false vacuum expands, destroying everything in its path until the universe is destroyed."

"How on God's green earth are we supposed to stop that?" Emily said.

"We can't stop it," Heisenberg said. "Once unleashed, if I understand this right, it keeps spreading."

"Exactly," Chou said. "The theory is that the expanding Higgs field would rewrite the laws of physics. Our universe would be annihilated and replaced."

"Where is it?" Albert asked, genuine fear in his voice, the first time since I had met him. I know Silas told us all that somehow the Architect changed our body chemistry to avoid panic, but even that had its limits, I suppose.

"If it exists at all, we don't know. Somehow, though, the Architect has determined it exists. That's why Silas keeps warning us the field has collapsed."

Heads swiveled toward the robot, who said, *"Confirmed."* Chou looked at it for a moment longer.

"What about Einstein's theory of the universe expanding?" Miko asked.

"Actually, that was Alexander Friedmann, who built on Einstein's theories," Heisenberg corrected. "At least in my time-line that was the case."

"Mine too. By my time, all astronomy confirms that theory," Chou said. "Which means the universe is expanding at the same time it is also being devoured by the false vacuum."

"So what was the Architect's plan?" Emily asked.

"And we're back to that core question," Michael said.

"The sun has, what, a few billion years to go before it novas," I said. "Are you saying the false vacuum might get here first?"

"It might," Chou said. "There were other things happening in space, which is what I was doing when my ship was damaged. These vagrant particles, we called them."

"Which are?" Heisenberg asked, genuinely interested.

"Not important right now," Emily said, interrupting.

"Silas, what were the collectors doing? There are how many on the planet?" Chou asked.

"We know there are four visible from this part of the continent," Amelia said, seemingly glad to finally have something to contribute.

"Silas?" I asked.

"There are 218 collectors on Earth," he said.

"What are they collecting?" Heisenberg asked.

"Energy."

"For what purpose?" Emily asked.

"To power the machines. Once they powered all the SILAS units and the machines like Blue Alpha, they enabled the Architect to bring you all forward and to terraform the planet to protect the collector network. If it is doing more, I am not programmed with that knowledge."

"It's like he was operating on a need-to-know basis," I said, more to myself than anyone.

"Does each collector have the layered biomes as we saw?" Chou asked.

"I am uncertain, but would believe so," Silas replied. *"It was an elegant way to preserve diversity for the future use of Earth's new inhabitants."*

"Wait, they're not collecting power," I said loudly. "The Adversary took control of the SILAS units and Blue Alpha told us a gamma burst was used to stop the robots. But it also did something to the collector network."

"That is right, Meredith. The release triggered a simultaneous cascade effect across the network. Every collector was activated at once. The effect destroyed everything for several miles around each unit. The network was then interrupted."

"Is that what we're to fix: the network?" Emily asked.

"Maybe," I said.

The conversation went on for a while, long after the food was cleared, as we debated how to share this news and what was our next step. At one point, though, I noticed Albert's chair was empty. I thought he excused himself for the latrine, but clearly, he was gone. It was also clear that no one had a clear idea what to do. Lots of theories, lots of speculation, and way too many questions. I was finally feeling tired and needed some sleep, maybe letting my mind process all of this.

Emily had a similar thought and said we'd adjourn for the night and resume discussion in the morning, but also made it quite clear we needed a plan of action. Everyone felt a ticking clock, be it the collapse of the known universe or the impending threat of Abernathy's army. And who knew what the Adversary would produce next, all in an attempt to find me.

As the group broke up, Emily brought Carolyn over to me and we stood near an edge of the long hut. Carolyn came up to my nose, so after all this time looking up to Chou and Silas, this was different.

"Carolyn's a political science professor," Emily said.

"I was teaching at the University of Maryland when there was an epidemic. It traveled fast and hit hard. I was sent home with a raging fever, my lungs filling up. As I fought for breath, I was invited, well, here."

"From when?" I asked.

"It was June 2, 2254. Your presidency was still remembered, all the work you did. I'd love to discuss it with you."

"I'm the 2018 model and haven't done jack shit," I said. I'd love to hear about me too, I realized, but now was certainly not the time. It would actually be interesting to have Michael and Carolyn compare their recollections of my deeds and see if they were identical. At least both thought kindly of me. That had to account for something.

"I invited Carolyn to be a part of this meeting because we need someone thinking about the two billion of us. We're scattered, which I gather wasn't the plan. I wanted her perspective about what might come next for us all."

"Hey, I'm happy to have all the help I can get," I said and meant it. Of course, until we had a plan of action, thinking about what comes next is as vague as everything else going on. We chatted for a few more minutes, as I tried to stifle yawning, and my eyes caught Chou studying Silas, who remained still in the back of the hut. Finally, I ended the chitchat and made my good nights.

The sun had set, the stars twinkled in the cloudless sky, and most everyone had already turned in. We'd been here just over a month and the nightly arrival of pixie dust seemed old hat. People were no longer staying up to watch them rain down on us, rejuvenating our bodies with nanotechnology that felt more like magic. That was fine; there would be time to marvel all over again when we finished our job...whatever that turned out to be.

My cabin was in a direct diagonal from the dining hut, so I made a bee line for it, but just before I entered it, I heard a whimper from the shadows in the back. As I feared, it was the huddled form of Albert, who was crouched down, arms wrapped about his legs, gently rocking back and forth.

"Hey, Albert, can I join you?" Without waiting for his answer, I slid down to his level and rested my back against the hut. We sat in companionable silence and I waited him out, fighting the urge to yawn loudly.

"Are we going to die?"

"Not today, Albert," I said as I slid an arm around him. Our discussion must have really spooked him because, normally, he was courageous, sometimes recklessly so, and he was so damned smart. Without the Internet, he was my source for all things natural and he was proud of that knowledge.

"Why am I here, what purpose am I supposed to serve? Why was I given a second chance?" Each question was punctuated by a hiccupping sob as he tried to control himself while still getting out the issues on his mind. We all get these moments, all wondering why we're here. I abandoned any pretense of asking those very questions as I sank deeper into my addiction. But here, here I wasn't addicted. I was clearheaded and was rolling with the punches so much so, I still hadn't stopped to ask the same questions.

"You're here because you can translate for everyone. And the Adversary wants you. Wild Bill was here, I guess, to keep the peace. Freuchen was...Freuchen was..."

"Freuchen was here to make sure we were safe," I finished for him. Who would do that now?

"So what is my untapped potential?"

"You're twelve; it's somewhere within you. There's plenty of time for us to find out."

He let that hang in the air as he continued to not meet my eyes, focusing on the ground instead. He was watching something and I looked down and saw a dark shape emerging from the dirt between his feet. There were two antennae followed by thin legs and the segmented head and body. Leaning lower, he watched and started to speak, then said clearly, "*Gryllus bimaculatus*, African field cricket."

"That's pretty impressive. Do you know them all?"

"I don't know. I haven't been stumped yet, but it's a pretty big planet. We've seen only a fraction of the world, and while I can recognize the trees and the animals, I don't recognize the land. We've seen nothing that matches my textbooks."

"Okay." Then I think I began to see the world from his point of view. It's been exciting and scary, but it's all so overwhelming. He's half a billion years away from anything and anyone familiar to him. We've seen precious few children in our travels, the price we pay for all the parental vigilance, I suppose. Yay, helicopter parenting.

"So, here's the thing, Albert. You're twelve, but we're not treating you like a little boy. We've kept nothing from you and have counted on you to tell us what we're seeing. It may not be why you're here yet, but I want to be around to find out. You're a pretty impressive young man now, so when you find your reason, I bet it will be pretty amazing."

He let that sink in. Then he looked up at me, right into my soul and asked, "Do you really think so?"

"Yes. Maybe not as amazing as instant translation, but we'll find out."

The choked crying ended and a small chuckle came out.

"Look, I'm exhausted, so I can imagine you're tired too. Get some sleep so you can be a part of the talk tomorrow."

"You still want me there? Even when I don't understand it all?"

"None of us do, Albert, which is why we need one another. You've been with me from the start, so I'm not doing this without you."

That did the trick. He threw his arms around me in a fierce hug, and I returned it. It made me wonder how I hugged, would hug, Michael as a child, and that just started me thinking in too many directions. Instead, I helped Albert up and walked him to the cabin where he would spend the night. Silas was nearby and accompanied me as I got him ready for bed, going so far as to tuck him in. It felt right.

I finally got to lie down a few minutes later, and as I began thinking about the conversation and the questions, my mind went blank and I fell into a deep sleep.

The following morning was already hot and humid when I woke up, making me immediately long for a bath, but there were decisions to be made. I washed up, ran my hand through my hair, which I began to think could use a trim, and headed for breakfast. Michael, Miko, Carolyn, and Bartholomew were already eating when I walked in, so I grabbed some fruit juice and nuts, and headed for them.

"It turns out, Madame President," Carolyn began, a twinkle in her eye, "that your son and I come from different realities."

"Oh?"

"Yes, during your first term, you negotiated a lasting truce between China and Taiwan," Michael said.

"While it was one of your deepest regrets at the end of your second term," Carolyn added.

"So what am I remembered for?" I asked her. She had intimated it was something positive, so I was okay with whatever she would say.

"You brought back bipartisanship as a good thing," she said with a smile.

"My timeline too," Michael said.

"It helped get you on the top ten presidents list," Carolyn added.

"Now that's a miracle," I said and we all laughed. It felt good, a brief moment, but a promising one for a day when serious decisions were going to be needed. This morning, refreshed, Michael looked stronger, less ill. I'd take that, since he clearly had a part to play Speaking of play, I saw over his shoulder that, outside, Albert found another youth, someone to play catch with. I guess a good night's sleep and no one trying to kill us did us all a world of good.

Still, I could see a sense of hope in Carolyn and Michael, their gazes directed at me. They saw a president who accomplished things, but I was still a twenty-seven year old who just flunked out of law school and hadn't accomplished much of anything. Once I knew I was here for a reason, I swore to change that, so today would be the start of that process. We'd been reacting too much, going off half-cocked with insufficient information and under-prepared for the Adversary. It was what cost Freuchen his life and no doubt we'd lose others along the way. But we had to go on offense, and as a sports fan, I know that meant we needed a playbook.

All of us, Albert included, reconvened in the long hut for a morning council. It was nothing like the grand dining hall where Dumbledore would address the Hogwarts students, but it would have to do.

As everyone took their seats, I overheard Bartholomew and Albert discussing where all the humans had gone, something Silas knew nothing about.

"Just before the fire, I had read *War of the Worlds*, and I wonder if the Martians attacked Earth," Albert said excitedly.

"I remember that movie," Bartholomew said.

"They made a film version? Wow," he said.

"But I think maybe they look like us, but with copper skin and can read minds," the older man said. "It was also a book from my youth."

"I was always partial to Marvin," I said as I took my seat.

"Martians had human names?"

"Just that one, Albert. He was always trying to conquer the Earth and was regularly stopped."

"Like us and the Adversary," Albert said.

"Something like that," Chou said as she joined us. "Martians were the stuff of fiction until we got there for real and found it dry and dusty. If it ever had life, it was long gone." She sure knew how to break the spell.

"It does raise an interesting question about where mankind went and how long ago it happened," Amelia said. "Everywhere I flew, there were always people. Now I pilot the *Brimstone,* and other than you guys, nothing."

"Where are we? Do you know?" I asked her.

She shook her head, brown hair waving in the process. "Don't recognize the coastline or the terrain. I look at the stars and even the constellations feel fuzzy."

"It could have something to do with being in the future," Michael said.

"The moon's drag on Earth isn't obvious day to day," said Werner Heisenberg. "But, if you say we're half a billion years forward, the drag would have a change. That amount of time would also mean the Earth's relative position to other stars would have changed, altering the constellations." Amelia nodded her head in understanding.

"Even a shattered moon would do that," Miko asked.

"Yes. I've been doing some calculations since we arrived, which is hard without my slide rule, but I have arrived at an approximate conclusion. The Earth's rotation has markedly slowed down so each day is now approximately 25 and a half hours long."

"Such a sudden change from what we're familiar with means our circadian rhythms are thrown off," Chou said.

"So that's why I haven't felt right or slept well," Emily said.

.

"Now that you mention it—" Carolyn began, but I cut her off.

"Silas, what shattered the moon?"

"I do not have that knowledge in my memory banks. It was filled with whatever I needed for my tasks. It is a mistake to think that my memory banks has elastic walls and can distend to any extent."

"What an odd way to explain it," Michael said.

"No, not odd at all," Chou said, continuing to eye Silas. "Silas is paraphrasing Sherlock Holmes."

"Really? I read his stories. Cracking good," Albert exclaimed.

"Me too. Well, that goes to explain your keen observations," Amelia told him with a smile.

I was looking at Chou, who seemed to be fighting her emotions. "What's wrong?" I asked her.

"Ever since Blue Alpha repaired Silas, the things he's been saying, like that old 'new car smell' comment to how he's been saying them, were nagging at me. That last exchange, about his data storage, it originated with Sherlock Holmes, but it was also an analogy often used by my husband."

"Your husband?" Emily asked. "What happened to him?"

"I last saw him among the stars. You see, Emily, my husband was the artificial intelligence that operated the *Shining Light*. He survived whatever happened and I believe that he did more than survive. I think he outgrew the starship and somehow became the Architect."

Eyes popped, jaws dropped, and everyone stared at Chou. Even Thor yipped at that. I forced myself to look to Silas for confirmation, but he remained motionless, his eye bar observing, but that was it.

Chou steadily met our gazes and explained, "Your stories all involve hearing a voice offering you a chance for life. It was disembodied. In my own experience, it was my husband asking me. And now here is Silas speaking that way. It has to be."

"How can we be sure?" Michael asked.

"By finding him and asking," I said. "Silas, is the Architect in one of the collectors?"

"No, Meredith. The space and power required by the Architect for all his works could not be contained in a single citadel."

"Was he part of the interrupted network?" Michael probed.

"No, but when the network was disrupted, the Architect must have lost control or contact with them."

"Michael, if you were something as all-powerful as the Architect and needed that amount of energy to operate, where would you be housed?"

Michael had clearly been thinking along the same lines and his brow furrowed in concentration, exposing a thick, horizontal vein. "There'd have to be constant cooling, room for expansion, and a power supply that couldn't be interrupted. Given the kind of unlimited resources we've seen used so far, the most logical place would be to house him on the moon."

The words settled over the room and everyone was quiet, contemplating what they'd just heard. For several, man hadn't reach the moon yet. For others, it seemed entirely reasonable.

"How are we going to get to the moon?" Albert asked.

THREE

CHOU'S HUSBAND, the Architect, was on the moon. Or at least that was what we thought, but now we needed to communicate directly. We had several threats to resolve and no road map. Once more, several were looking to me like I had all the answers. All I had were questions and a growing sense that we had rested long enough. It was time to execute the plan, whatever the plan became. For every moment we discussed things was another moment Abernathy's army, or some other threat, was nearing us. And the longer I stayed here, the more I was endangering the residents of New Manhattan.

"Silas, how can we get to the moon?" I asked him.

"*There are no rockets on Earth,*" he replied. The Architect might have provided us with some starter materials, but I doubt he left behind a spare Saturn V rocket and fuel. We were quite some time away from being able to create our own metals and space travel was definitely low on the priority list. Nails, needles, and other day-to-day goods were required first. Not only was the Architect giving us a chance to start over as a people, but a chance to start society all over again. No doubt there wasn't any fossil fuels left, so we'd have to go really old school. That'd take time to figure out, time I needed to buy everyone by finding out the answers.

"Can one of the collectors make contact with the moon? Or wherever the Architect was?"

"Presumably, the systems properly rebooted after the energy surge, then yes, such contact could be attempted," Silas said.

"Do you know where one capable of communication might be?" Chou asked. No doubt, she really wanted to speak with her husband. Hell, I didn't even know what she called him.

"There is one I am certain could do this, but it is located closer to the other coast."

"You point the way, I can fly us there," Amelia said, ready to go, just like that. I appreciated her spunk, but we needed to learn from the last few weeks and travel far better prepared. I also needed to figure out who was best suited to accompany us. Chou and Michael for certain and Amelia to fly us. She'd need backup and I'd need some more muscle, which meant Bartholomew. I debated over Albert. He was so young and I might not have been feeling particularly maternal, but he was a liability. Then again, if I left him here, he'd probably try and stow aboard, like he did earlier on the *Alexa Rae*. I also promised him a chance at finding his destiny, so maybe I owed that to him. Besides, I just promised him last night he'd be a part of this, and I wasn't going to renege on that.

Would I need an astrophysicist? Maybe. Miko could also help scale the mountains likely buttressing the collector. Vihaan didn't look to be in great shape, but we'd been dealing with nanotech all along, so his expertise might come in handy.

Carolyn had interesting insights, but I didn't need a poly-sci professor at this point. Her thoughts about the differing communities, though, would be needed when this was all done. Better she remain behind, although she seemed ready and raring to come along. Well, we would all have to deal with some disappointment.

I could also put out a call for volunteers, but it meant getting to know people cold, assessing skills, and figuring out how they could help. That required time I instinctively felt we didn't have. Instead, I went with my gut and said to go with those I knew. Emily would have to brief the growing community.

"Silas, can you program a map into the *Brimstone*?" I asked.

"No, as I do not have a map in my programming."

"We need a map," I said. "Could you print one on metal like you did your daily data log?" Before his memory was repaired, he would imprint the vital information on scrap metal and scan it each day as he awoke. Thankfully, those days were over.

"There is no map or metal to use."

"I have an idea," Emily said.

I gestured at her, even though she was the mayor or governor of the community and my host. Yet, everyone kept deferring to me when it should have been her. Her poise and confidence – and her grit – was everything I saw a leader being and I didn't feel like that at all.

"Just outside our compound are papyrus trees. We've been stripping some to make rope for construction, but wasn't their skin used to fashion paper?"

"Yes," exclaimed Albert.

"Does anyone know how?" I asked.

"It's too time consuming," my walking encyclopedia said glumly. "You soak it and stretch it and dry it and it takes days and days."

"Alternatively," Miko spoke up. "There are trees we can peel the bark off of and use the inside."

"I can calibrate my laser to etch the bark without burning it," Silas added helpfully.

"Silas, why don't you and Albert go find some and get us a

map we can use?" I suggested. Like a shot, Albert was out of his chair, and thankfully, Silas' long limbs let him easily catch up.

"Well, good to know we can make paper," Emily said. "We'll need it."

"For record keeping?" I asked.

"No, for communications," Carolyn said. "In time, we will want to talk to the other communities. Unless we want to rely strictly on oral interpretation, we need paper."

"And pens and ink," Amelia added.

"Anyone know which birds provide the best quills?" Emily said.

"Okay, once Silas gives us a roadmap, we need to stock the *Brimstone* and get out of here. If they want me, it'll be a chase. All morning, I've felt like a sitting duck. If you'll come, I want Chou, Amelia, Michael, Vihaan, Miko, and Bartholomew to come. I'll be taking Silas and Albert too."

"Isn't it too dangerous for the boy?" Heisenberg asked.

"Try keeping him here," I said. "No, he's been with me from the beginning and he is better off coming along." He nodded and I caught a look of disappointment from Carolyn.

"Agreed," Chou said in confirmation.

"Okay, you'll need food and water, some medical gear," Emily ticked off. "Not that we have a lot of anything, but we can spare you some."

It was agreed, and everyone scattered. I took a moment to myself and reviewed the contents of my bag. Much as I liked the soap, it could stay behind, as could much of the canned goods. It'd make a fair trade for the stuff Emily would be providing. I checked my canteen for damage.

Then I saw Chou standing alone, observing the community come to life with purpose. People were bustling as Emily shouted out orders, which were relayed. Yeah, with no cell service in the future, we really were back at square one. *That's okay,* I thought, *my phone is out of battery life.* I walked beside her, looking up once more, trying to read her eyes.

"Come with me," she said and started off toward a pile of stones which had been collected to help with drainage. Someone around here must have been an engineer or even a plumber. We walked to the pile in silence and then she crouched low, examining several with her hands before selecting one.

"Your scimitar, please," she said.

"You want to practice?"

"No." I pulled it from my belt and handed it to her. She then balanced the blade on the largest rock while using one in her hand to scrape along the edge, sharpening it. The grinding sound was unpleasant, but she was right, I needed to be prepared.

"How are you?"

"Relieved my husband is alive. Wanting to speak with him. Worried we don't have the answers we need."

"It's a lot to absorb," I agreed.

"It is, but I was trained to analyze data and make determinations."

"Right, I keep thinking about you being the security officer, but it was security and research officer," I said. She nodded and continued honing the blade.

"Your training must continue. If there is time, we can continue to drill en route to the collector."

"You know I made myself a promise, well, one to you and your husband, that I would try and live the life he envisioned for us. I don't want to take any more lives."

"You can still use this without killing and I won't let you go into battle unarmed," Chou said matter-of-factly. "It makes an excellent deterrent."

She worked and I watched for a while. Then I asked her,

"What is his name? 'Architect' is more of a title and it's not what you called him. It's not HAL, is it?"

"Hal?"

"Old joke, never mind."

"He was my beloved," she said and continued to work, occasionally pausing to check the progress. Satisfied after a time, she flipped it in her hand, and returned it to me, pommel first. I gingerly placed my hand along the edge and saw how much sharper it felt. With care, I placed it back in my belt and rose.

I started to speak, but a shrill cry in the distance interrupted us. We headed toward the sound, which definitely had the tone of an alarm. "Get everyone on the *Brimstone*," I said. "I'll find out what's happening."

I hurried my steps toward the running figure of a dark-skinned woman, her hair flying behind her head. The look of panic was evident even from a distance. My stomach dropped, fearing the worst. I didn't even dare try hoping for the best.

"Lots of them!" she said.

Emily got to her before I did and the woman was babbling, but as I got closer, Emily's confused look cleared. I was translating for them. And as I neared, I could make out an approximate count of four dozen figures, all black, all sort of human. It had to be Abernathy, finally finding us. How? I shoved the question aside for later. It was time to leave and fast.

"He wants me," I shouted. "Get everyone to the opposite side of the compound, and he'll head for me. Maybe he'll leave you all alone."

"We can fight," she suggested.

"Anyone who falls gets coated in the nanobots. You'd just make the army bigger."

"Analise, go warn the others," Emily said. The long-haired woman took off, shouting and waving her arms, motioning for everyone to move to the south. As she did that, Emily and I looked to see the team assembling by the *Brimstone*. I could hear the engine coming to life and hoped Amelia wasn't one for going through the pre-flight checklist.

Silas appeared from between two huts, carrying Albert, who was holding a rolled piece of wood in his hands. I gestured for the airship and they pivoted and headed in that direction. I could hear the rising voices of panic as it spread across the population. Whoever Emily tapped as her lieutenants were clearly trying to direct the herd. The hierarchy had been well established as no one argued and people were following the direction of a half-dozen people.

I swiveled my head, looking around to see the black blob approaching, but thankfully, they were still a distance away. Then I turned back and met Emily's eyes. She gave me a brief, fierce hug, whispering, "Godspeed. Now get out of here."

Going from zero to sixty, I sprinted for the *Brimstone* just as Silas was entering it. I could hear the crunch of trees breaking. The army was here and the destruction was going to be bad. Forcing myself to look forward, I dug in for the cabin door, trying to ignore the screams behind me. We should have left earlier. We needed better sentries. A better warning system. How did they do it back then?

Scrabbling inside, I found an empty chair and hung on, shouting, "Take off, take off!"

"Already on it," Amelia yelled over her shoulder.

Moments later, I saw the first figures, vaguely human. There, in the center, was Abernathy. His silhouette, with the cobra-like hood shape and now-triangular head, was distinct. I imagined he was radiating sheer hatred, and as he entered the compound, he saw the *Brimstone* and began heading for us.

"Up!" I cried.

"You know another way to fly?" Amelia cracked, flipping a few more switches, and then I felt us slowly begin to rise. The last time I saw him, he could extend his limbs and I didn't know how far that went,. We needed altitude and fast. He was already coming into focus and I saw glossy black eyes amidst the oily blackness. I feared he'd leap and latch on to us, or pierce the helium bladders.

"What on Earth is that?" Vihaan exclaimed.

I let out a mirthless chuckle, since those were my exact words when I saw the black orb in the collector. It hovered over dead ground and rippled, building up momentum as Tommy Two-Thumbs neared it. Then, it speared him like a marlin. Within seconds, the orb reduced itself in size as it transferred its mass to Abernathy. In time, it covered his body, distending his form, remaking it, following some hideous design. He was still following the Adversary's commands, seeking me out, seeking Candidate 1.

"Nanobots," I said, catching my breath. "Nanobots tuned to some network of the Adversary's. He was human once, but now he's a walking, talking mass of nanobots. With everyone he touches, he passes it on like a disease."

"Self-replicating," Vihaan said in a whisper, his eyes darting right to left, thinking furiously. "They use the organic material to fuel reproduction on an accelerated scale."

"Yeah, well, he's been building an army and they still want me."

"Why?" he asked.

All I could was shrug. We'd been over this and still had no answers. I stared out the window, watching Abernathy arrive just beneath us. He couldn't reach us much as he tried; he couldn't leap at us, or fly, thank goodness. But he was in New Manhattan. As Amelia banked left, the cabins and huts fell away, but black fog seemed to envelop a portion of it. I prayed Emily and the others were able to get away faster than Abernathy could follow. The problem was, he seemed tireless while the others were merely human.

"Where to?" Amelia called out.

Albert rushed forward, unrolling the bark. "Silas says we're to go here." His finger stabbed at a point. "And we're here." His finger moved to the opposite edge.

"Aye aye, navigator," she said. "North by northwest it is."

"We need speed," I said. "I thought he didn't have a map."

"I was able to make extrapolations based on a review of our exploits since we met," he told me.

"Aye aye, captain," she said with a grin. Despite all the dangers, she was enjoying herself. She lived to be in the air so was in her element. Not so much Vihaan, who seemed to dislike heights. He was going to have to suck it up since we had no other choice.

I brooded with worry, staring at the land beneath us. The forest we'd previously traveled, the Evergreen, was beneath us already. At least it was progress.

Chou worked her way forward and sat beside me.

"Where do you think the others were?"

"Others?" I asked.

"When we last saw Abernathy, he had maybe a thousand humans already turned into his nanobot army. They overwhelmed and took apart Blue Alpha. There were at best four dozen here in New Manhattan."

"Michael theorized they were looking for me," I said. "Maybe they split up. When we left...the collector..." And Freuchen.

"Logical," she said. "We must devise a way to stop Abernathy, find a way to disrupt his network."

"That sounds like Vihaan's world, not mine," I said, still replaying my friend's death in my mind's eye. She left me alone to brood and spoke quietly with Vihaan and Michael. Miko and

Bartholomew were peering through the glass encasing the gondola, enjoying the view.

After a few minutes to wallow, I swallowed hard, refusing to cry again, and made a decision. I worked my way to the front, admiring the thin clouds and bright blue ahead of us. To Amelia's right was the etched map, dark brown lines against the tan lining of the bark. On it was an outline of the continent, although it was not one I recognized. There were fragments that resembled Africa or South America, but it was alien to me. Still, it was something and I saw Albert had used a charred twig to make marks. In one place was a star with "NM" under it. New Manhattan. Okay, it was a start. Then I saw what I needed.

"Silas, can you direct Amelia to get us to Avalon?"

"*Of course,*" he said.

"What's there?" our pilot asked.

"We're a handful against an army. If we're going into war, I need a general."

"Not you?"

"No, I promised myself I would honor the Architect's desires. Besides, I've no training. I need someone who can handle a gun. And can command men."

"It's a half day out of our way. Are you sure?"

I nodded. "We're facing an army, so it's time to build our own."

FOUR

THE GARRISON at Avalon had grown, much as New Manhattan had. Its leader, Edward James Hubbard, had gone for a hub and spoke design, using the center for a meeting place. There were six segments, each nearly identical, a series of long structures, several with a steady plume of smoke rising. As we neared, I could see people moving about, everyone assigned a job, each to their own talents. Hubbard was fighting during World War I and nearly died before the Architect rescued him. In my world, he survived and became one of the 20th Century's great poets. Here, he was a man of wisdom and enterprise, overseeing the construction on an island, its placid waters protection from Abernathy's army. Along the shore, I could see felled trees being hollowed out, the beginnings of canoes. A few people could be seen further down the coast, fishing.

A part of me longed to just land and rejoin this community. But newfound duty and obligation won out, especially since anywhere I laid my head was going to put a target on them and I couldn't presume the water would be enough protection. I long ago learned what happens when you presume.

More than a few people had spotted our approach, our

shadow looming large on the land with the lowering sun behind us. I had told my new companions about these people, the ones I first arrived with, and I looked forward to seeing them again. But I didn't want us shot at, couldn't afford the helium to escape or explode.

Once more, I moved to the front and asked about a microphone. Amelia cocked her head to her left and there was a mic on a coiled line. Then I reached into my backpack and withdrew the paper Hubbard had given me when I left Avalon. I thumbed the mic to life and began to read.

"The war's maiden walks the bloody path,

And pauses here and there,

To kiss a cold forehead, caress a pale cheek.

Her heart beats in its wrath,

But forces herself instead to care

For one of these may have been her Greek..."

"What is that?" Miko asked. Before I could reply, Michael chimed in with "The Maiden."

I gave him a surprised look. He shrugged. "You loved that poem and recited it to me now and then."

Well, it was good to know I was consistent. The recitation had the desired effect and I recognized Hubbard's figure running toward us, his arms waving away those brandishing whatever they had for defensive weapons. He was still in his torn and well-worn British uniform.

"Okay, Amelia, it's safe to land."

She nodded and maneuvered a few controls, slowing the engines and bringing us down. We'd gathered quite the crowd by the time we settled on the land, keeping a respectful distance from the garrison. A small knot of people surrounded him and I recognized Jacquetta, Evita, and the man I came to see: Wild Bill Hickock.

Wild Bill was standing awfully close to Jacquetta, so I

hoped their flirtation moved forward. He'd lost his horse to the Nazis and I could tell just how lonely he had been before arriving here. And here I was, asking him to leave her.

We disembarked and Edward was beaming at me. Once everyone was off the *Brimstone*, I made a quick round of introductions, followed by Edward's side. He craned his head, looking around.

"He's gone," I said softly.

His face fell at that and Wild Bill dipped his head in acknowledgement. They'd both seen enough death to understand the loss but also that we had to go on.

"Is there somewhere we can talk?"

"Of course," Edward said. "Oliver and Sarah, please take our guests for refreshments." He eyed Chou. "I suppose you're coming with us? You two are never far apart."

"She needs constant protection," she said and fell into step.

He brought us to his cabin, which doubled as his operations center. It was spartan since no one had much, but there was a wide tree trunk that served as a table, a good portion of its root system still in place so it wobbled a bit. Edward gestured to two additional slices of tree that acted as chairs. As he poured water, Wild Bill leaned in the doorway, his thin frame backlit by the setting sun.

As quickly as I could, and interrupted only a few times by Chou, I outlined the last few weeks. I summed up with the threat to our lives from Abernathy, not bothering him with the false vacuum, which might or might not be coming our way. There was only so much time and there were things to do.

"I can't do this alone, Edward," I said after taking a long drink from the cool cup of water. "We need to get organized and I need a force to stop Abernathy."

He nodded and prepared to respond when Wild Bill interrupted. "You got a way to stop this thing?"

"Not yet."

"You want cannon fodder then," he said bluntly. "You got no way to stop him, so you just need a wall of people. I reckon that's asking a lot."

"We have to fight and stop him, so I can get to the collector and speak with the Architect."

"I got that part. It's the robot army I don't have settled," he drawled.

"That's why I'm here," I admitted. "I need you, Bill. I need someone to lead the force we will build."

He shook his head. "Hold on there, Meredith. Sure, I can shoot some. But I'm no leader of men..."

"And women," Chou cut in.

"If you say so. But I don't have the first clue about half of what you just said. I'm no military man, and Edward, he's seen far worse battle than I ever have, but we need him here."

"And I've seen too much," Edward said quietly.

"Clearly, you need protection. I can do that. I can come along and watch your back, but I can't...I won't be leadin' people into a hopeless fight. You show me where to aim, I'll take my best shot."

"First you tell me about parallel realities, and now you're telling me these nanobits..." Edward began.

"Nanobots," Chou corrected.

"Nanobots can take us over, take away our humanity. At least you've identified the threat; we just need a solution. Now, if Bill wants to go with you, I can't stop him. I'd advise against it, because we're building something good here, and it too needs protecting."

"If I don't stop Abernathy and his puppet master, you will eventually be destroyed," I said. I looked at Wild Bill, who was thinking deeply.

"We have to go. We have many miles to cross to reach our destination," Chou said.

"How do you even know where to go? The tinman? Silas?"

"Yes. In fact, let Albert show you the map," I said with a smile.

"Map?"

"Yes, come see the world we're on."

He followed me from the cabin and we found Albert being fussed over by Evita, Sarah, and Jacquetta. The boy was showing them the very map we were there to see. Edward stood behind him and Albert showed off where we had been, describing the forest, and the mountains surrounding the citadel, the remains of which could be seen from Avalon. He then showed them New Manhattan and his finger traced our path. He took out his stick and added an A to the island, the largest on that shore.

"We've seen other settlements," I said. "Everyone seems to have found places to call home."

"They're all threatened, aren't they?" Edward asked, frowning. As I nodded, I also noticed Wild Bill had taken Jacquetta away from the group. In the growing shadows of the impending evening, I saw them huddled close, him talking, her shaking her head. I could fill in the dialogue for myself. When they returned to the group, she had tears in her eyes and then she glared at me, and I didn't blame her. But Wild Bill came from a time when a man did what he thought was best, even if it hurt the ones he loved. It was a simpler time, I guess, and one I admired.

Edward convinced us to at least stay for a meal, which was warm, tasty, and filling. We restocked our canteens and made our farewells. I gave Edward a tight hug while Albert blushed at the ones he was receiving. Wild Bill and Jacquetta were saying their farewells in private and he met us at the airship by himself. He looked ready for war with a Nazi machine gun, two Lugers, boxes of ammunition, and his own trusty six-shooter. He nodded at me once and then went aboard, Albert right behind him to show him around.

Less than five hours after arriving, we were leaving Avalon. I dearly hoped it would not be the last time I would visit the island.

Wild Bill watched Avalon fade in the distance as we flew higher and the coastline gave way to trees, scrub, and sand. He sat like a statue, gazing, until I saw him flex his hands, spreading his fingers then clenching them into fists.

"Never been so high, have you?"

"Nope."

"Scared of heights? It's pretty common," I reassured him.

"I don't know. Never been so damned high up," Wild Bill said. "Gives you a whole new way of looking at things."

I left him to his thoughts and settled beside Chou to see how she was doing. There had to be some relief in knowing her husband had survived and was near. If you can call the moon near.

"You okay?" I prompted.

"Fine."

"Fine doesn't really cover what you're going through," I said.

She looked at me and exhaled a long breath. The fierceness that was her general demeanor faded, revealing a vulnerability I hadn't seen before.

"What does a half billion years of existence do to you? Is he still the same? Was he isolated; did he have friends?"

"You worried if he cheated..."

"Nothing like that. But I've seen what long voyages like ours did to people and that was just a decade or two of space flight. This is on an entirely different scale."

"How much can he really have changed if you recognized him from Silas' speech?"

She paused at that thought. "What if we reconnect and it's not the same?"

"It can't be, can it? A month here has changed you in some ways, so half a billion years will definitely have changed him. But into what remains to be seen."

I placed my hand over hers and gave her a light squeeze. Chou wasn't touchy-feely, but I suspected she needed some human contact. It lasted a beat, then two before she moved her hand away.

"We need to assess our supplies," she said, as if the previous conversation hadn't happened. "We left New Manhattan before we could fully load up and all we received in Avalon was water and fruit."

She rose and began opening cabinets, making a mental inventory. In one, she found what looked like a tablet, and it powered on at her touch. It was thinner than anything I had seen before and curled at one edge. Returning to the first bin, she began rapidly typing with one hand, moving at speeds I thought only teenage girls could manage.

Methodically, she examined all the supplies, and then began speaking with our complement, which I had begun to think of as the IMF, *Mission: Impossible*'s Impossible Missions Force, because if saving the planet, and maybe the universe, wasn't an impossible mission, I didn't know what was. Which made me Ethan Hunt and I looked nothing like Tom Cruise. People continued to look at me as the leader while I still didn't feel it was earned but handed to me because I was the object of the Adversary's desire for reasons that continue to elude us.

Chou returned to my side, her serious expression in place. So much for girl talk. "We have vegetables, fruit, and water for at least a week. We lack protein beyond that. We're also short on medical supplies, notably bandages."

"Any good news?"

"We have plenty of ammunition for the machine gun and pistols, plus we have assorted knives for the others."

"Not enough food to properly sustain us, but plenty to kill us," I said. "Sounds like the America I left behind."

"We can stop each day for fishing and maybe some hunting," Chou suggested.

"Well, it's not like we can stop at Walmart, so let's make that the plan." My reference went right by her, but she didn't inquire. Instead, she rose and started forward, where Bartholomew was taking a turn piloting the airship. She and Silas consulted over the crude and far too incomplete map. I know she was asking about places to fish, but I wished it could tell me where the Adversary or at least where Abernathy's army might be. The Architect brought just under two billion people forward in time, and in less than a month, we lost who knows how many people to violence, let alone the thousand or more that were now Abernathy's Army. And how many people did the Adversary bring forward and how were they integrating into this brave new world? If they were violent killers, they would remain a threat to the Architect's utopia. Well, one threat at a time.

It was determined that the following day we were likely to reach a river that should have good fishing. What Silas didn't tell us, and which we were surprised to discover after the sun rose the following morning was how deep the river was in relation to where we could land the *Brimstone*. The barren territory seemed devoid of life, not even plants, just rocky terrain and deep fissures that led down to the river, which looked wide and I could see was running at a good clip. The taupe ground was cracked, in need of a good rain, and some scrub seemed to be growing here and there. Down below was the river and lush green foliage. At least Wild Bill would be happy about going down. I had made sure everyone got some sleep as the airship ate miles, although I was disappointed when I saw how little we moved on the makeshift map.

"You're letting the scale bother you," Michael said from over my shoulder. "Trust me, we're on course and making reasonable time. All the stops for food will slow us a bit, maybe cost us a day all told."

"A day we don't have," I said,.

"You don't know that. It's just another unknown, so we keep going forward."

His reassurance helped a bit, even if it still felt weird talking to my son. He was certainly handling it better than me. I shoved those thoughts aside and studied the map. There were several new marks that I asked Albert about.

He was eating a peach, juice already on his chin, but was grinning, which made me happy. "I saw fires big enough to tell us there were villages, compounds, garrisons...what are we calling these places? Everyone has a different name for it."

"Villages will do," I said. Compound and garrison sounded too military for my taste. I spotted six new signs of civilization, which I took to be a good thing. It made me wonder, though, about just how many there were and would they soon be fighting over resources or imaginary lines in the sand. There was enough unrest being stirred up by the Adversary and his scattering us meant there was more than a bit of confusion down there. Another issue for a later time.

"I found us a place to land. Silas' eyes tell me it'll be the easiest way to make it to the river," Bartholomew said.

"Have you ever landed this?" I honestly couldn't remember.

"There is a first time for everything, is there not?" he said with a big grin.

"Just don't land us too close to the edge," I said.

"Where's the fun in that?" he said but was keeping his eyes on the controls, maneuvering us lower and not near the edge.

I made sure everyone was awake and prepared to go for a hike. We had some spears made from branches and our knives, but I wished we had a good fishing pole. We'd make do and hopefully find some dead wood to use for cooking as opposed to chopping down a tree, the kind of thing Freuchen would do with gusto. I wished I had that axe of his.

After we landed, the party began making its way down with the more experienced Miko in the lead, something that took over an hour. The rock formations gave us plenty of places for our hands and feet, but it was slow going and I wasn't looking forward to the climb back up. She was making it look easy and I was jealous. I maybe rock-wall climbed a few times at birthday parties when I was much younger, but this was new to me, and even with developing muscles, I was achy long before I got to the bottom. It was hot and I tried to comfort myself with the old joke about it was at least a dry heat. Still, my shirt stuck to my back and I felt the sweat running down my neck. I tried to remember to regularly drink from the canteen, something I could easily refill from the river.

Michael, the oldest in our group and in the worst physical shape, chose to remain behind, so I was thankful for that. One less thing to worry about. Albert, though, was happily scrabbling down, taking the lead with Miko while Silas was in the rear, his metallic form digging deep into the rock to support his greater weight.

When we finally reached the bottom, it was noticeably cooler and the sound of the rushing river was actually pleasant. Both sides of the bank were shaded by trees that looked old based on how thick their trunks were. Between the rock wall and the nearest bank was a good thirty yards, so plants and grasses grew. From what I saw in the sky, the river traveled quite a ways, crookedly bisecting this portion of the continent, eventually curving to the west. No doubt there'd be animal life down here, so maybe we'd have some surf and turf tonight.

We spread out along the bank, some stopping to pour water over their heads, and used our spears to try and catch some of the fish we saw. They were large and I had no idea what type they were, but no doubt Albert could tell me. First, they had to be caught. Amelia was poking away with gusto, not hitting a thing but having a fine time trying. Albert crouched low, studying the fish for a bit, before rearing back and piercing the cold water. Vihaan and Bartholomew were equally unable to catch anything. So of course it was Chou, she of the superior physique and reflexes, who caught the first fish. She'd observed the others and then studied the water, and with one smooth movement, struck deep into the water and pulled back with a wriggling silvery blue fish affixed to the tip. She completed the arc over her shoulder, dislodging her catch onto the dirt. Wild Bill promptly brought down a stone, crushing its head.

There was banter and laughter, so for a brief moment, the dread up above wasn't pressing on us. I actually laughed and even saw Chou smile.

We were like this for at least a quarter of an hour, but then birds, ones we hadn't noticed in the trees, suddenly flew up, made frantic circles, and rushed across the river. Wild Bill dropped the fish he was cleaning and reached for his pistol, fingers still dripping with guts. Chou twisted around, the spear point dripping but empty. From somewhere deep between the trees that formed a barrier between the rock wall and the river bank, I saw a flash of fur and heard the low growl.

"Oh, shit," I said to myself. "Albert, get back."

Moments later, a second sabretooth tiger padded into view. Like the one we saw early in our visit, this was large, prehistoric, and according to Silas, not supposed to be here. It was one of the predators brought forward by the Adversary to act as a counterbalance of sorts. Regardless of reason, it was here and it was clearly a threat we hadn't prepared for. This one was spotted, more like a cheetah than the one we saw weeks before. Its white fangs were stained yellow, saliva making one glisten in the sunlight. Given how large it was, easily six feet long, the tail seemed ridiculously short, but it was upright, curling.

Its friends appeared behind it and I quickly counted five, so it was hunting in a pack. Swell. We had spears and Chou made one work earlier, killing the first one we encountered. But none of us matched her in skill, except maybe Bartholomew. He was tightly gripping his spear, keeping it before him in a defensive posture. All had been tattooed with blood and gore, so we must have somehow interfered with their lunch.

"*Smilodon fatalis*," Albert said from somewhere behind me. "How many do you think there are here?"

"Too many," Wild Bill said, studying them with his experienced eyes, his pistols in both hands. He was calculating, I could tell, determining if he could shoot all five before someone died. His not immediately firing didn't bode well for us.

"What do we do?" I asked Chou, who was a little bit behind me now and to my left. I felt powerless until I remembered I had the scimitar. But if I went for it, I'd be a moving target sure to attract attention and I considered they were within leaping distance.

"Keep watch and be ready to react," was all she said in a low voice.

The group of animals stood before us, studying us, sniffing the air, the lead one pawing at the ground beneath it.

"They're sated from eating, slower to move, which will give us an advantage," Chou said.

"To do what?"

As the words left my lips, the lead sabretooth crouched and sprang forward, right at Bartholomew. His reflexes were good and he was swinging the spear in both fists like a baseball bat, making contact. The wood splintered, but the shift in momentum sent the big cat onto its side. As it scrambled upright to his paws, another leapt over him, right at the now defenseless man. Before it could make contact, Silas had reached over Bartholomew's head and grasped the attacker around the throat and then swung it around in an arc, releasing the cat so it sailed into the river and was swept away, its cries angry and plaintive.

The others charged forward, but by then, Bill had taken aim and fired twice, taking down another, the shots echoing back and forth between the stone walls. I had my scimitar out and stood still, the blade vertical before me, ready to strike, but only defensively. That changed when one of the cats made for Vihaan, who tried to spear him, but it glanced off the spotted fur. It knocked the older man down, slicing open his forearm, forcing me to act. I came up behind it and aimed for the head, but my first swing missed. Instead, I had to alter my position as the cat reared back a paw to swipe again at Vihaan. I came along its flank and made a horizontal cut that went through fur into muscle, causing the cat to roll over and howl. It was a horrible sound, one I'd be happy not hear again. With no choice, since it loomed over Vihaan, I swung again, cutting deeper, striking bone, as it staggered, moving aside.

Chou and Bartholomew were cornering one cat, each striking with their knives, slicing into the cat, each accompanied by a growl. If I remembered right, cornering an animal was never a good idea, but then Amelia joined them, and they kept at the cat, not letting it attack. It was death by a thousand stabs, and it was terrible. Behind me, Bill fired again, emptying a pistol into the fourth cat.

I heard the fifth cat before I saw it, and by then, it was in the air headed directly for me. I didn't move swiftly enough and it forced me to the ground, one paw slicing into my arm. I let out a shriek of pain and tried to wriggle away, but this thing easily outweighed me. I wasn't going anywhere and certainly couldn't use the scimitar. Its breath was horrible, saliva dripping on me as it studied me for a moment, figuring out where best to attack. Humans, I gathered, were not on its regular menu. I kicked my feet, which merely made it wobble once.

Behind me, Miko and Chou had their spears at the ready, taking careful aim as the sabretooth settled on my chest for its attack. Its growl signaled his intent, which was when the two women stabbed at it. Each pierced its fur and the cat howled and shrieked, writhing in pain, its forepaws slicing away at me. It scrabbled off of me and turned its ferocity at the women, which was when Wild Bill, coming up from behind us, took aim and fired once. The beast collapsed atop my legs. Miko helped roll it off me as Bartholomew helped me to my feet, my own blood mixing with the sabretooth's, staining the ground.

"Anyone hurt?" I asked, my breath ragged, my heart still pounding against my ribs.

"Yeah, you," Wild Bill said. Vihaan had already pulled out a cloth to wrap around himself and Bill did the same for me.

Amelia was already at Vihaan's side, reaching into her bag for the first aid supplies. Of course, it was the airplane pilot who thought to bring that stuff on a hike. It didn't occur to me we'd need it. She applied pressure, causing the older man to wince. We had to staunch the wound and wait until nightfall for our daily pixie dust treatment.

As she got to work, everyone else seemed fine, if rattled.

"You want I should go find it?" Wild Bill asked, reloading his gun.

"Are there more?" I asked.

"We won't know until we go looking, but if there are five, there may be none or six," he said.

"Bartholomew, go with him," I said. "Chou will keep us

safe." There were nods and the two men paused at the tree line, listening, then went in. As they disappeared, I went to see where Amelia was wrapping Vihaan's right arm.

"He'll live," she said.

"I should hope so," he said, trying to force a smile, but he was seriously scared and it'd be a while before he felt normal. "Meredith, you look worse than I do."

"It feels that way too," I said, trying not to grimace. Miko fussed over me before Amelia could bring her supplies.

Albert came near me, and in a small voice, asked, "Do you think Abernathy heard the gun shots?" The fight scared him and the brave lad I had come to rely on was seriously rattled.

"He'd have to be very close to hear that," Chou said. "We haven't seen him on our journey, so no, Albert, he did not hear us."

"What about those nano-bugs?"

"We haven't seen any of those in days, weeks," I reassured him. "We're fine." For now.

"Silas, were you able to hear their approach?" I asked.

"No, Meredith. My systems were focused on our fishing. I was not in a security mode."

"You have different modes?"

"They are backup subroutines, used as required."

"How come I never knew that?"

"You never asked."

"That's not funny," Chou snapped.

"They were suppressed by previous damage, but Blue Alpha's repairs allowed me access."

"Good to know." Once Amelia finished with me, I went to the river bank and knelt down. With both hands cupping the water, I drank some and then refilled my hands and poured it down my back, wincing with every move. The variety of threats was making it hard to feel prepared. In a war, it's usually a mass of guys in uniform shooting at another mass of guys in uniform. Red coats versus independent blue, blue versus gray, and so on. Here, it was Nazis and sabretooths and nanobots. You couldn't possibly be ready for them all, especially on unfamiliar ground. We were going to be in a constant disadvantage until this got resolved. If this got resolved.

As my breathing returned to normal, I could see Amelia and Albert cleaning up the debris, retrieving our fish and making a small pile. We were going to have to leave and resume the trip.

It was another fifteen minutes before I heard rustling then Wild Bill announcing his presence. He and Bartholomew emerged into the sunlight, looking no worse for wear.

"Never did see another cat," he said.

"Good."

"But we found their lunch. Looked like bison, two of them," Bartholomew added.

"What are bison doing down here?" I asked.

"Couldn't rightly say, but we interrupted their meal and they came looking for us," Wild Bill said.

"The bison were likely brought here to be part of the food supply," Chou said from behind me.

"Not for us," Wild Bill said.

"No, they were victims of the Adversary. Multiple paths of chaos the Architect warned about. Upsetting the ecosystem and the food chain the Architect designed is one such path. And if the food supply is compromised, our ability to sustain nearly two billion people will be a problem."

"Okay, let's gather fish and get back to the *Brimstone*. We have miles to go before we sleep," I said.

As everyone busied themselves, I absorbed Chou's warning. Our problems were mounting and our solutions were not keeping up. Hell, we had no solutions yet.

FIVE

THANKFULLY, the next two days were uneventful. We flew, noting the changing terrain, from forests to fields, to deserts. Silas helped Albert add to the map, noting other rivers and a cluster of seven mammoth lakes, patterned like a starburst. We saw birds in flocks and small clusters of animals. I even saw two packs of wild horses running free, their dark forms nearly outracing us, it seemed.

Just no signs of civilization. The further inland we went, there was no evidence the Architect brought anyone here. He seemed to have brought us to the coasts, with plentiful water and land in equal proportion. Still, it would have been like the Adversary to divert people to a dry desert and let them die of dehydration.

We played *I Spy* and other games to pass the time and keep Albert entertained. In turn, he happily recited facts about the environment beneath us. Amelia was also teaching Michael and Vihaan the basics of flying the *Brimstone* so we had more options. Both were doing pretty well and I know it gave Michael a greater sense of purpose, especially after being left behind when we went fishing. But then again, it also meant he wasn't a sabretooth's dinner option.

There was a tedium to the flight, even though the sense of dread and tension remained in the background. I busied myself, learning how to clean a gun, helping Wild Bill work with the materials we had on hand. I made sure to spend time with everyone, getting to know them better, one by one, and in the back of my mind, assessing how best they could contribute under various scenarios. If the Adversary was going to bring the chaos, I was going to counter him as best I could.

We had entered a region of low, grassy land, reminding me of the prairies men like Wild Bill were associated with. Albert explained we were entering a veldt, which I knew to be a term for African land. It was a large plateau region, with small rivers and relatively dry, hot weather punctuated by a rainy season. About thirty minutes into this region, Amelia summoned me to the pilothouse. She gestured to her right and I looked through the dusty window. There were a cluster of structures, the first sign of human life we'd seen since leaving Avalon.

I called for Albert so he could add it to our map. He and Amelia discussed the scale and they approximated the best they could. All the training on longitude and latitude, all my reliance on GPS, all gone.

"Take us down. Safely away so we don't seem threatening."

"Really?" she asked, surprised.

"Yes. If we're building an army, we'll need allies. We need friends, and they need to be warned."

"Makes sense to me," she said and began adjusting the controls and I immediately felt us turn and begin a descent. As we neared, I could see numerous thatched huts, several in each circle, each circle surrounding cook fires. Trails of smoke emerged from each, lazily wafting into the sky. Wooden racks had been constructed, clothing and grasses drying. I could see new homes being built along with other large objects I could identify. It was certainly an industrious group, although everyone seemed to be craning their necks to look at us or start jogging in our direction.

By the time we settled, a gathering awaited us, easily several dozen people. I saw all skin tones, sizes, and shapes, just like everywhere else. I wondered when and where they came from and if they'd managed to speak to one another. I asked everyone but Wild Bill to leave weapons aboard the ship. We had to appear nonthreatening and I also asked Silas to remain aboard until I explained the situation. No one argued, clearly having accepted me as their leader, such as it was.

As a result, I was the first to emerge from the airship, smiling and hands open. A tall, whippet-thin man, his face weathered and tanned by sun, draped in what might be a dun-colored sari, led his group forward until we met in the middle.

"Hello," I said.

"Forgive, but you speak Tsonga," he said.

"No, English," I said, grinning as his eyes flew wide.

"How can you..."

"It's a gift. My name is Meredith, and if your people gather around, say thirty feet, they will all understand me."

He gaped at that for a moment then nodded. "I am Isabis," the man said. "Welcome to Idolobhana."

By then, my IMF team assembled beside me and Michael gave me a look. "It means village."

"Where are you from?"

I sighed. I was going to be doing this a lot and I had prepared my speech, rehearsing it the last few days, knowing it would come in handy. "We all come from somewhere else, from different lands. Recently, we came from the coast," and I gestured in the general direction. "There is a lot to explain, including answers to some of your questions and a warning of dangers ahead."

"What sort of danger, luv?" a bearded Australian wearing clothes that suggested the 18th century asked.

"Can everyone hear me?" With surprised looks, there were nods and yeses heard. I launched into the who, what, where, when, and why, skipping the how, since that remained a mystery. At the mention of parallel universes, the Aussie, who was named George, exclaimed, "That explains that. I thought I had my history all wrong when Isabis said Napoleon conquered all of Europe."

"Even Russia?" I asked Isabis, who nodded.

"How can we trust what you're saying?" asked a dark-skinned man, maybe sixty, with eyes that said he'd seen plenty in his life. Several others nodded their heads. There will always be skeptics, I thought, even with my mysterious gift as evidence that things weren't as "normal."

I waved my arm dramatically, and emerging from the cockpit door came Silas, all nine feet of gleaming metal and those twinkling blue eyes. Gasps were audible and more than a few backed away as he came closer, looming over the crowd. He stood at the rear of our team, a safe distance from the residents of Idolobhana. "Everyone, say hello to Silas, one of the last remaining robots built by the Architect." A few actually murmured hello, especially the children, who were more fascinated than frightened.

"Hello, everyone," he said, his metallic voice translating into easily a dozen different languages.

"Okay, I'm sold," said a man, who seemed dressed in the remains of a zoot suit, the jacket long gone in the heat, but the green-striped wool pants remained, splattered with mud.

"Have you seen any others?" Chou asked.

"The first week or two, we'd get a few stragglers who were

disoriented. Really lost. We've stabilized the last three weeks maybe. We number 126."

"Soon to be 127," a woman, small, with long blonde hair, called from the back and others near her parted, as she patted her swollen abdomen.

"Congratulations," I called. People were still amazed that they could understand me and each other.

"How can you do that?" Isabis asked.

"One of the great mysteries," I said and he nodded.

Then he broke into a grin, showing crooked teeth, and gestured at Idolobhana. "Come, let me show you what we've built."

We followed in a cluster, with a few of the villagers staying with us, as others drifted back to their work. The huts were ingeniously woven from natural materials, each holding four people, maybe five with children. The center fires had meats and vegetables on spits slowly roasting over low-burning wood. Children chased one another, and it was good to finally see children again.

As we neared the rear of the village, I saw men and boys digging while women were dampening the earth using water from woven baskets. They formed brick shapes and set each to bake in the sun. Over to one side, an animal-like shape was being carved out of similar wet dirt.

"What're these?" I asked.

"If this is to be our home," Isabis explained, "then we wanted it to look like our home. We're building animal monuments to act as a gateway, a front door if you will."

"These are like the ones I saw once in Great Zimbabwe," Bartholomew said, clearly impressed. "They designate authority."

"This is our land now, right," Isabis said.

"I suppose so," I said, the uncertainty clear, causing him to frown. "I mean, we were all brought here at once, more or less, to restart the human race. I'm not sure the plan called for separate settlements."

"But where is everyone else?"

I called Albert over, and he unrolled the map and began pointing out our journey, making certain to show the unidentified settlements between Avalon and Idolobhana. Isabis let out a slow whistle at that. "How many you say we were?"

"Nearly two billion," I said

"All on one continent?"

"Can I get back to you on that?"

"Another unanswered question?"

"One of too many," I admitted.

He called out for a woman, Mei Ling, who hurried over and paused as soon as she saw the map. The woman was delicate in appearance, her brightly colored robes starting to fade in the constant sunlight. "Where are we?" she demanded and Albert approximated it with his forefinger.

"Can we copy this?" she asked in a light voice.

"Of course. As far as I am concerned, there are no secrets," I told her and got a smile in return. As it happened, she had arrived with paper and ink, not enough to spare us any, but she rummaged and found a sheet approximately the size of the bark. We left her to copy the work and were shown where completely dried bricks were being stacked to fashion an oven.

Of course they wanted to host us for a meal, to share information, compare timelines, and just have someone new to speak with. I got it and had to fight my impatience to get back on the road.

"Ready to move on?" Wild Bill asked, coming up so quietly, I didn't hear him.

"Something like that. Sure, I wanted to make contact, but if we stop and eat everywhere we go..."

"You worried about gaining weight?" I had to look at him and catch the gleam in his eye telling me he was kidding.

"Every stop is vital, but lingering not so much," I said.

"Where I come from, you want allies, you break bread with them," he told me, and it made sense. How many deals were made over food? I had to actually put into practice all the tried and true methods I only heard about in school. Already, Isabis was treating me as the leader of a foreign land. He had been a banker and understand how corporate alliances worked. I was playing catch up.

When I stifled a yawn a few hours later, he saw it and nodded.

"You need to sleep."

"And we need to do it from the air. We have so much more territory to cover."

"Then let me tell you this, Meredith. I like what the Architect is trying to do. I like the idea that we're starting over and that I have some unfulfilled potential. I'd like to be around long enough to figure out what that is. I now know I will need allies to do that. So I am pledging you my support. We will continue to build, but with an eye on fortifications, not statuary. We'll also build, sad to say, weapons."

"They'll do little good against the nanobots," I reminded him. He was from 1866, so nanotechnology was still unfathomable to him. Thankfully, there were others from uptime that could support him.

"You've said there are more than one kind of danger."

"True enough."

"We must warn the others, the ones you haven't visited," Isabis said. "Can you or Chou or Silas tell it over again so we may write it down? I have fast runners we've used to carry messages from one end of Idolobhana to the next. We can outfit them with copies of the map, make contact now that we know they're out there. I have to be honest, I didn't think we were the only ones here, especially as people joined us early on. But I had no idea where here is. Everything looks and feels different."

"It is," I assured him, explaining about the lengthening day.

I asked Chou to brief Mei Ling, who seemed the most adept at taking the notes, and as they spoke, I took one more walk around the village. It was so different than the garrison at Avalon or New Manhattan, but these were now new communities, new homes and fresh beginnings. I silently repeated my pledge to the Architect to be worthy of this opportunity.

As we walked, the nightly ritual began and everyone paused, arms outstretched, smiles on their face. "Mojo time," one cried and everyone let out a ritualistic cheer. Everyone had a name for the nanobots that repaired tissue, regrew limbs, and rejuvenated one and all. I spread my arms, welcoming the wash of positive nanobots on my sore, lacerated limbs. Within minutes, I felt good as new, although the yawns kept coming.

It was then that I realized this was a moment to kiss cheeks or hug or shake hands or swap spit or something to signify the alliance. But we were different places and the rules were nonexistent. I settled for a simple "thank you" before gathering the team and heading out. As we returned to the *Brimstone*, Amelia let Bartholomew handle liftoff since she imbibed a bit too much during the feast. I was amazed at how quickly alcohol had been reintroduced in the world. When I mentioned that aloud, it was Vihaan who explained how quickly the fermentation process could work.

"Well, that was easy enough," I said once we were in the air, feeling drowsier by the moment.

"They will not always be so welcoming," Chou said.

"Especially if Abernathy has already paid them a visit."

"He is behind us, so that won't be the reason. People arrived scattered and scared, with no one like Silas to welcome them and explain the situation. They're surviving but asking more questions than the ones we've been posing."

"The Adversary really messed with your husband, didn't he?"

She nodded and brooded as I rose to go find a bunk to lie down in. The sleep was deep and peaceful, the relaxed atmosphere of Idolobhana pushing away the threats and my own fears.

As we continued across the continent, I instructed whoever was piloting that any habitat within an hour's flight off course was to be visited, without question. We needed to spread the word, make alliances, and have them ready, because if Abernathy and his icky goons were after us, they'd get to them eventually. By flying straight through the day, we were certainly gaining ground or at least maintaining our lead, which would be essential when we got to the collector. From the air, I could see the distant silhouette of others, each one dutifully added by Albert, who was delighted with his assignment. I hadn't realize how invaluable it would become.

Our second stop was possibly even more welcoming than Idolobhana. We found them about eighteen hours away, with a small series of lean-tos in neat rows before a large platform with an awning of some sort. We landed and were met by one person, a stunning, almond-eyed, older woman named Bich. She welcomed us to Mới Bắt Đầu, which meant New Beginning, and its inhabitants fell under her influence, going for a minimalist approach in the moderate temperatures as they were located at the edge of a massive lake. There were rings of trees that were old and had full foliage, providing welcome shade. Wild animal life, which delighted Albert as he rapidly named all he could spot, roamed freely.

The six dozen or so people were told by Bich, whose name translated to Jade, that they were all given a gift of life and it should not be squandered. Once they climbed out of the lake, where most had arrived, she began speaking to them about the moment. The moment of being, the moment of existing with all things in harmony. While the people came from different cultures and times, her easy acceptance of their differences apparently worked to calm their fears. Day by day, she directed the construction of minimalist structures, taking time throughout the day to rest and meditate. She directed the work, picking up bits and pieces of the varying languages, integrating them into her instructions.

She was a disciple of Buddha, a practitioner of Zen, something I never really knew much about but accepted that it was working. Everyone seemed serene when we arrived. Between the mild climate and the general vibe of community, it felt ideal, pretty much what the Architect might have expected from all of us. Which meant I had to bring evil into their lives with news from the rest of the world.

When their leader let out a loud whistle, all work stopped and people looked at Bich and then us. Wisely, I kept Silas aboard the *Brimstone* as I did before. No need to shatter their calm with a nine-foot-tall robot. I had enough bad news for them.

I spoke, as did Chou, once more outlining the problems threatening their lives. Few doubted us and Bich calmly accepted the notion of the multiverse and her attitude was replicated by the others. She nodded with approval of the Architect's plans for mankind, but her eyes darkened when I explained how those plans were upended by the Adversary. She compared it with the snake in Eden and I couldn't disagree.

What surprised me, though, was how she rejected the notion of building fortifications or training people to fight, although she admitted to having practiced judo as a youth and could be their teacher. I was running out of arguments, my tone getting shriller. Some diplomat I was going to be if it was going to be like this.

It was Albert, though, who got her attention.

"Please, ma'am," he began. "I've never seen so beautiful a place. If the Adversary's army marches through here, it will be destroyed. You will all lose your selves, becoming just pieces of a machine. I don't think that's why you're here."

"No, we are not," she said, lowering herself to meet his eyes. "But we have foresworn violence. We will not fight, but we are also not without a sense of self-preservation. We can post sentries and make plans to move out of the way." The Architect didn't even have to explain it to her; she understood what this arrival meant. Good for her.

"We need messengers, people to spread the word," Chou said.

Bich paused, considering the pros and cons of further contact with other communities. She appeared conflicted and the silence was drawing out, making me worried. Finally, she nodded her head once and said, "We can help with that should it be required."

That would have to do. There wasn't much to tour, but we walked about, meeting people, and Albert showed off the map to those who seemed interested. No one chose to copy it, preferring their isolation. I prayed it would still be here when everything was said and done.

She had found plants that could be brewed for tea and served us each. It was more bitter than I expected, but it did allow us to peacefully end the visit. On our walk back to the *Brimstone*, I mused to Michael, "What I wouldn't give for a walkie-talkie." I then heard a buzzing nearby and swatted away what I thought was a fly, only to feel the more solid frame of a robo-bug. It wasn't alone, as I then saw it was part of a small swarm. Where they'd come from, I didn't know, but it meant the Adversary was watching. Worse, he now knew of Mới Bắt Dâu.

"They're everywhere," I complained, but Vihaan carefully scooped it out of the dirt. He held it close to his eye, marveling at the construction.

Once aboard the airship, Amelia gently lifted us into the sky; she'd gotten really good at those takeoffs and landings, something Bartholomew needed to practice. Vihaan and Michael went into the rear to use the equipment available there to study the robo-bug. Once again, Chou sat next to me, her face grim.

"They will be the first to fall," she said flatly. "If they truly have renounced violence as part of their new start, they will be ill-prepared for Abernathy. Not even the pixie dust can save them."

"But they're off the course. If he's trailing, he'll make a straight line for the collector. It should save them."

She did not look convinced and I instinctively knew it myself.

Thankfully, later in the day, we had a more receptive welcome in the settlement of Llibertat, run by Elazar, a handsome man with ebony skin, maybe a little younger than me. He was from 2079, in a reality that didn't know me as president, which felt like kind of a relief. I didn't bother to ask who won instead. His name translated to Help of God and he was far more practical than Bich. They lived just within a dense forest, fashioning platforms among the thick trees, in a place that felt like the California redwoods. When we arrived, they had already begun work on weapons: bows and arrows for hunting, but those would make handy weapons, if an arrow could pierce the nanobots that coated and transformed humans into unspeakable horrors.

He was full of bravado, which the people around him

seemed to echo. They sat at the base of a tree and let Chou explain the world they had arrived in. It went on silently for several minutes until she was interrupted by an older man in the middle.

"So we kill them," he bellowed, a trace of Irish accent in his voice.

"And drink their blood," a young goth girl shouted from further back.

"No, thank you," said the motherly type beside her, getting a chuckle from the crowd.

"We will fight them, ya," Elazar said. "We will protect our new home. Tell us how."

"We're working on that," Michael said and the Irishman called out, "Work faster!"

Their machismo, which may not be the right word since men and women were in agreement, was encouraging. They might have conquered a forest, but Abernathy would be something else entirely. They already had scouts in place, keeping an eye out for the wild animals about, which apparently included predatory wolves and always hungry bears. Others among the two hundred residents had also formed exploration parties and brought back enough information that they had their own crude map of the area. Silas found more dried bark and etched a copy of their map to add to Albert's collection as he transferred the information.

"What we wouldn't give for a good laser?" Elazar said in admiration. "We could make more precise weapons."

"*I am sorry, but those do not appear to have been provided you,*" Silas told him.

"Ya, we make do with what God, or the Architect, gives us," he said with his ever-present smile. He was a man used to working with his hands, a landscaper who was in a horrible truck accident, when he was offered a chance to live.

He was standing closer to me than should be normal and I suddenly realized he was hitting on me. I was so out of practice and hadn't felt normal in so long that his behavior felt more threatening than enticing. His interest became evident as he fingered a loose lock of my hair.

"Such a vibrant color," he said, then actually sniffed it. I'd barely washed it since we left New Manhattan and I doubt it had an enticing fragrance. Still, attention without deadly intent was actually a relief.

"Can you stay longer?" he whispered in my ear. I winced, aware how close my "son" was along with Chou, who I felt frowning with disapproval.

I merely shook my head, freeing my hair from his fingers.

"Next time, ya?"

I let the question remain unanswered. If this was my future, and I survived this insane situation, then and only then could I let myself think about plans. Sure, it'd be nice to settle down with someone and start a new world together, but those were luxuries that would have to wait. My only scheduled date right now was meeting the Architect.

The visit was mostly a pleasant one, even if it meant climbing several trees to see their accommodations. It was cooler than I personally preferred, but Michael and Amelia seemed to appreciate it, while Miko and Albert were delighted to be climbing freely. The Llibertatans' work was good and precise, very secure among the thick branches, with enough limbs close enough to practically cross from one tree to the next. There were some vines used to secure the platforms and a woman was weaving a ladder with impressive dexterity. If anything, they were among the more secure places we had seen so far. No doubt, Abernathy's army could climb, but these people scampered like monkeys, practiced at climbing after a month of tree living. I'd put my money on this lot surviving.

When we left, I considered it another victory, another outpost we could rely on, and so the network was growing.

My confidence took a blow, though, at our next stop, disconcertingly named Peron, led by Sergio Pereyra, a survivor of many a revolution in Argentina during the middle of the 20th century. Pereyra, with graying and thinning hair, and clothes hanging off his body suggesting he lost his paunch, had tired eyes. He'd seen enough and didn't want to see more. There were easily over two hundred residents here, situated in an almost parallel line to a river, well stocked with fish. Construction of homes was ongoing, but they already had several low, long structures, with thatched roofs over a mix of wood and mud brick. They were serviceable if crude and certainly lacking in furniture, unlike Avalon's garrison. I heard sawing in the distance along with splashes in the river from people gathering water for cooking.

"I have seen enough war," he told me, his voice conveying the weariness.

"I don't think you will have a choice," Chou told him.

"Let the robot fight; he's big enough," Pereyra said.

"He wasn't designed to fight but will if pressed, like you must," I said.

"Must I?" he asked.

"I think you must," a woman, with steel gray hair said, coming up and sliding her arm beside his.

"I am Isabelle," she said by way of introduction. Pereyra hadn't much of the social graces beyond shaking our hands and letting Chou repeat the news of the world. Most listened and kept their own thoughts on this. Having her support seemed important as he looked at her kindly. It was nice to see people who had found not only a fresh start but even new romance.

"Why? Why fight again? I'd rather we build ping-pong tables than weapons."

"Why can't you build both?"

He brooded.

"I understand, I read about what you went through. You were one of the Disappeared, weren't you?" I asked. I'd read about them in a world history class and was horrified at the military taking hundreds of people with no warning, no explanation, and few being ever seen again.

"Si. My work for Peron made me suspect, even if I was just a clerk," Pereyra said. "I was being beaten and I was certain I was going to die in a puddle of my own blood. They never sent a doctor to check on me after their 'interrogation'. I was hemorrhaging when I was invited here."

"Then defend this, protect these people," I implored.

He leaned his head against Isabelle's and they communed in silence. Then, with a heavy sigh, he nodded. "Messengers."

"Scouts," I countered.

He nodded again.

"Weapons," Chou added.

"Must we?" he said.

"It's wisest to be prepared," his mate told him.

"Si."

After some more talk and, yes, another meal, although the fish was wonderful, we made our farewells and resumed our course in search of answers.

As we inched across the continent, the contacts continued. The pattern took hold: a wary meeting, disbelief or immediate acceptance of our situation, concern over Abernathy and the Adversary, and most pledging physical support, from runners to riders to soldiers. Silas was often confirmation we weren't making this up or they were hallucinating. We'd have to polish him after some visits, his metallic casing smudged with fingerprints or worse. Only one other community like Mới Bắt Dầu refused outright support, taking a severe isolationist stance.

Fortunately for them, they were not in what should be Abernathy's direct line. Still. I worried about them and their small yurts. We found them in an arid desert region, and they had already moved twice before. Their leader hoped the nomadic life they'd accepted would protect them.

I was gaining newfound appreciation for how large a land mass we were crossing. What was it Isabella Teresita Galindez told me a few weeks back? They'd found twenty-seven redheads in a single day and yet, redheads were only two percent of the population. I remember memorizing that fact for an elementary school report and it stuck with me. People made presumptions about me being a redhead, such as having a fiery temper or was somehow lucky. I hated being called a ginger and didn't like the idea that being a rarity made me more desirable, although stats said we had sex more often, and certainly in college, it felt that way. I did look forward to retaining this color for some time, watching it go to silver or white, not gray. While mutations like Tommy Two-Thumbs were unpleasant to look at, I was always reminded my red hair is also a mutation, hence it being so uncommon.

Back aboard the *Brimstone*, Amelia had estimated we were still several days away from our target, and then we could save the world. At that point, Wild Bill commented that this world, or at least the continent, needed a name.

"Bill, there's just the one continent," Albert said at that point.

"No, there are seven. I am sure I learned that in my younger days," he said.

"Not anymore. Did you ever hear of Pangaea?"

"Can't say that I have," he replied. Albert looked over to Chou to help explain it.

"Geologists have theorized that before the seven continents you know, the entire land mass of the world was one or maybe more super-continents that broke up over time as the tectonic plates shifted."

"What plates are those?" he asked Chou.

"Under the surface, the world rests on massive formations we call plates, and as they moved and shifted, rubbing against one another caused mountains to form or islands to sink. They're what causes the earthquakes."

"Now that's something I do know," Wild Bill said. "Never liked those tremors."

"The plates continued to shift for the last half billion years, and as our rotation has slowed, the continents were brought back together," Chou said.

"Let me see that map of yours," he asked Albert. Dutifully, the boy unfurled it and we all looked at it with new understanding.

"So you mean to say this is all seven continents now pushed together?" Bill said.

"That's right," Albert said. "Silas helped me figure some of it out." His fingers traced and showed us what had once been Africa and how Australia was now somehow part of the Japanese islands. Greenland was an odd attachment off the Canadian coast. It was one thing to consider this an altered continent, but if this was the inhabitable world, everything was so much more massive. Our trip, which seemed huge, now seemed smaller while no less urgent.

The map itself had a variety of annotations, the different communities, deserts, forests, and more biomes were labeled. Each collector, spied from a distance, was also here, totaling thirty-two, nearly 15 percent of the total. Not bad for a few days' flight.

While we were all in agreement, no one was ready to affix something so permanent as a name when it could all go away should we fail.

"I got another sighting," Amelia called out a little bit later. Albert and I headed for the cockpit and she gestured to the left and we could see it. A semicircle fence defined part of the structures, what might be wooden cabins. The nearby forest had provided the timber, but what was that mass of people doing off to one edge? It wasn't work; more like a formation.

And that was when the first bullets bounced off the ship's frame.

SIX

AMELIA WAS swift and precise in her action, getting us higher in the sky to avoid the gunfire. Had the Adversary brought an entire army here? They had guns, which not one Architect-provided group seemed to have possessed. I guess the law of averages would suggest some guns were brought over, but who thought firing first was a proper way to say hello?

I studied the group below me: two well-ordered lines of men, seemingly in uniform of some sort, taking turns aiming and firing while a stout, bearded man stood behind them, clearly giving commands.

The gun fire stopped when it was evident we were too high, but the men remained in position with others gathered behind them, forming a third then a fourth line. They were well-trained. But were they here at the Architect's invitation or the Adversary's?

"Can you land us away from the gunfire?" I asked Amelia. She nodded and flipped a few controls, angling us away, toward a flat spot far from the men and the fence.

As we descended, I figured it might be best to present ourselves as anything but a threat. We'd emerge and stay in line by the airship, letting them come to us. That would suggest we weren't aggressors and then I'd let my translation gift do its thing. No one argued, and once again, Silas would act as our trump card. I decided Bartholomew should remain aboard, in the pilot's seat, should we need to make a hasty retreat. I had already decided, maybe to convince myself more than anything else, that if the Adversary brought them here, it was to hunt me, so a settlement wouldn't make sense. However, if I thought Edward had done a fine job building the garrison at Avalon, this was larger and much more complete.

Sure enough, no sooner did we touch down than the troops were in motion, making good speed while staying in formation, and I was pleased to see the bearded man in the lead, taking charge, not cowering behind them. He had a round, full face, covered in a thick, full brown beard. He may have been stout but also fit, as there was little jiggle to his torso as he trotted forward. He acted like a man in control with dark eyes and a serious expression. He held up a fist and let out a sound I couldn't actually translate, more of a guttural "hunh," but the men and women stopped in place. Those with rifles had them at the ready but weren't aiming at us. His troops, I could now see, had all used some berry juice to dye their tops a grape-jelly color to simulate uniforms. The people, judging from their hair styles, ranged across the years, but all were in their twenties to forties, many with sun-tanned faces long before they got here. One had a long scar across a cheek, another was missing part of an ear. But they shared a determined look, awaiting a command.

The bearded man took one step forward, so I matched him. That caught his attention with some surprise, because he had been looking at Michael. Then Wild Bill took a step behind me; my protection detail.

"What do you want?" His voice was deep, used to command, and had an accent I couldn't place.

So many answers to that one. For this to be over, a Nathan's hot dog, a hot bath. For someone else to be in charge...

"We come in peace," I said, sounding like an alien making first contact with humanity. Depending on his era, I just might strike him as otherworldly.

His eyes went wide, as did most everyone else's when we first met. "You speak Turkish?"

"Not really," I said and explained about my unique talent. He eyed me suspiciously as a result, but then I ignored that and introduced my people.

In return, he identified himself as Osman Nuri, and when his name didn't register, he said with pride, "Pasha of the Ottoman Empire, and somehow here with all these people." Okay, I remembered the Ottoman Empire as long gone by my day, but a powerful force in the Middle East and Asia, gone by World War I – I think.

"Me too. I have some information you may want to hear. After that, I have need of your help." As I said all along, if I was going to face Abernathy's army, I would need one of my own. The Pasha seemed to have one already in training. His expression altered when I said I needed his help; appealing to his pride seemed to be useful.

"Come to my Kale," he said of his community, which was indeed a stronghold.

"Wait, I have one more thing to show you, to help convince you that what we are here to explain is the truth." I gave a practiced gesture and both Silas and Bartholomew emerged. If the Pasha's eyes went wide at my translation, they went wider for a moment at the sight of the nine-foot-tall robot. But that lasted for a second, and I could see the eyes switch to calculation, assessing the dangers Silas represented and if he could be stopped by his forces. This was a military man, the kind of commander I wanted Bill to be. This Osman Nuri could well be the final piece I needed. I made the final introductions and then gestured for him to lead the way.

As we entered the stronghold, as the word translated, I marveled at how much he and his people had accomplished. It didn't hurt that there had to be nearly three hundred, the most I'd see in one place. But there was no meandering about, no easy pace to the work as I saw in New Manhattan and elsewhere. No, these people were working hard, following directives that must have come from the Pasha, who exuded authority. I even heard the neighing of horses, and as part of the tour, we saw a rough corral, where three people were working with horses, breaking them from the looks of it. Structures included homes and a barn where I heard other horses. There was a hen house of some sort, and large turkeys were wandering free nearby. This was rapidly transforming itself into a small city. The boxy grid pattern to the structures was orderly, each cabin with some sort of outhouse in a straight line behind them. One building had great plumes of smoke emerging, which had to be the cookhouse, strategically placed near the animals.

Osman was taking great pride in showing what they had accomplished in the month they had been here. He quickly assumed control of the people after the startling arrival from three hundred separate near-death experiences. His mastery of multiple languages allowed him to find a network of translators so everyone could be heard and he could be understood. His bearing and experience made him a natural, and within forty-eight hours of their arrival, trees were being felled and calisthenics were required at the start of each day. Once everyone's skill set was determined, he set about work details, sketching in the dirt his plans for the stronghold.

"Why so much emphasis on defense?" Michael asked.

"No one recognized where we were or what was happening," Osman said. "There was fear and uncertainty, but I was convinced we could not be the last humans alive. Until we knew more, it made perfect sense to protect ourselves. The Ottoman Empire had many enemies surrounding us at all times, so fortifications were, of course, a priority."

There was no doubt he was the right man to help us, but he was so accustomed to command that I worried already. We needed a defense until the mission was accomplished and he saw everything in military terms. At one point during the tour, I leaned over to Albert and asked in a whisper, "Do you know this man?"

He shook his head, whispering back, "I really like plants and animals, never bothered to memorize as much history."

"So much for my personal Google," I murmured.

"You keep calling me that. What is it?"

"Later." I focused on the Pasha, noticing he had bothered to learn everyone's names, having already memorized ours. He asked questions, answered them from his workers, and exchanged short pleasantries with all. The people were visibly deferential and Osman seemed to enjoy it all. He definitely was paying more attention to Wild Bill, Michael, Miko, Vihaan, and Bartholomew than Amelia, Chou, or me. A product of his era, sadly. Interestingly, he never spoke to Silas, who took up his accustomed position in the rear.

During our walk, when he wasn't talking and showing off, we'd begin filling him in. When we got to the part of about parallel universes, he stopped in his tracks. Time travel didn't seem to bother him and he took readily to the idea since it explained so much. He asked it be repeated for him, so Michael tried to refine what Chou had said. Finally, he nodded.

"So, in some other reality, I bested the Russians," he said, mostly to himself.

"What do you mean?" prompted Vihaan.

"It was 1877 and we had recently defeated the Serbians,

who had proclaimed their independence then waged war on us. In April, Russia decided it was their turn, crossing the Danube River and entering through Bulgaria. I was assigned to defend the Nikopol fortress, given 15,000 men and 174 cannons, but the Russians, damn their eyes, the city fell in July before I could arrive.

"They were heading for Constantinople, crossing the Balkans, so I moved my men south and met them in battle at Plevan. They ran home to their mothers and we dug in before they could return. I was right and they returned on the 30th. By then, we were fortified and I had reinforcements, so we met them in battle. It was there, in my headquarters, a cannonball crushed the roof and I was buried in debris. I was dying when I was spoken to. I thought it was God welcoming me to heaven." He stopped and barked a laugh. "Instead, I'm here."

We were invited for another meal, a grand feast, for they had caught several deer in the nearby woods. I could already smell the roasting meat and realized we had skipped lunch. Likely, they would eat before sundown since there was scant evening light available. It would be there that I intended to outline our needs.

Like other settlements, alcohol had already been made and this was a tangy mixture I couldn't identify. They were short on anything resembling utensils, so we got our fingers dirty with the greasy, but delicious, game and root vegetables. He boasted of other military exploits in his colorful career, but seemed to confine his comments to the men, barely sweeping his eyes over us. I was doing a slow burn over that, while the blatant sexism didn't bother Amelia, who grew up with it, and Chou, who chose to ignore it.

"What do you call this drink?" Miko asked.

"Tanrıların nektarı," Osman said with pride.

"Nectar of the gods?" I said with a laugh. The Pasha

frowned at this. "I mean, it's very good, but it's not the best liquor I've had."

"I miss whiskey," Wild Bill said.

"Oh, I'm sure we'll get back to making it," Michael assured him.

"Give me an Old-fashioned," Miko said. "Sweet and it goes down so easily."

"You know, before spirits, man developed beer," Bartholomew said and began to lecture on its history, although only Albert seemed interested. The others began chatting about other things, taking their minds off their favorite luxuries. We'd invent new ones, I was sure, just as soon as we got a few more things accomplished.

Finally, I spoke up, as he completed a tale of how he stopped Yusuf Ekrem in Syria, establishing himself as a fixer of problems. "That's what we need," I interrupted.

His eyes made their way to me and he licked his grease-stained lips.

"I told you how we have to stop the Adversary," I continued.

"Your unseen mechanical enemy."

"That's our belief. Like the Architect, even like Silas, we think he is an artificial construct, a powerful, malevolent machine."

"Blow it up," Osman said and some of his followers laughed.

"We have no bombs, nor do you, I see. Once we see the Adversary, we'll know how to stop him. But we have a different kind of mechanical army coming after us."

"Men?"

"Men, women, and children have been taken over by the machines," I said, trying to simplify things for a 19th Century soldier. Shrewd on the battlefield he might be, but his scientific interest seemed to end with weapons. "They stopped being human and now act on behalf of the Adversary. I need an army to fight them, hold them at bay, while we," and I paused to gesture at my IMF team, "fight the Adversary directly."

"How big is this army?"

"I estimate over a thousand strong," Chou said.

"We are but three hundred and not everyone here is a fighter. I don't like the odds," Osman said. "And if they're machines, that gives them an advantage."

"You wouldn't believe how much of one," I said.

He waved a hand before his face, trying to swat a fly. His expression seemed dubious, although his eyes blazed at the idea of a fight, finishing one here that he could not finish in his time.

"We have been recruiting help," I said. "Albert."

Dutifully, Albert arrived with the map at the ready. He unrolled it and began explaining the highlights to Osman, whose eyes narrowed as he seemed to be absorbing every bit of information, trying to memorize the details in a glance.

"Did you make this?" he asked the boy.

"Silas helped, but I've been adding to it every day," he said with pride. That earned him a chuckle and ruffle of his hair from stained, slick fingers.

"Most are willing to send people to help, others will only act as messengers. But, with your horses, we can be in touch with each community faster than I had hoped," I told Osman.

"Where did you last see this Abernathy?"

I studied the map and showed him New Manhattan. "That was a week or more back," I said.

"How fast do these machine people travel?"

"The few times we saw them, they appeared to be no faster than your average human," Chou allowed.

"So, twenty miles a day or so? You should have quite the lead on them," the Pasha said.

"If they paused to sleep and eat," I said. "There's no

evidence they need either, so we're estimating closer to sixty miles a day."

"Sixty, on foot? What powers them, then?"

"We have surmised that the tiny machines that infest the bodies convert the organic matter into energy," Chou said.

"And what happens when they run out of organic matter?"

Chou looked over to Silas, who had been silently watching the exchange. "I do not know." More information he didn't need to know and had no access to.

Osman swatted another fly as he studied the map. His eyes went from to side to side, his mind turning over the variables as he understood them.

"Humanity was given a second chance," Michael said. "We have to protect that chance and it seems we cannot do it without you."

"I would agree, since your Architect has not seen fit to send many soldiers," Osman said.

"Well, you haven't met all two billion of us yet," Wild Bill said, a twinkle in those eyes of his. "I'd wager there are more than a few who know their way around a rifle. Where'd you get all your weapons?"

"They were here, with us," Osman said as if it was an odd question.

"Got much ammunition?"

"No, and I bet we'll use it all on this army and that will leave Kale vulnerable."

"To what?" I asked.

"To whoever comes marching through next, wanting our land or animals," Osman said matter-of-factly.

I shook my head at his mindset. I had so hoped we'd grow out of it, but not yet apparently. "You don't get it, yet?"

"Get what?"

"My...Michael said we have a second chance. Our fresh

start and maybe this time we can do it without territorial disputes."

His eyes showed that he didn't agree, but rather than argue, he held his tongue. "A discussion for another day," he finally said. "You will have runners, and we will have an army. We will face this Abernathy so you can do whatever must be done."

He picked up his wooden cup, which had been miraculously refilled by someone when we weren't watching, and he drained it in one long pull. Then he swiftly slammed it down, crushing an insect. At the last second, I recognized it as one of the Adversary's robo-bugs.

He knows where we are.

PART TWO

We are what we pretend to be, so we must be careful about
what we pretend to be.
–*Kurt Vonnegut*

SEVEN

THE FOLLOWING MORNING, we got to work. While several of us stayed aboard the *Brimstone*, a few of us stayed within the Kale. Osman couldn't have been more gracious, but he fussed more over Michael, Vihaan, and Bartholomew than anyone else. Wild Bill, being a fellow gunman, got extra attention, much to Bill's discomfort. He seemed to tolerate Albert, even though he had the best command of the map and its intelligence. That nectar of the gods packed enough of a punch, that I went to bed buzzed and now felt slightly hungover. By the time I emerged from the airship, the Pasha informed me that he had already dispatched two riders to make contact with the nearest settlements and begin the process of building an army. I had to give him credit for taking decisive action.

After we breakfasted, with some very weak tea that made me seriously miss coffee, Osman addressed the assembled community. In brusque terms, he detailed the facts and the threat. He insisted that at least a third accompany us to the collector, and a third remain to fortify the Kale. The remainder would decide for themselves, whether to act as messengers or weapons makers or soldiers. His voice was strong, and as I stood by him, the translation washed over everyone with ease. The full gamut of reactions could be read on their faces and my heart went out to them; just as they were settling, now the new home was imperiled.

It was agreed that the riders would be in constant rotation and motion. Wild Bill told Osman how it would work, using his own experiences with the Pony Express back in his time. The name stuck, which pleased me. Copies of the map were created that morning as horses were readied and a party went out to secure and break more.

"Ah, to have a cavalry once more," the Turkish military man mused as the riders left later. "In time, I suppose."

In time, I had hope, we wouldn't need a cavalry of any sort, but kept that to myself. He busied himself with his people, so I took the time to help a few of the people finish work on a new building. It was as much to do something with my hands than fret over the time ticking and Abernathy's impending approach. I was concerned about the robot-bugs last night and wished there was something that could be done about them. Vihaan had remained on the *Brimstone* most of the day, studying the one we caught intact.

Late in the day, as the selected soldiers finished drilling in formation, which Osman told me would be as much for discipline as it was for order, there was a cry from a sentry. I feared the army had arrived, so I hurried with the Pasha to the fencing and saw it was a lone figure, a rider on a white horse. Since Osman had no white horses, this was cause for suspicion. This man was riding bareback, using some sort of rope or vine for a harness. The horse seemed fatigued, the rider increasingly animated as he drew closer, an arm waving in greeting. He was Asian, with black hair, a flat face, and high cheekbones, looking maybe twenty. His clothing was nondescript, with a torn sleeve and either blood or mud caking his shoes.

Osman had the guards keep watching, with several holding drawn knives but I instinctively knew this was a not a threat.

"Red hair...it's you, Meredith..." he panted as he dismounted.

"Get the horse to water," Osman instructed as the man drew close.

"Yes, I'm Meredith."

"Somtow," he said, head bopping in greeting. "I've come from Peron. Sergio Pereyra says the army is coming."

My fears made manifest. He was getting closer with every hour we were stationary, but this could not be helped. Not here, not now.

"Tell me," I said, a reassuring hand on his arm.

"We got word from Llibertat that the black army had been seen in the distance. They knew you were on your way to Peron, so they sent a runner, a runner on his feet, to warn us. And Pereya sent me ahead to warn you."

Osman frowned at this. "Where's that damned map?" he growled. "Find me Albert."

"Has Pereyra warned anyone else?"

The head bopped once more. "He sent runners in all directions, following the map. He has also sent two dozen soldiers to join up with you. They're a day or so behind me."

Shit's become real, I thought. *I am building an army and they will be protecting us, which means people will be dying – on my behalf.* That freaked me out and I was lost in thought, considering these terrible, unasked for consequences, when Osman's voice grew louder, breaking the spell.

"This is not ideal, but it's been done before," he said. "We can work this in stages." His next words were interrupted by Albert's arrival with the map. The worn bark was unrolled and Somtow traced his finger, showing where he had traveled, where he lost half a day making a wrong turn, and where the runners had gone. Several had been dispatched to places we saw only from the sky and hadn't stopped to visit. Would they send help or remain isolationist? How many would come to fight and die for a vague idea of freedom?

"Prepare to depart," Osman ordered me. I gaped, but he cut me off. "You need to be in the air – ah, to have a chance to fly – and put distance between here and your destination. We will march tonight."

"How will we communicate?" I asked.

"Your ship will land at sundown each day, giving us a chance to catch up. Ah, what I wouldn't give for wagons. Each night, we will review and make adjustments. I will leave a small force here to guide whoever arrives from the other places. Riders will continue to carry news."

He had already devised a battle plan and a strategy, which was impressive. Less impressive was his ordering me around. I came in search of a general to work with, not serve. But he was right about one thing: the sooner we got in the air, the better.

"Albert, round everyone up. Refill the canteens and tell Amelia to power up the *Brimstone*." He threw me a salute and rushed off, earning him a pleased harrumph from Osman.

Somtow continued to address me, which I could see made my commander bristle, but it would have to do. "How can I help?"

"Rest here, tend to your horse, join us when you feel ready or go home," I told him. "It's entirely your choice."

He considered that and replied, "You say you need help to save us all, right?"

"Something like that, yes."

"Then I will join the army and march after you." There was a youthful bravado in the voice despite its weariness. It sounded like me in my undergrad days, fervent about whatever cause caught my fancy.

Osman gestured to the largest building. "There's food there. Eat, rest, and let the starstuff do its work. Then we'll put you back to work." He paused. "Well done, Somtow."

The words from the Turkish Pasha seemed to energize Somtow and he straightened a bit, nodded, and walked off.

It wasn't that much later that I too walked off, away from the Kale and aboard the *Brimstone*. Osman came to see us off, craning his head to study the technology that he had never dreamed could be possible. His day was decades before flight and clearly hot air balloons hadn't been part of his military experience. Michael offered to show him around, but Osman declared himself too busy, bade us good fortune, and hurried away.

"I actually think this spooked him," Michael said as we closed the hatch.

"He is a man out of time, holding on to what he knows, which is war," Chou said. "He's forty-five and has been fighting his entire adult life. He sees this and recognizes it as a threat he cannot hope to defeat."

We took off and made good time, as the Kale dwindled behind us. Chou and Albert went over the map, estimating our daily itinerary. Inwardly, I chafed at the idea we'd be stopping for eight or ten hours a day, but it was necessary. Before we left, Silas helped us select sizeable stones that had been unearthed during the Kale's construction. Albert happily smeared each stone with berry juice, staining his hands and pants in the process. Each hour, a stone would be dropped from the airship, marking our path, helping guide Osman's force.

"Do we stop for any more towns?" Amelia asked. She gestured to the right at what appeared to be a small cluster of huts and a central fire, smoking lazily, moving upward.

"Not now," I said. Before leaving, I told Osman he needed to send a rider to each town with the news, warning, and request. A lot to process in a short time, but it had to be done. I couldn't live with myself knowing a thousand-strong army could descend on them with no warning. There was a part of myself that preferred we remain the target and that Abernathy wouldn't deviate from his course. We'd know soon enough, I supposed.

"Are you certain?" Vihaan asked.

"It has to be done," I said, although I was feeling a twinge of second-guessing myself. I moved to just behind Amelia and said softly, "Right?"

"The most difficult thing is the decision to act. The rest is merely tenacity." Amelia told me. "You strike me as tenacious enough. You got us this far. You've made a decision, so let's stick with it."

Yeah, I needed to have more conviction, but I've never faced anything with such consequence. People kept seeing the more adult me, not the real person, a struggling twenty-seven-year-old who didn't ask for any of this. But, I told myself, I did accept the offer for a second chance. That was also a decision to act, so now I had to see it through, which meant forging ahead.

Tension was palpable aboard the *Brimstone,* so Chou took me to the rear to continue training me, forcing me to get better with the scimitar. Wild Bill watched, his eyes rarely leaving my blade, assessing and silently judging me. Vihaan and Michael were huddled together over the now-disassembled nanobot but didn't say anything to us, speaking in a jargon even my translating skills couldn't always parse. That's what I get for going to law school, I suppose. Miko took one of the ship's tablets and was doing something with the stars, studying the night sky with incredible intensity. Miko remained focused on the tablet and the map. Bartholomew and Albert were playing a makeshift version of checkers, so at least we had ways to stay occupied and not go crazy with what ifs.

On the second day, we touched down by a lake and I let everyone dive in to refresh themselves. Such luxuries would be harder to come by in the coming days. Whereas Chou had little modesty, running in without her clothes, most of the others were more circumspect, wading in with some of their clothes on. I got down to my underwear and joined in, a diminishing bar of soap in my hand. Once I finished with it, I tossed it to Albert and the talisman of our collective past continued its rounds. Chou was brief and efficient with it then resumed doing laps, training to stay in combat-ready shape, ever the security officer. Just floating was nice and I lingered despite the rising chill as the sun was setting.

As I emerged from the lake, wishing desperately for a thick towel, the first rider from the troops arrived on a panting horse. He gaped at me in my bra and panties, someone clearly unaccustomed to seeing a woman like this, and I willed myself to stand straight and not be embarrassed. After all, I was developing a toned, buff body, so I should be proud.

"The others are maybe an hour away," he told me and then looked away, moving his horse to the edge for a drink.

"Thank you. Jump in if you want," I said, then, bravado rapidly fading, hurried to the ship for clothes. I wished I had more than the one outfit, something to worry about later, but I was getting tired of the clothes I'd worn since "borrowing" them from the *Titanic*.

As promised, Osman, astride a big, coal-black horse, led his forces, easily over a hundred strong, to the airship. By then, I was dry and clothed, ready to receive my general. We'd already started a fire and had gathered fruit from the trees that had grown near the edge. It was only berries but would have to do. I knew he'd brought whatever provisions the Kale could spare, hunting and gathering along the trail. From the air, we'd seen packs of horses, deer, even beavers building a dam on a river. No doubt, several had already been caught, killed, skinned, and turned into jerky or whatever they ate while marching.

"Pasha," I said, using his honorific to show respect. "I am happy to see you and the others. Let them use the lake while we talk."

Osman nodded gravely then over his shoulder shouted orders that, thankfully, were easily understood for the first few rows of haggard-looking men. The marching had been hard on them already, so all that drilling no doubt helped ready them. What would they be like when it came time to fight? He was already looking grave, which I took to be a bad sign.

Without preamble, he said, "The army is making up ground; two days behind us is my best guess." That was not good at all. We had nearly a week to go before reaching the collector, so by the end, it would be a real race if he continued to make up time.

"What news from the Pony Express?"

"The word is spreading and most everyone is sending men... and women, anyone willing to fight for our world," he said. "We told them to look for the marker rocks and our trail, although that tells Abernathy the same information."

"It can't be helped. Do we have new allies, new villages we've contacted?"

"Yes, yes, when Albert's here, one of my men can help him update the map." He paused, then turned and snapped out more orders to those who didn't immediately head for the lake. He was perspiring despite the cooling air and looked worn but refused to yield, ever the leader.

Later, he had gone to the lake, splashing water on his face and down the collar of his shirt. His men had added fresh venison to the fire, so it was roasting slowly. While his generation lived on meat, I was longing for vegetables, even a salad. Osman toured his men, offering reassurances, comforting the really tired, and spoke to several about caring for the horses.

When he finished his rounds, he returned to the fire, settling next to Wild Bill and Bartholomew. Chou gave me a quizzical look, unaccustomed to the blatant slight, but I shrugged and resumed my own meandering walk, with Silas and Michael. I was still trying to get comfortable around my son.

"He's everything I heard about the military," Michael mused.

"Oh, come on, there have to be armies in your time," I said.

"There are. But he's from such a different era. As I recall, the Ottoman Empire lasted as long as it did thanks to the strength of their army and men like Osman. They lived for war, constantly battling one another for territory. In my world, the armies were small, more like rapid deployment squads based around the world. There were still border skirmishes, especially with rogue states, but we didn't need all the fire power and bluster." Some fire power would actually be wonderful, given what was following us.

"Sounds great, almost ideal. In this world, I would prefer no army at all. Sharing the resources would immediately deprive people from warring over them."

He looked at me, his eyes serious and dark in the dim light. "You've given this a lot of thought, haven't you?"

"I remember why we're here, what the Architect's goals are for mankind. Once the Adversary is handled, I don't want borders, no imaginary dotted lines on maps, no fighting for land or water."

"You want a utopia," he teased me. "Those plans never work. I've read the books."

"Look, I know I'm being idealistic and maybe unrealistic. But this fresh start means we can learn from history, not repeat it, and do better."

"We can do better," he repeated.

"What about it?"

100 PAUL ANTONY JONES & ROBERT GREENBERGER

"It was your campaign slogan for your second term," he said. "You made clear you weren't satisfied with the job in the first term and told the voters you wanted to do better, making them want to do better. You actually took forty-eight states in a rout."

"Really?"

"Can't lie to my mother, can I?" he said and I know he was teasing and I know he was well aware we're only dimensionally-related, but it made my heart flutter a moment.

"This is weird, isn't it?" I asked.

"Damn straight," he replied and I laughed. "It's like I'm getting to watch you become the woman I know, the one who did so much for me and then the nation. I've missed that version of you."

"What happened?"

"A combination of old age and a pandemic. You had the loveliest state funeral. I even got to walk with your casket."

I had to ask. "What about my...your father?"

"Dad was there, right beside me. He lasted a few more years, but never got over losing you. He was a little lost without you there. He finally died about fifteen years before...well, before I was here.

"That was another reality, a world that is probably facing its own false vacuum event. It makes me glad I'm here, and to see you again."

"But I'm not your mother, and I am not a president. I'm an ex-addict making the best of a crappy hand I've been dealt."

Michael shook his head, disagreement on his face. "It may feel like that right now, but look at what you've accomplished so far. The Adversary scattered us intentionally, but with each contact, you're undoing that. We're reconnecting and together. That should mean something."

He'd thought about this too, and was right, of course. I was so focused on the next step, the next decision, that I hadn't paused to reflect on what had happened. I dwelt so much on the errors, the choices that should have gone differently. The life I took.

He put his hand in mine and I squeezed it once as we walked.

The next day was uneventful; as we flew, scouting for rivers, lakes, animal life, and signs of civilization, Osman marched, and we met up. The forces had swelled as more groups – squads? – joined up. His army had just about doubled, and once the troops stopped marching and ate, Osman had them drill together, forging the rag-tag men and women into a unified whole. I sat watching, impressed at his skill, his natural ability to command, admiring it, wishing I had some of that. I stayed close to silently lend my talents to make his job easier. Every night, the starstuff, or pixie dust, revitalized the troops, readying them for the next day, so we at least had that in our favor. Osman used that to his advantage, pushing them hard each and every day.

Albert and Silas took all the new information and the bark map was getting crowded. One of the newly arrived men had brought me a gift from his village. It was a roll of paper and some pens. It felt like Christmas having this, and Albert gleefully went to work. He and Silas carefully copied over the shape of the continent, but before they filled in the details, Albert came to me.

"We should use a scale," he said.

"Okay."

"Metric or Imperial?"

"Metric versus..." And it hit me. Americans used the Imperial system for feet, inches, and pounds. Was there even a choice? Growing up, there was always talk of adopting the metric system for uniformity, but it never happened. Now we could set the standard for a world since this map was the key, even if it meant who knows how many of us would have to learn to convert inches to millimeters and so on. Scientists, even in America, used metric; it had to be that.

"Metric," I said definitively.

"Righty-oh," he said happily and scampered off. Hours later, he and Silas returned, with a far more sophisticated-looking map. In his delicate hand, the names of each community were listed, our path a series of red dotted lines. His penmanship was a reminder that he came from an earlier time, where such things were required. Me, I was a whiz with my thumbs, my hand-writing okay, but nothing like his. The lakes, mountain ranges, and forests were identified but unnamed, as were the large islands similar to Avalon. Silas' memory actually had the numbering for the various collectors and we were up to 78 of the 218 identified and named.

Amelia stood over my shoulder and admired the newly revised map. She traced a finger from our lake to the destination. "Looks to me we have three or four days to go."

"Make it four; we don't need a worn-out army," I said. My pilot nodded and began planning the next day's flight as I sought out Osman to bring him up to speed. He remained stiff and formal with me, clearly uncomfortable with a woman as his ostensible leader.

"Four days," he repeated.

"Can your men manage?"

"They must," he said. "You continue to chart the path and we will keep Abernathy at bay," he said.

"You can't forget, he is a machine. He won't rust in the rain, he seems to have inexhaustible energy, and if he touches a soldier, they're as good as dead," I said.

"So you've told me already. I don't forget vital intelligence," he said. "They have been warned, and they are training to protect one another. We're doing this without armaments, minimal ammunition, and nothing to protect ourselves with. We don't even have Roman shields. If I had a few days and a forest, we could fashion more weapons and defenses."

"We don't have more time!" I said more loudly than I intended. It attracted attention when I meant this to be private. "Every day you stand still, Abernathy comes closer."

"I am well aware," he said coldly.

"You think I want to risk their lives like this? It's certainly why the Architect brought you and them forward. They each deserve their second chances, same as everyone else."

"It's war and people die in battle," Osman said. "It has always been that way."

"That wasn't the plan for here and now! Sure, in your day, you measured glory by the body count. But here, there wasn't supposed to be war."

"Conflict is part of human nature, Meredith," he said. "It's how we were born. Look to your history. There has been conflict in every culture's history. Some wars were fought for lands. Some for wealth. Some because of praying to different god. But aggression is born within us, so it takes discipline to answer our better angels and choose when to fight and when to offer an open hand. If I were to face Abernathy, would he take my hand?"

"He'd swallow you whole," I said softly.

"So we must fight. But I know your country, Meredith. Less than a century before my time, your ancestors fought for something other than land or wealth. They fought for an idea and I don't know of anyone else who did that. Your country showed us there might be another way. You even survived a civil war that would have torn other countries in two. If you hail from such a people, it makes sense you are fighting for the Architect's ideal world. It is I, I think, who will have to adapt."

Many of the troops came near us, openly watching the exchange, staring more at me since I was translating. He shot them a warning look, but I countermanded it with a gesture and they stayed, which irritated him.

"Without you..." I began.

"You can't save the world," he finished, irritated once more at being reminded and I felt silly. At least I hadn't told him about the field failing, since that would have blown his mind. That vital piece of quantum physics was left out of the explanations, since it could detract from the core mission of stopping the Adversary. By doing that, I thought it would buy us time.

"Madame President?" a woman said from the back of the crowd.

Osman cocked an eye at me.

"Not yet," I called out. As there was a murmur, I looked steadily at Osman. "Pasha, in several of these parallel realities, it appears that when I am older, I will be elected President of the United States."

"A woman?" he said in awe.

"You were alive when Victoria ruled England, so why can't I be president?" I asked, some humor in my voice.

He had no answer for me.

"Madame President, what happens after you reach your target?" She meant the collector and restoring the power network. She appeared to be in Puritan garb, black and white clothing, a white bonnet protecting her head. For a woman like her, everything we'd talked about must have sounded too fantastical to believe.

"What happens? We will have that conversation together. All of us," I said, my voice rising. "Once we defeat the enemy, every man and woman will have a say." There were scoffing sounds and skeptical looks, others nodding in agreement.

"You know, a large percentage of the people we've encountered so far come from times and places where they answered to a king, queen, dictator, or some other authority. Few had a say, so what you're suggesting sounds like a fantasy, much like parallel worlds," Chou said, coming to my side.

"Good thing none hail from a time when a watery tart threw a sword at you," I said with a grin. She gave me such a perplexed look that I laughed out loud, changing the mood in an instant.

And so it went for the next several days without significant incident. Then came the night before we anticipated reaching the collector, which was already looming into view, suggesting its massive size. We had all gathered around the fire, the troops singing and horsing around as Osman joined me and the others for additional strategizing. It had been raining, which made the terrain challenging. Our general suggested they slow a bit and confront Abernathy away from the mountains that ringed the collector. We debated the cover the mountains and hills would provide versus a confrontation on the flat, exposed ground we were currently on.

We hadn't concluded anything when the night sentries announced an arriving messenger. One had already arrived earlier with positive news as more forces were on their way, taking routes to avoid Abernathy. This man, though, was bleeding profusely, his clothes soaked black with his blood. Several rushed to the horse to steady it as two others grabbed the rider, an older man with snow white hair against his dark skin.

"Mer-meredith," he whispered.

"Water! Blankets!" Osman shouted.

I rushed for the figure, taking his slick hand in mind. "I'm here."

"Abernathy...his army is a day away. They've grown...towns destroyed..."

"Towns? Which ones?"

He named one I didn't recognize then said Mới Bắt Dầu, which made my heart sink. I knew it. I warned Bich, but she refused to listen, which was her choice. But it meant all those gentle people, the ones who turned against violence, were now part of an army bent on that very thing. Flying about his head was another of those damned robo-bugs. I swung and missed.

The rider was carried off to be tended to, although we had no blood supplies or ability to transfuse him as I feared he needed. Could he hold on until the night's sky filled with color?

As I learned before taking off in the morning, he barely made it, and even with the nanobots' help, he was weak. He'd come that close to death, a death in my name. I carried that thought with me as we ascended into the morning sky, the cloudy day promising rain. Amelia would need instruments to determine her course as the darkening mountains and gleaming collector were directly ahead, already beginning to fill the cockpit windows. In the gray morning sky, the mountains were draped with foreboding.

The next two hours were easy, quiet ones. I had my morning tutorial with Chou, who was finally starting to be satisfied with my progress. Bartholomew and Michael were taking turns telling stories to Albert, who was greedily soaking up information about what could have been his future had he survived the boarding school fire in 1910. He'd have likely served in World War I and had he survived that, would be around the Blitz, by then raising his own family. Instead, he was 12 with a bright new world awaiting him, if we could be successful.

Silas was the first to raise the alarm. *"Amelia, there is something in the air,"* he said. I then heard it too, a buzzing of some sort, and at first, I thought it might be a swarm of robo-bugs, but we were too high for them.

That was when the first bullets struck the airship.

Amelia tried to maneuver us away from the attacker, banking hard, and throwing some of us against the walls. As I tumbled to my knees, I looked out a port window and cursed loudly.

"What is it?" Wild Bill asked, amazed at the sight. We were both staring at an oncoming red biplane, the kind flown during World War I. Funny, I had just been musing about that time. The plane was a single propellered rectangular box, with wings above and below the fuselage. The nose and tail were white, while the wings and body were cherry red. There were black crosses on the top wings, on the body toward the rear, and the tail. These plus-signs indicated this was a German war plane. And the red was the tipoff.

"Holy shit, it's the Red Baron!" I exclaimed.

"You have got to be kidding me," Amelia shouted from the front, frantically trying to evade the oncoming approach. Its twin machine guns sparked in the gray sky, and moments later, I heard the impacts. As he grew closer, the reverberations increased. The *Brimstone* had no armory. The tasers Abernathy's men used on me and Freuchen were still here, but how on Earth could they help?

"The red what now?"

"He's nicknamed the Red Baron, the most celebrated German fighter pilot during the first World War," I said, still peeking out the window. All I could remember was Snoopy imitating a Yankee fighter pilot in constant combat with the Red Baron, but damned if I could remember his real name or much about him. What was it with the Adversary and German attackers? At least the Red Baroness, Isabella Teresita Galindez, wasn't German, just inspired by the man trying to kill us.

"First?" Wild Bill asked, some surprise in his voice.

"He's Manfred von Richthofen," Amelia called. "A truly great pilot, and he's seriously strafing us. Sooner or later, he's going to damage the solar batteries or the helium bladders."

I wanted to say something encouraging, but how could I? I didn't know aerial combat; I didn't know how to fight a trained killer of the skies. This was Amelia Earhart's world, sort of; she was an explorer not a fighter. The best I could do was stay quiet and let her fly us to safety, if that was even possible.

He swung by the airship again, firing rapidly and then looped beneath us. A red light blazed in the pilothouse and I heard Amelia curse. We then rocked back and forth.

"He's hit one of the compartments. It's collapsed!" she cried.

When Chou sliced all four helium compartments to free me and Freuchen, there was an engineering team to do the repairs. The best we had was Michael and Vihaan, yet neither were exactly mechanical engineers. Still, they had rushed to the upper compartments to try and do something. The compartments were designed as a failsafe to keep us aloft, but this was not reassuring as long as the Red Baron continued firing on us.

As he looped around again, Wild Bill pulled out the Luger, having learned it was deadlier than his trusty six-gun, and headed for a port window. With steely nerves, he flipped it open and waited. He was tracking the biplane by sound, his hands and gun steady. It swooped down from above, coming through the thickening, gray clouds, a rumble of thunder now in the distance. The German war hero flew closer to us and Bill took aim, then squeezed the trigger once. The crack of the gun was loud enough to momentarily drown out the plane's approach.

"Well, shit," he said, evidently having missed his moving target. He rose and moved off, leaving me along to watch the attack. I wanted to suggest the machine gun, but we had no real way to mount it in time. Bill hadn't even trained with it, trying to preserve ammunition.

The Red Baron was luckier, hitting a second compartment, and the shrill alarms were louder, along with Amelia's curses. The ship began tilting, tipping us over to the right, as Amelia tried to level us off, but failing at it.

He flew into the clouds but his engine was distinct, even

through the alarm, which was screaming at us. Amelia told it to shut up.

"He gets a third one, we're definitely going down," she called over her shoulder. Her look was grim and determined, as if sheer will would keep us in the sky. With the biplane buzzing us, I wasn't sure that was the best place for us to be.

Aware we had no weapons to fire at him, he boldly next appeared straight ahead, an aerial game of chicken that his nimbler plane would win. The guns fired once more and a new alarm replaced the other one, so we must have been critically hit.

He wanted us down and was giving us no choice, because my stomach dropped along with the *Brimstone*. "Can you land us?" I cried, not daring to move.

"Trying," was all she said. There might have been other things the computerized pilothouse contained, which might have helped, but even with all the time spent flying, she didn't know it all. She was at first confused by the computer interfaces until Miko walked her through the touchscreen controls. She'd been making a greater study of them, but she was in the back, trying to repair the damage to the helium bladders.

Once again, the Red Baron was approaching, this time from a sharp angle, diving right for the final bladder, aware this was his killing blow. Did the Adversary really now want me dead or had the thrill of the fight gotten to the German pilot? We were rapidly descending and I could see the ground begin to rush up at us, already slick with rain, which had begun to fall in waves. A wind was buffeting us like a punctured balloon, which was certainly an apt description right now.

"Best we level the playing field, don't you think?"

Wild Bill gently nudged me aside and he leaned toward the German machine gun through the window, precariously balancing its legs on the sloping deck, taking aim. I shuffled over to the next window and could see the Red Baron's plane was growing in size, its engine roaring in the growing wind. We were shaking, both from the descent and the increasing winds, both of which gave Bill trouble as he kept adjusting his angle to line up his shot.

When he was satisfied with the alien weapon in his calloused hands, he opened fire in a long burst, the recoil pushing him back until he leaned against our cabin wall. He was quiet, focused entirely on adjusting his aim as he fired. The sound was more than deafening because, for a few moments, I could hear nothing at all, white noise filling both ears. And then things grew quiet, time felt suspended, and I had no idea what was happening. I could hear nothing, but I saw Wild Bill's mouth curl into a satisfied smile. His hands dropped the weapon, which smoked from its sustained discharge.

I got back onto my knees and cautiously peered out the window, catching a glimpse of a column of smoke, lighter against the storm clouds, dwindling.

"Got 'im," he said with certainty.

We were still descending and it appeared that no matter what Amelia was doing in the front, or Michael and Miko in the rear, was going to change that. It meant we needed to brace for impact and my eyes darted around, seeking things to cushion ourselves. There wasn't much. Silas was toward the back, helping Albert get below the seats while Bartholomew and Chou were grabbing cushions and blankets, anything to help absorb the inevitable impact.

"It's going to get bumpy," Amelia cried from her pilot's chair, hands slamming against controls.

"Get?" Wild Bill said.

It got bumpier. A lot bumpier as the ground rushed to meet us. We hadn't reached the base of the mountain range, the land beneath us rocky but flat. If anything, the muddy surface might help as we continued downward.

The lower we got, the more the winds seemed to knock us about, and I grew nauseous but refused to vomit. Instead, I tucked myself into a ball beside Wild Bill, whose arms were wrapped around his knees, back to the wall, and we waited.

I so didn't want to die because death meant failure, and if we died, then the Adversary would win on Earth and the false vacuum would then consume the planet and all else in our reality.

Impact was worse than I imagined as I heard metal groan as it twisted out of shape and glass was breaking all around us. I was wet, thinking it was blood at first, but it was actually rain and I was instantly drenched. We hit the ground hard and tumbled over and over, getting the gondola caught up in the ruined 200-foot span of balloon. I bit my lip as I was turned upside down and the aches and bruises kept coming as I spun about, freely slamming into one wall, then a table. Bodies flew by me and I could barely make out one before another sailed after it. For a moment, my head hit something hard and the world went black.

We skidded, bumping over stones, our momentum slowing as the wreckage filled with water. Then we were gently rocking from side to side until the gondola grew still. As I opened my eyes, my stomach won out, and I threw up, narrowly avoiding my tattered pants. I felt sore but whole. Nothing seemed broken. I looked around the scrap heap of the airship and watched as Silas began moving debris from the huddled form of Chou, who had wrapped herself around Albert. Both lacerated and Albert's right hand seemed swollen and blue. I continued scanning, happy to see Vihaan emerge from the ladder shaft where he had sheltered during the crash. My heart beat wildly, as I didn't see Michael, and my fear was bordering on panic. But then Vihaan looked up and helped Michael and Miko climb down. My elder son was cradling an arm that must be broken and he was cut on both cheeks, laughably symmetrical, making his bloody face look like your stereotypical Indian.

Bartholomew emerged from a rear room, also whole but bloody. He gave me a thumbs-up, which I returned. My ears were ringing fiercely, obscuring most sounds, which might have been for the best. To my right, I saw Wild Bill, dazed or maybe even unconscious, but the steady rise and fall of his chest was reassuring. Carefully, I opened one eyelid, uncertain exactly what I was looking for, but the pupil responded to the dim light, so I took that as a good sign.

It hurt to move, but I rose from my knees to unsteadily balance against a bent portion of the gondola. I looked ahead, but Amelia was out cold. Every window in the glass-covered pilothouse was shattered and the wind blew the rain in sheets, adding a hazy screen. I continued to carefully move forward, aware that there was glass below, the footing precarious, and my body complained with every step. I was beginning to discern sounds through the buzzing, so that was progress. What I heard, though, wasn't great, the electronic buzz of exposed wires, sizzling in the rain. We'd all have to be careful until one of us figured out how to safely power down the remains of the *Brimstone*.

When I reached the front, I moved to Amelia's right and peered at her, letting out a loud gasp followed immediately by a sob. Still strapped in, Amelia was still, eyes fixed, and a large shard of glass neatly bisecting her neck, wedged into the back of the chair. Blood was seeping downward, staining her leather jacket, mixing with the rain to appear pale pink. The great aviator was dead and the nightly pixie dust couldn't do a damned thing about it.

The tears mixed with the blowing rain and I slumped

against the pilot's chair, cutting my pants open on more glass. There was so much glass, so much blood, and I couldn't stop any of it. How was I supposed to fulfill the Architect's plan when I couldn't keep my team alive?

I felt a hand on my shoulder and thought it might be Chou, but I looked up to see Michael. His eyes were filled with sympathy, sharing my grief, and I was reminded I was not alone. There were others and the job could still be done. We communed silently for a moment, a horrid tableau, and there would be no time for a proper funeral and burial. After enough time, and I had stopped crying, I rose and turned to the others. They were fanned across the remains of the gondola, each looking so incredibly sad. Were they all crying? The rain made that impossible to tell.

"We have to finish this on foot," Chou said.

"Can we?"

"There's no choice," Wild Bill said. "You want to face this Adversary, we have to find him, and to do that, we need your friend the Architect."

The way I was feeling, the Architect was no friend of mine, but I wasn't going to say that about Chou's husband. He had provided so much and it wasn't he who brought the Red Baron to this new world. Wild Bill was right, so I told everyone to scavenge what they could and be ready to move out in five minutes. I joined the hunt, even managing to find my backpack, torn and worse for wear, but at least it was mine and could complete the trip with me. Wisely, Chou grabbed the two tablets and found something to protect the paper map, which looked wilted, much as I felt. Bartholomew and Wild Bill grabbed the tasers, the machine gun, and whatever else looked useful. Knives were distributed so everyone had a form of protection.

As we assembled, I looked to Silas and asked his estimate to reach the collector on foot.

"*Presuming you require eight hours sleep and rest breaks not lasting more than half an hour, it should take approximately one and a three-quarter days.*"

If Abernathy and his nano-army were catching up, it was now a foot race.

EIGHT

THE RAIN MADE the going slow and difficult, the muddy terrain slowing us down, but apparently, Silas had calculated for that. Not that it made me feel any better. We walked in miserable silence, the rain pounding on us and everyone thinking about poor Amelia. I hadn't really gotten to know her well, but she was up for the adventure and for the cause. If this worked, she deserved a lot of credit.

We had trudged for maybe four hours when we saw shapes in the distance; low, boxy shapes. From the air, we hadn't spotted a community so close to the mountains, but I was delighted. It meant possible warmth and more allies. I signaled to everyone and we formed up in a single line so we appeared less threatening. There was no sign of sentries or much life; the rain and wind saw to that. But there were flickers of light here and there, so someone was home. We carefully approached the first building, something made from stone and...grass? I'd heard about grass homes but had never seen one before. There was no real door, just some wood in the doorway.

"Hello?"

A young boy, maybe seven, with a soot-smeared face, peered up at me. "Hello."

"Who's there?" an older male voice called.

"New arrivals," I said, and then a burly man, easily forty years old with already thinning hair and a bulbous nose, stood over the boy. He eyed me then saw the others behind, and let out a grunt.

"Too many of ye to fit in here," he said. His fat fingers pointed to a larger building. "Boss' house." And with that, he backed away into the gloom.

The boss' house was easily the largest in the area, which numbered maybe ten or twelve buildings. The same workman-like construction, same dimness thanks to the rain. The key difference was that there was an honest-to-goodness door. I knocked.

Without hesitation, the door was opened and a woman, maybe thirty, with dark, curly brown hair, wide set eyes, and freckles dancing across her face stood in the doorway, holding a lantern. The light flickered in the breeze, casting wild shadows everywhere, but the look of surprise then recognition was plain on her face, confusing me. We hadn't met, at least not in my reality.

"Meredith Gale?"

I nodded and she burst into motion, waving everyone in and directing us to the large stone hearth that blazed with fire, casting light in that corner of the building. As I stood there, welcoming the warmth, I studied the surroundings. Like so many other places I visited, it was a work in progress. There was a large, flat stone atop other stones that seemed to serve as a desk. At this end, there were benches of wood, held up by more stone. The floor was only half muddy, mainly from our tracks, and the grass ceiling seemed to hold the water at bay. In the shadows, I could make out a sleeping palette of some sort, so she lived and worked here, hence the size afforded her.

"You all look pretty wretched," she said with a laugh. Her good humor and welcoming way was certainly nice, but how she knew me gnawed on my mind. "Get cozy and I will see if there's anything warm for you." She hurried into the shadowy half and returned shortly with some blankets, which we shared, with me and Chou huddled together.

"Who are you? How do you know me?" I finally had a chance to ask once we were all circling the fire.

"My name is Janelle Rivera. Welcome to Don Bosco. It's not much, but for now, it's home," she said. "And I know you because we've been on the lookout. We received word from Bahay, the village about half a day from here. Not long after we both began our bases, we found pigeons and one of their people knew how to train them. For the last three weeks, we've been sending back regular messages, as much to stay in touch as to get the birds accustomed to us.

"They'd heard from a horseman about what was happening. That you were headed in this general direction, so we've been looking for a redhead and her army."

I didn't like to think of us as an army, too violent, and that was why I kept thinking of us as the IMF.

She laughed. "You're the first redhead I've seen since we arrived, so it had to be Meredith, the walking translator. I'm speaking Tagalog, but all your companions understand me."

"So you know about my mission," I said.

"Something about finding the source of how we got here and saving us from a bad guy." That's what happens when you play telephone. The message always gets somewhat garbled. I corrected some of her misinformation, filled in other blanks, and then launched into my prepared speech about the need for allies, resources, and most importantly, warning her of Abernathy. As I spoke, a few people had drifted in and helped Janelle serve us some sort of hot vegetable soup, which was honestly bland, but it filled me, and for that, I was grateful. A few gaped at Silas, who stood silently conserving his power given the lack of sunlight for quite a few hours now.

"I know you're building an army of some sort and you want my help. We're just forty-three people, so I can't spare much. We can ferry messages and I can spare a medic. She's already volunteered."

After the scrapes and injuries we've had, I was thankful for someone with genuine medical knowledge. I had lost all sense of time and suspected we were behind Silas' schedule. But the rain continued and we were finally drying off while still processing Amelia's loss. Being stationary would also allow Osman to catch up, even though he had only a general sense of where we were. Muddy tracks in lieu of stones would have to do. That, and the wrecked *Brimstone*. We would stay here, sleep, dry off, and start fresh in the morning, and hope for the best.

With that decision made, I felt myself unwind a bit. Janelle and her people had plenty of questions and I let the others provide the answers for a change, sitting so my presence facilitated the dialogue. I stretched my legs out, feet toward the fire, and leaned against the wall, appreciating the sturdiness. I assessed myself: there was a pulled muscle in my back, I was deeply bruised all over, my head ached, and my heart was heavy. The pixie dust had its work cut out tonight, which was coming soon, I realized. The grayness was getting deeper, at least charcoal, soon to be coal black, and a moonless night awaited.

I was drifting off, when Janelle came to me, her smile in place, and a woman beside her. She was tall, somewhere between me and Chou, thin and muscular, hair buzzed short even after a month here, so she had to have been nearly bald to start. She wore a tank top over a torn t-shirt and was wearing cargo pants and well-worn boots. This was a soldier if I ever saw one, a regular G.I. Jane.

"This is Corporal Corinne Levy," Janelle said. "Our medic now assigned to your team."

"So formal," I mused. I struggled to my feet and extended a hand. Her grip was firm, with slightly more pressure than necessary, as if proving her worth. "Is the rank necessary?"

"Just who I am, ma'am," she said in a surprisingly light voice.

"Well, I don't think of myself as a ma'am. Meredith will do fine. What shall I call you?"

"Corporal Levy. Don't like Cory much."

"What have you heard about our goal?"

"Just the basics," she said, all business, little warmth. She was definitely more Chou than me. I filled her in a bit and explained we'd leave in the morning. I received a curt nod and then she spun on her heel and marched, yes marched, off. Well, if I needed an army, I got myself one solid soldier there.

The sun was shining the following day, attempting to wash away our pain and sorrow. The thick, white clouds complemented the blue sky and I already felt my shirt beginning to stick to my back. The *Brimstone* had air conditioning of a sort, so I had been spoiled, and now I was going to march like everyone else. Even as Don Bosco was fading in the distance, I glimpsed, far to the right, the next one, closer to the base of the mountains.

The ground was drying but still challenging to traverse, my feet continuing to adhere to the ground. There was little conversation as we moved along, and I noted Corporal Levy had taken her place toward the rear, behind Michael and Vihaan, who occasionally whispered back and forth. Silas, as always, took the rear so as not to outpace us with his far longer legs. I was glad for the sun because I needed him fully charged for whatever came next. We were a dirty, tired group when we broke for a light meal under the shade of trees. By then, the next village was easily seen, a series of log cabin-like structures, maybe fifteen in all, suggesting a small community.

Before we got much closer, a runner came directly toward us, a woman in shorts, ponytail flying behind her lean form. "Welcome to Fale!" she shouted more than once. It appeared we were expected, as Janelle had dispatched a messenger overnight as we slept. She directed us to the community, and once more, there was the pleasant sound of people at work. I heard a saw and some pounding that might have been a hammer but turned out to be people tenderizing meat before slipping the pieces on skewers.

A broad, muscular Maori, his blue tattoos crisscrossing his body, welcomed us literally with open arms. "You are Meredith Gale, and I am..."

"John Ah Kuoi!" shouted Bartholomew with a wide grin.

"You know me?" Kuoi was genuinely surprised.

"Know you? You are a rugby superstar!" Bartholomew said and the other man seemed even more surprised.

"I had a nice career, but superstar?"

"Well, where I came from, you were huge. You singlehandedly won the championship for Samoa '80. It was brilliant."

"We lost that year," Kuoi said, confused.

"I don't know what you have been told, but we're not all from the same place," I said and briefly covered parallel worlds, a concept he was familiar with from television, so was more accepting than others. As people worked, I noted they were happy and friendly, more communal than some of the others.

We accepted his hospitality, happy to have somewhere shady to sit and drink cool water. As quickly as I could, I answered Kuoi's rapid fire questions and then he answered several fanboy questions from Bartholomew. He happily told us how every day he had them doing physical work but also time for organized play. He longed for a rugby ball or even football, but apparently, the Architect couldn't provide everything we needed.

"I have sent runners to Themélio, which is about two hours that way," he said, gesturing round the curve of the mountain base. "We've been trading meat for vegetables since their land is somehow better."

"Maybe they have a green thumb and you don't," Bartholomew teased, noting the nearly black dirt caking one of Kuoi's hands. He'd been earlier tapping trees for sap to use as a sealant on a new cabin.

"Are you sure you won't spend the night?"

"We'd love to, Kuoi, but the sooner we make contact with the Architect, the sooner I think we'll be safer."

He nodded with a knowing smile and then tilted his head back and let out what could best be described as a lusty war cry. But in moments, a dozen men and women jogged into sight and stood in two rows. Several had long knives, machetes, and even a lasso.

"I hear you're building an army," Kuoi said with a laugh. "Well, when they get here, these will join them. Our contribution to the cause."

We made some additional chit-chat as I welcomed each to the "cause" and Silas dutifully noted them by Candidate number and registered them in some database he was building. Feeling refreshed enough, it was time for farewells. I looked at the sun, now on its descent, and knew we'd make it to Themélio before dark and could camp there for the night. Hopefully, the following day would get us actually into the mountains and to the collector.

We followed a path that had been well worn from the

messengers who had gone back and forth over the weeks. The first real road of a sort, but too small for the map. With the base of the mountains to our left, we followed the path, which was barely wide enough for two abreast, and we chatted amongst ourselves, looking ahead for the first glimpses of the next port of call. As a result, we missed any possible warning sounds. Instead, an arrow flew over my shoulder and embedded itself in the smooth ground two feet before me.

"Scatter!" Chou cried, and everyone dashed out of the way, backing away and hoping to stay out of range of the archer or archers. No, definitely archers, as a small volley flew from behind a rocky outcropping from the nearest mountain. I spotted hats and helmets peeking from behind their cover, clearly out of range of my scimitar and one of the tasers Chou managed to secure from the *Brimstone*. We were outgunned for certain, but that didn't mean we were doomed. Instead, we had our own brand of fire power. Wild Bill immediately withdrew his pistol, ready to fire when a target presented itself. His first shot chipped rock right before an archer.

From their clothing, they were either really pissed off Renaissance players or people from somewhere back in time, before gunpowder was in regular use. They wore dark tunics, no real armor that I could tell, and loose pants. If they were soldiers, they certainly didn't look it. Their wooden bows were curved at the grip, almost scalloped as it fanned out to the tips where the string was tied tightly at both ends. They were easily six feet long, giving them power but also exposing them every time they wanted to shoot. The arrow that missed me was simple enough, a two-foot shaft of wood and a wide metallic arrowhead, with bird feathers at the tail.

As I was studying our opponents, I noticed Chou, Wild Bill, and Levy inch forward, getting just below them. Bartholomew dodged one shaft and joined them, then all four began climbing the mountain, each making certain they had a safe place for hands and feet. As they climbed, I needed to keep the archers focused on me, so I stood up, hoping I had calculated right and was really out of range. The first two arrows fell short and then the third went over my head, causing me to back up, where I tripped over a stone and fell on my ass. The next shot, which I never saw coming, pierced my thigh and I howled in pain, so much that Chou was distracted from her climb and took her eyes away from the attackers above her. I daren't indicate where she was, so I just sat there, staring at the arrow sticking out from my leg, pants leg soaking up the blood.

A shadow loomed over me as Silas became my shield before bending down and carefully lifting me in his massive, multifaceted arms and moved me to a far safer distance.

"I am sorry, Meredith, but I have no field medicine training," he told me apologetically.

"Good thing we brought a medic along," I said between huffing breaths as I tried to control the pain radiating from the wound.

"But Corporal Levy is not able to tend to you," he said.

"I'll live. She's a soldier and is up there trying to neutralize the enemy." At that, I scanned the flat terrain and saw everyone else also backed up, just far more gracefully than I had. Albert waved, and I weakly waved back. To him, this must have all been terribly exciting, even as I saw the look of concern on his soft features.

Then I turned my attention to the rock wall and saw that Chou and Levy had moved above the attackers and out of their sight, ready to pounce such as one could bounce from rock to rock. Speaking of which, Bartholomew hefted a good-sized stone and hurled it laterally toward the four archers, who were now entirely exposed, taking aim at us. His throw hit one in the shoulder and as two others turned in their direction, Wild Bill opened fire, the cracks magnified as they bounced off the mountain wall, and they crumpled. Chou and Levy then made their move, making the short leap to the outcropping they had used to await us. The living archers were surprised to see them attacked, by women no less. Quickly, Chou tasered one while Levy delivered an uppercut and downward strike that brought the man to his knees. His hands went up in an act of surrender.

While Levy was gathering up their bows and arrows, and relieving the four of their knives and even a sword, Chou led the two captives back down, with Bartholomew and Wild Bill taking the rear, six-gun out and gesturing menacingly since they didn't recognize the pistol. Once on the ground, Levy rushed to me, her kit in her hands, and examined my wound, which was throbbing, each pulse a new wave of agony. I was handed a stick and told to bite down on it while she worked. Then, with her bare hands, she snapped the wooden shaft in half, one piece about a fist's width remaining in my leg. Her practiced fingers probed around the wound and then she doused a knife in alcohol and very carefully cut into my leg to widen the entry wound and retrieve the shaft's remains. If I thought being pierced by a medieval arrow was painful, this was several magnitudes worse. The shaft and the arrow head slid out with a sickening slurping sound and she tossed it over her shoulder before bandaging me up.

A part of me wanted a painkiller, but I knew better. That craving dragged me down and put me in the place where I wanted to take my life, and in turn arrived here, where I had been regularly hunted, this time like an animal. That made me angry as I had had my fill of being a target.

Chou helped me rise, unsteady as I was. We ambled over to the four men, who sat back to back on the ground, watched over by Bartholomew and Silas, who scared the living hell out them, just looming over them. Good.

"Who sent you?" I asked, sounding as in command as was possible, channeling my anger.

They were silent and Wild Bill wandered over and gently prodded one with his boot, a promise that the next one would hurt. Finally, the older of the two looked at me and said, "We were under fire, nearly burned by barbarians. Then we heard a voice offer us freedom and savior. We agreed and were suddenly here, yn the wild. Each of us had an ymage of the redhead woman, told to fynd hire, and kill the others. For oure lives, we wolde gladly kill anyone."

Well, apparently, my translation skills were not exactly perfect for Middle English, but we all got the gist of it since it so closely resembled what the Nazi told us four weeks earlier. The question now became what to do with them and I had no idea, having never captured a prisoner of war before, and by then, it felt very much like a war.

"How far from Themélio?" I asked the others.

"Maybe an hour," Chou said. "You can't go that far on your own."

"Want to bet?" I said through clenched teeth. Well, not on my own; I'd need to lean on others for help, so we divided up the weapons while Bill trussed the four archers as best he could. He walked behind them and Bartholomew in front, positioning them in the middle of our group to minimize their chance of fleeing. They seemed dazed and more than a little confused by their surroundings and they repeatedly looked over their shoulders at Silas, unable to figure out what he was.

Michael and Vihaan took turns helping me limp my way across the ground, every step a small burst of agony. We managed, but our pace was certainly slowed by me and I refused to waste time having them try and cut down a tree and fashion a litter. After all, I'd be good as new in under twelve hours.

Closer to two hours later, we arrived at Themélio and its cluster of circular homes in a series of concentric circles. This was far larger than any community we'd seen in days, but it made sense. They were near a river, with trees, plants, the beginnings of a garden, and another horse corral. It was a thriving village, and as we were spotted, activity stopped. Several rushed forward to help me limp into town, shouting greetings in various accents. I was taken into the third hut we passed and laid down on a fresh bed of what might have been straw. A young woman came and offered me water, which I greedily drank.

Nicholas Ariti, tall, aristocratic in bearing, with white streaks at the temples and a weathered look to his serious face, greeted me. He'd been named leader and had modeled Themélio on the Greeks, he told me, emphasizing science, philosophy, and combat. Two different messengers had reached them, one from neighboring Fale and another from a community I hadn't even visited. "We took both messages and studied them, divining the truth and adding it to what we believed to be truth. The collector you seek, it was to be explored once our homes were built and our community stabilized. It wasn't going anywhere."

He summoned two of his better athletes to take the bewildered archers prisoner, having them given food and drink but then secured so they could not escape, not that they had anywhere to go. In fact, I thought once things were explained to them, they might actually help us. But that would be later.

As Levy rewrapped my wound, Ariti proudly told me of this community. How every night, while awaiting the pixie dust, they speculated on everything, from where on Earth they might be, what the dust was all about, and who built something as massive as the collector. Everyone was encouraged to join in the discussion and no idea dismissed as too outlandish. To some of his community, it smacked of witch-craft; to others, the stuff of science fiction. They had already compared enough of their personal histories to understand they were not only from separate times and places but parallel realities. This meant there weren't too many questions for us beyond the practical concerns of surviving Abernathy's approaching forces and how best they could support Osman's own army.

As I faded away in much needed sleep, I heard Chou begin to discuss options, secure in the knowledge that, for a change, I wasn't needed at that moment.

When I awoke, it was Albert sitting beside me, a cup of water at the ready. The sun had already set and the others had eaten with our hosts. He ran to tell Corporal Levy I was awake and then Michael walked in with a plate of still warm vegetables.

"How do you feel?"

"Like crap," I admitted. I stuffed a pepper in my mouth, surprised at the burst of heat in my mouth. He chuckled and handed me the water.

"We'll move you outside for the pixie dust show. Ariti is fully on our side and ready to help. Something like four dozen of his people want to fight. We've given them some of our spare weapons, including the bows and arrows. Those four are dealing with definite future shock and aren't going anywhere. Ariti's also giving us horses to finish the trip, so we will definitely reach the collector tomorrow."

"Bows, arrows, pistols; none of that is going to make a differ-ence against Abernathy's nanotechnology. Does Vihaan have a clue how to combat that?"

"He's been giving everything else short shrift, totally devoting that keen mind of his to the problem. There are theo-ries and having briefly studied the robo-bug certainly helped.

He's been looking for the root technology, the platform everything's been built on."

"Any luck?" I asked, starting to feel way out of my league.

"Theories and nothing we can test," he admitted, his shoulders slumping.

"It's something, I suppose," I finally said. Then I finished my dinner, feeling slightly better. The leg was nothing but a solid dull ache making the time feel glacial.

I was taken outside, placed in a prime position, near their fire and to Ariti's right. The area felt like the beginnings of an amphitheater, complete with platform for speeches. There were few decorative touches in sight, but what there was suggested Greek columns and filigree. He had been an archeologist before an earthquake triggered a cave-in, trapping him in the remains of an Aztec temple when his invitation arrived. So much tragedy was replaced with so much promise, but it was clear, the vast majority of the people I had met in the last six-seven weeks – I was clearly losing track of time – recognized and embraced this second chance. They shared my questions but also my resolve to start over and do better.

I silently promised myself as the first trickle of pixie dust colored the night sky, we would endure. The answers would be found, humanity saved, and if necessary, so would the world.

NINE

WHEN I AWOKE, I heard quite the commotion outside the cabin, so I rushed out, marveling all over again about the pixie dust's amazing restorative abilities. A messenger had come running with word that our path was blocked by an armed group, but not Abernathy. These clearly were more time-displaced menaces from the Adversary. Two in rapid succession suggested he was getting desperate to stop us and was upping the stakes if it was any more than four.

As it turned out, it was more like a hundred and four. Swarthy, dark-skinned men and women in mostly leather armor had massed on the path leading into the mountains, blocking our way. While we could look for an alternative route, they would still be a presence, a threat that was not easily dispatched. The four dozen Ariti promised us would be handy but meant we were outnumbered more than two to one and I did not like those odds. That they hadn't charged the village was an interesting sign, but I couldn't worry about that now, just be thankful.

"What do we do?" Vihaan asked me when I emerged from the cabin.

"This is why I recruited Osman; he's the tactical genius," I said in frustration. My heart was already beating faster and my need for coffee was growing exponentially.

Ariti briskly headed my way, announcing, "They're Mongols, 13th century warriors."

"Is Genghis Khan among them?" If the famed general was, we were probably dead.

He shook his head, but we were still outmanned and out-armed. His four dozen had fallen in and Levy was reviewing their weapons and formation. She'd have to act as our military commander until something better happened. Chou joined us, looking graver than usual.

"This is a most unfortunate turn of events," she said by way of greeting.

"No shit," I grumbled. "We can't meet them here; it has to be outside and away from Themélio. Suggestions?"

"I agree. I would suggest the forces here engage the Mongols and allow our core group to find an alternative path. There are options."

"No," I said firmly. "I will not use humans like cannon fodder." I paused, remembering my arguments with Osman just days ago. Well, any more than I had to. "It's not why they were brought here and I won't rob them of their chance. Not unless I take the same risks. It wouldn't be right."

Chou nodded, eyes not meeting mine.

I was resigning myself to this grisly risk, calculating my low odds of survival. I dispatched Chou to find a safe place for Albert, who I refused to let fight. As she left, Wild Bill, Bartholomew, and Miko appeared, their game faces in place. They weren't going anywhere and for that I was grateful. Michael and Vihaan weren't fighters and would also be sitting this one out. I instructed Silas to remain behind as well, too valuable to lose in this fight. That left five of us to join the four dozen Themélions. With luck, someone would write a song about this battle.

Chou returned and we silently nodded to one another, ready to wade into war.

We were interrupted with a new cry from a different section of the village. Ariti hurried in that direction and I signaled we should wait to see what was happening. Soon, he was running toward us.

"A large force is on the horizon. Could it be your army?"

Chou and I followed him to the top of a hut roof, where a sentry had spied the shapes. It was a mass of human beings, clouds of dust or smoke rising from different sections. They were huge and growing larger by the step. It had to be Osman, finally catching up with us.

"I have an idea," I told Chou and Ariti as we hit the ground. They listened and nodded and then he summoned a messenger. The instructions were given and the young man threw off some sort of salute and ran for a horse and was gone. Chou had gone to relay the instructions to Levy and I filled the others in. I received a few skeptical looks, but no one argued.

Within fifteen minutes, Levy was leading the four dozen away from Themélio and toward the Mongols. We'd been told few were on horseback, most were infantry, but each carried a scimitar, like mine, or a halberd. There were also lances and longbows, so they had a greater reach and could pick us off as we approached. It helped we knew where they were positioned, awaiting us, barring our path and daring us to challenge them. To me, it felt like the Adversary was getting a bit nervous. Good.

The scouts were good and provided us with a path that would take us away from the mountain, an oblong arc that would bring the Mongols toward our position, away from the mountains' protection, and hopefully open up a flank to be exploited. We just had to act like we were on our planned destination and let them come charging. It would be risky, what with their arrows, but if Silas' keen vision could keep us out of range, we'd be fine. I hated to bring Albert along, hell, even Michael, but we were heading forward, so there was little choice. What I wouldn't give for a forcefield.

Ariti wished us luck and saw our group off, the four dozen troops departing fifteen minutes later, so it appeared we were alone and unaware. I felt like a sitting duck out in the open, but trusted my instincts and everyone else trusted me. That Chou, with her security training, didn't object to the plan was a positive; not that she approved of it, but she followed my lead. By the time we left, it had to have been mid-morning and the sun was rising high in the cloudless sky, casting a bright light on everything, which hopefully meant no one would have the benefit of surprise.

Given our arc and the enemy's position, Silas estimated it would take seventy-seven minutes to reach them, and every minute felt tense. The ground was dry now, dusty even, with patches of scrub growing here and there. The trees were closer to the base of the mountains and acted as a barrier between the village and the Mongols, which was fine by me since I wasn't a big fan of raping and pillaging.

Around the seventy-minute mark, I slowed our pace and asked Silas to scan ahead. He could see nothing, so we trudged ahead, secure in the knowledge that the troops were behind us. Our arc was taking us into view of the enemy and we were finally spotted. Even from this distance, I could hear a war cry with fainter cries in reply. Okay, we were spotted, now to draw them out.

"We've been spotted; everyone get ready," I commanded. Michael and Albert dropped back, closer to Silas, whose huge metallic form should provide some shielding. I heard steel slide from leather scabbards and the cocking of two pistols. Vihaan even chambered a shell in the rifle he had been given by Ariti. While not a marksman, he was willing to fire into a mass of humanity, presuming the odds would ever be in his favor. No sooner did we get ready, then there was another air-splitting scream. From behind the curve of a mountain came four horsemen, two with lances, two with bows. They charged us with the other seven dozen running behind them doing their best imitation of the rebel yell.

"Get ready!" I cried as they neared us incredibly fast. One of the archers stood in his stirrups and took aim, letting fly the first arrow. It wound up falling considerably short of us. I was already getting pretty tired of people firing arrows at me.

As far as an arrow could fly, a bullet went further. Wild Bill positioned himself, took aim at the approaching second archer, and fired. The man was thrown backward and he tumbled from his horse to the dusty ground. The other three riders veered away from us, having never seen a gun before. To make his point, Bill took aim a second time and fired, hitting one of the lancers, who dropped the weapon, clutching his right arm. He reversed course and headed away from us. The others were less certain what to do, waiting for the sheer numbers to bolster their bravado.

"Vihaan, now!" I called as he raised the rifle to his shoulder, steadied himself, and after a very long beat, squeezed the trigger. The bullet whizzed past the horsemen and actually struck one of the front line soldiers, a short, wide woman, who fell to her knees. Not that it stopped them entirely, but they slowed, uncertain how to manage a more powerful enemy.

Ariti warned us that his recollection was that the Mongols were so successful because they prepared for war, using spies and intelligence, along with fierce discipline and training since practically birth. When they went into battle, it was with superior numbers, and even though this was a fraction of what they were used to, they no doubt imagined we would be easy pickings.

Their leader, looking resplendent in his quilted red coat, his coned helmet, and plume, gleamed in the bright sun. He was surrounded by at least five loyal soldiers, while he could be seen shouting commands. Obeying, the forces split into five columns, ten men each, each stalking us from different angles, already having figured we couldn't fire on all of them at once. They were marching, not running, either hoping to chase us or cause paralysis. They approached and I was counting the minutes, with at least five having passed. We'd need no more than ten minutes more before our surprise arrived.

The men continued forward, steadily, and their formation was impressive to watch. Each man brandished axes, hooked lances, and spears. A few held swords in their hands, just waiting for the order to start swinging. We need to slow them down.

"Bill!" I shouted, and understanding my meaning, he aimed at one column and fired, hitting one. He fired at another and missed, but the message was clear. Then Vihaan, on his own, raised the rifle and fired at a third column. He, too, missed. But it had the desired effect as cries were raised and the marching slowed but did not stop. Bullets were clearly alien to them all, which worked for us. For all they knew, we were sorcerers hurling magic at them.

We also began to retreat a bit, putting distance between us and buying more time. In the distance, I heard the first pounding hoofbeats and hoped the sight of our nascent cavalry would help break their spirit. While the rising plumes of dust the horses caused was seen and commented on, it did not stop the Mongols, who continued to come after us. A field commander, though, his long, drooping mustache glistening with oil, directed the farthest column to set up a human wall, and be prepared. Here's where things were going to get tricky. The Mongols were remembered nearly a millennia later because of their successes, a lot of which went to their training and preparation. The forces Levy was leading weren't anything you could call polished, more *Stripes* than Seal Team Six.

The two forces neared one another, gaining momentum, and as they came into sight, I saw our forces brandish their own bladed weapons. What our people knew, and the Mongols did not, was that as long as they lived, they would be repaired tonight. That gave them the ability to be a little more reckless and I hoped that would be an advantage.

Then, just like that, our horse riders met the Mongols. Swords flashed, horses whinnied in fright, and human cries that needed no translation filled the air. I took a brief moment to make certain Silas had Albert protected then withdrew my own scimitar and stood side by side with Chou. We didn't approach the nearest column and made them come to us. Wild Bill was to my side, his six-shooters loaded and ready. He didn't have an unlimited supply of bullets, but with luck, this would be the last time they'd be needed. Then he shot the first man to take a swing at us, and Chou scooped low to pick up his lance. She whirled it fast, getting below a lance strike headed for her, and drove the tip into a gap between the coat and arm.

I noted one of the other columns came toward us, so we had to hurry. I really, really didn't want to take a life again, but there was little choice afforded us. I swung low, trying to wound and disable my attacker while Bill delivered an uppercut that knocked another aside. Behind me, I heard the sounds of struggle and Vihaan's rifle go off again, which actually caused all the Mongols to reflexively flinch. There was a buzzing sound as Miko, using the second taser, stunned a soldier.

One Mongol soldier, who couldn't have been more than eighteen, rushed me, only to be knocked aside by Bartholomew, who rushed him from the side. Grabbing the man's sword, Bartholomew hamstrung him, and then swung upward at another attacker. Wild Bill backed away from the melee long enough to assess where he was needed and then fired three more shots before using the butt of one pistol to bludgeon someone trying to grab at him.

No one was charging me for a moment, so I looked over to see Levy and the others had kept their attackers at bay. But I also saw the reserves were now coming from the Mongol side, the rest of the horde, save those protecting the leader, who kept shouting commands, arms gesticulating like a football coach during the Super Bowl.

We kept at this for several minutes, although it felt more like several hours. If it was like this fighting humans, what could we do against Abernathy and the nanobot army? That train of thought made me shudder and I was genuinely thankful I was distracted from that as I swung my scimitar upward, blocking a blow I nearly missed seeing.

A fresh cry of alarm was heard to one side, a rousing cheer from another. I whirled about to see giant plumes of dust being kicked up at the horizon. Everything was falling into place and the Mongols actually paused, studying the dark line approaching then looking back to their leader.

With renewed vigor, Levy's troops made their way toward us, forcing the Mongols to follow, keeping them somewhat contained. As they passed Silas, Michael joined them, using the taser Chou had given him to take down more than a few surprised Mongols.

Osman's forces came into view, hundreds strong, now clearly outnumbering the Mongols. We had taken some hits as Chou and Bartholomew suffered serious cuts, and Vihaan, when I wasn't looking, took a fierce blow, his entire right leg covered in blood. Levy had rushed to tend to him while Ariti's people kept moving, swinging, punching, and even biting as needed.

It wasn't long before Osman rode forward and reached me, a dripping sword at his side. This was a man who appeared to be in his element, a wolfish grin on his face, dark eyes bright with intensity.

"Pasha," I said.

"Meredith," he replied. "Your message spurred us on, and I have to admit, it was a fine strategy. We now have the best of them."

"You're not going to like the next part," I said. He eyed me warily. When I explained what I had in mind, his face darkened and he shook his head. "Do you know the concept that the enemy of my enemy is my friend?"

"No." But he ran it around in his mind, understanding the general idea, which seemed to sway him.

He summoned two soldiers, ones I didn't recognize, and he dispatched them to watch over Albert, who had been complaining about being coddled, but right then, I didn't care. I then signaled for Silas to join us while Osman called for more men. Osman dismounted, sword still in his right hand, and stood beside me. I told Silas what the plan was, and at first, he actually seemed reluctant to participate but accepted the goal. Standing before us, he began walking in a straight line. Osman and I walked side by side behind our nine-foot-tall guardian, his men behind. When one Mongol attempted to slice into Silas, he swiveled about, and with superior strength, plucked the sword from the man's astonished grasp and tossed it far away. Undaunted, the man tried to punch Silas, only to cradle his hand in pain.

The line of five soldiers stood fast between us and their leader, but we paused about a dozen feet away, and we stepped out from behind our protector. He turned around, protecting our backs, and I addressed their leader.

"Good morning," I began mildly. "Is there a chance we can have a conversation?"

The man eyed me, clearly astonished to understand my words, but he didn't budge. His eyes never left mine and I thought I detected a moment of recognition since I was the only redhead in the group.

"Can you call a cessation of hostilities so maybe we can talk?"

He blinked but did not budge.

"I'm going to make this quick. You were trapped, probably outmanned, outgunned, or whatever. You heard a voice. It promised you a glorious battle. All you had to do was find me and kill the others. Something like that?"

The expression flickered for a moment, which was all the confirmation I needed.

"You don't know where you are or who we are. You can tell with your own eyes we're all dressed differently. We have different, deadlier weapons, which I bet you covet. You are less certain what happens after you complete your mission and I am in your hands."

The face was marble, but he was listening, as were the five before me, and their expressions were far easier to read.

"So, right now, you're outnumbered and the Pasha here," I paused to gesture to Osman, who nodded, following my lead, although I could sense his tense posture, ready to resume fighting. I imagined this galled him, "is as good a military man as you will find. I'll tell you something you don't know. There's a larger army coming, a deadlier one, and they want to stop me from saving the world. Now this is a pretty big place, plenty of room for everyone. All we have to do is survive. So here's the deal: you're not getting me. I'm going to head up to that metal construction up in the mountains and do what I need to do. You can either oppose me and probably die for your efforts, or accept the reality. Join forces with the Pasha. I promise, the next battle will be one for the ages. It would be more glorious than this one and it would let me do my job."

Two of the guards actually looked to see what their leader would say or do. The man remained impassive and just looked out at the carnage. He was losing, badly.

"Here's one more tidbit I bet the voice didn't tell you: every single one of your men who survive this fight will be healed tonight, ready to fight tomorrow. The dead will stay dead, but your wounded will be repaired. Do you want your men to live or die?"

Osman nodded at me, aware that a military leader's responsibility to his troops was paramount. I can't tell you if that last bit swayed him or it was the final number of an equation he was tabulating in his head. But the Mongol told the five to signal a ceasefire. Osman withdrew a bright red kerchief from a pocket and began to wave it.

"*If I may, Pasha,*" Silas said, taking the kerchief. Towering over the others, he waved it, and at first, Wild Bill saw it and signaled back, then punched an attacker and turned to relay the signal.

It took less than a minute for the fighting to stop. Everyone stood in place awaiting the next instructions. Everyone but Levy, who swung from soldier to medic and was attending to the most injured.

Over the next hour, we restored order and I asked the Mongol leader, whose name was Möngke, which aptly meant eternity, to gather his forces so I could explain where they were. The concepts sounded preposterous to one and all since the concepts of time travel and parallel realities was not something they had heard of before. However, they all heard the voice that offered them a mission, so if some powerful deity could take them from the steppes of Asia to here, then the rest was plausible. I then explained about the collector and how it would let us speak with the voices, the two forces that brought my people and Möngke's here. We would form an alliance to prepare for the great war to come and then they could choose their own destiny. I was secretly hoping that seeing all these different people from all these different places might make them want to integrate. I feared they'd be a future irritant, but I couldn't focus on tomorrow. We needed to get to the collector ahead of Abernathy, who was likely less than a day away.

It didn't take long for the Mongol forces to grasp that they could communicate with their enemies when I was nearby. Some thought me a powerful sorcerer or something and I couldn't allow that to go on. I explained I was singular in nature, and was otherwise flesh and blood like they were. I showed off my purpling bruises and bloodied knuckle to prove the point.

With the fighting over, we caught our collective breath. I asked Osman to bring us up to speed and he spoke of the villages visited, the long marches, and the spreading word of the nanobot army.

"And they spoke of you, Meredith," he said. "People have been looking for you. Some had been visited by the *Brimstone*; others had heard of the flame-haired woman being sought or who could translate any language. You're becoming quite the personality."

"It's nothing I asked for," I said.

"But you're this world's first celebrity," Bartholomew crowed. I grimaced at that.

Osman summoned several newcomers to the forces and they huddled with Albert and Silas (well, with him, huddle doesn't quite work), adding new information to the map, filling in gaps, adding names the locals had given their rivers and lakes, their villages. Later, I shared this with Möngke, tracing my path since arriving here nearly two months earlier. He'd only been there a day, waiting in the rocks, dealing with the cool night, everyone with an image of the redheaded woman burned into their minds.

"You share everything?" he asked me.

"This may be difficult for you, but we were all invited here, saved from lonely deaths, and offered a second chance. You were offered glory and life, but little seemed to have been said of what happened next. We're all here to start over and maybe, just maybe, build a better world."

He considered that, keeping his own counsel. His eyes traced the map, seeing vast swatches of open land, which might as well have been marked "Here there be Dragons," since it remained unexplored territory. I could imagine he was seeing lands to conquer while I was hoping he saw it as lands to settle. That might still come.

Chou approached me soon after and cocked her head toward the mountain. "It's still daylight. We have several hours before sunset and could be well into the mountains before we needed to make camp. This way, we could be at the collector tomorrow."

I was tired and saw Vihaan had been injured badly enough he couldn't walk without help, serving to slow us. In fact, other than Albert, no one was unscathed, but they'd come if called. Our goal was within sight and that would give us the drive to push on, especially knowing we'd all feel better overnight. I didn't even bother to put it to a debate. I nodded and Chou headed off to relay the news.

"You're going," Osman said flatly. Möngke stood nearby, uncertain of his new role in this situation.

"Yes, just my original group for now. You and Möngke need to blend the troops, get them ready for what's coming. It'll be tomorrow if your intelligence is correct. That's not a lot of time."

"We need to protect you too," Osman said, his voice full of pride and duty. "Let me send some troops."

"It is wise," Chou added.

I considered it then came to a decision. If everyone was looking to me as their leader, hopefully they would actually take direction. Even my proud, sexist Turk seemed to be coming around. "Take the day. Blend the forces, train as a single unit. Then, rather than sit here and wait for Abernathy, follow us into the mountain, for the collector."

Osman's craned his neck, looking at the ominous, unbelievably large collector, its powerful miles-wide trunk sucking energy from the sun. He'd heard about it but hadn't focused on it much as yet. He was certainly nonplussed if not outright freaked and I got that and was sympathetic.

Comically, Möngke followed his gaze and his jaw literally dropped. If Silas was big to him, something made by man was impossibly beyond his comprehension.

"Who made that?" he asked.

"The being who brought us here, the enemy of the being that brought you here." He absorbed those words and continued to stare.

"How will we communicate if you leave us?" Möngke asked.

"You're both brilliant military men; you speak your own language in a way. You will find a way, even if it's just hand gestures, but I can't stay."

Neither man looked happy but accepted the fact.

Within an hour, we had eaten and gathered our gear. Someone took a branch and turned it into a walking stick for Vihaan to lean on, Michael rarely away from his side. Wild Bill handed the now abandoned rifle to Levy, who took it readily. I had made my farewells to the two military men, happy to see that Möngke was making an honest effort to work with Osman. I caught them eyeing one another, sizing each other up, seeking weakness. Maybe they were two of a kind, which would only benefit us all

Our posse headed toward the mountains after Silas directed us in the direction where the geography would allow us the easiest passage. I hoped there would be constructs like Blue Alpha to greet us, but that was for tomorrow. Now we had to find out way through the mountains, toward the massive collector, and then up and in. It always sounded easier than it truly was, but we walked in single file, with little chatter among us. The sun beat mercilessly down on us and we were fairly exposed as we walked and climbed. Somewhere there had to be a road or even a path to access the collector, but Silas didn't know where it was, so we were left to amble along and hope a lot.

Our path wasn't overly arduous, just hot and tiring. The steep parts would come tomorrow, so now it was making distance, and then figuring out where to camp for the night. There were genuine insects buzzing about us and Michael seemed especially tasty to them, so he was constantly waving them away, complaining all the way.

Finally, we found a flat enough space that would accommodate us. We were tired and worn, so it made sense to camp here, eat, sleep, get a fresh coat of pixie dust, and push off at first light. Having the collector in sight was either taunting us or the carrot we needed to keep going; it depended on how tired I was feeling. I ignored the mental dilemma as we cleared space, gathered kindling for a fire, and got to work setting up camp. Our dinner was almost as quiet as the hike, which made sense given how worn out we were. Albert was still energized and went exploring with Silas as company and bodyguard. Finally, when I couldn't keep my eyes open anymore, I yelled for them to return.

Chou took the first watch, tending the fire and polishing her blade. Me, I was dead to the world, dreaming of sugar plums or something equally diverting, As a result, I was slow to rouse when I heard scuffling, then a cry of alarm. When I finally pried my eyes open, I was astonished to see Chou sword fighting someone clad entirely in black while an equally attired person was coming my way. Thankfully, the scimitar was within reach and I was on my knees by the time he approached. He swung, I countered, the two blades clanging in the cool, night air.

Ninjas. Really? There were maybe a dozen arriving from above, and our party was under assault. Once more, Wild Bill was fast to react, his six-gun raised and firing off a shot that nailed one looming over Vihaan. Bartholomew reared back and landed a powerful blow into the side of one's head, sending him reeling. Michael used the rifle as a club, taking one out that way before another landed a blow that staggered him. One of them threw a star that pierced Miko's shoulder, dropping her to her knees. Levy flipped one, bending backward to avoid a sword slicing through the air. There wasn't enough space for us to easily fight a dozen ninjas, and it was complicated with swinging blades and rifles.

A ninja leapt over one of his compatriots, something short and sharp in his right hand, and landed a blow to Michael, deeply cutting into his left arm. The pixie dust had already paid us a visit, so this needed immediate attention. He remained down, as did Miko.

I ducked under one blow, only to have my legs swept out from beneath me, and I lost my breath as I slammed into the ground. He was on me, pinning the arm holding the scimitar, and some sort of claw-like thing clutched in his right fist. I'd be shredded for sure and I wriggled, resisting and hoping to dislodge him, but he outweighed me and I wasn't going anywhere. I did manage to rock a bit and used that momentum to arch my back and throw my legs high enough to ram my knees into his back. That unsteadied him enough for me to twist to the right and get him off me before I became human confetti. He was faster than I was and reaching for me, when Wild Bill stepped between us, and those claws cut into his leg. He grunted once and stomped the ninja into senselessness.

By then, I was on my feet, the scimitar before me. Bill was in pain, as were Miko and Michael, so this had to be ended.

"Can we talk about this?" I cried out. If I could stop the Mongols with my words, maybe it could happen with ninjas.

The one nearest me cried "no" and swung an arm around Chou, who did a move so fast, I couldn't make it out, but I did hear the bone snap.

I didn't want to take more lives, but if it was us or them, it had to be us. Too much was at stake and I hated myself for the calculation when it came to human life. The Adversary was going to have so much to answer for when this was all over.

One approached Bartholomew, swinging something in his right hand. The staff was silver. At the top was a chain and at the end was some sort of spiked flail. It whistled as it gained speed, readying to land it. Bartholomew must have read my mind, because he now held the rifle, took aim, and fired. Another fell in a bloody heap, the flail falling uselessly to the ground.

Behind me, Bill's gun coughed twice and more ninjas fell, each punctuated with a barely suppressed grunt of pain.

Chou snapped the neck of another with a clean, efficient move.

To my surprise, Albert caught the drop on one ninja, who was making a move for Vihaan, coming up behind him and striking the legs with his bladed weapon. When he and I had discussed combat days before, I advised him to always go for the legs when possible. It hampered or stopped their mobility and gave you more of a chance. I hated seeing someone that young forced into this sort of violence, but that just went on the Adversary's bill. Levy came to his aid and reached out, grabbing the ninja's hand and breaking it.

The numbers diminished until the dozen were either unconscious or dead. There was an unpleasant odor from the blood and viscera of the injured and dead. I threw my arms around Albert, whose elation gave way to terror as the reality settled in on him. Chou helped Levy tend to Michael and Wild Bill as Bartholomew scoured the area, collecting weapons and stowing them in his rucksack. Better we have them because who knew what would be thrown at us next.

Later, Chou approached. "How's Albert?"

"Scared," I said and she nodded. "How's Michael?"

"The blade cut a vein, but Levy staunched it. He lost blood and we have none to give him, so he will be weak for the next day. Miko's a bit better than that. Wild Bill will limp for a bit. That weapon cut deeply, mangled skin and muscle."

"It's hours before dawn, but maybe we should get started and keep moving," she suggested.

"You're the security expert. What's your advice?" I was shaking, tired, and worried for Michael.

"A moving target is harder to hit," she said.

So we gathered our things, grabbing branches to light our way, and began our climb. We were probably all still tired, moreso thanks to the adrenaline flushing through our bodies. No one was hungry and we barely paused to eat as we trudged at a snail's pace. Ever so slowly, the ink-night sky lightened, and then there was color, the first pink hints of a new day. The lightening sky set the collector's massive form in an impressive silhouette, and it was looming larger, which meant we'd get there today.

About an hour after the sun peeked over the horizon, we found a path, narrow but well-trod by people in the recent past. We stepped on to it and kept moving, one step after the other.

"No further," a heavily-accented voice cried as two figures stepped before us. They were middle-eastern, bearded, their mismatched clothing was obscured under the dynamite-laden vests they wore. Was the Adversary that desperate, sending suicide bombers after us?

"What a wretched hive of scum and villainy," I muttered.

"What?" asked Chou from behind my right shoulder.

"Never mind," I whispered. I managed to talk the Mongols out of killing us, failed with the ninja, so this was the rubber game. I wasn't feeling too optimistic about this one because suicide bombers tended to be fanatics.

"Aren't you looking for me?" I asked, hoping to learn their true goal.

One looked ready to say something when the other shushed him. Then I heard something slipping out of leather behind me.

"The hell with this," Wild Bill said and shot them with such speed, neither man could react. While I couldn't see the bullet, I actually felt it whiz over my shoulder, getting a little close for comfort. But Bill had proven himself time and again as a crack shot, so I really shouldn't have been worried. However, I might never get used to any of this.

We looked at the two bodies, wary of the deadly vests, but saw they weren't going to help us much. Chou neatly removed the wires to ensure they didn't accidentally detonate. She retrieved the packs of C-4 and sticks of dynamite from their vests, along with two rusty pistols. She examined then tossed the pistols, but stowed some of the explosive material in her gear, handing the rest to Levy. Instead, though, we heard a distinct explosion behind us. Then another, further away, closer to the Pasha's army. We felt the vibration of the first explosion, and heard dirt and stone shift and then a rumble. Wherever the third man was, he had definitely blocked our trail back, giving us no choice but to keep moving. It also neatly cut us off from Osman, which I didn't like at all.

The latest threat spurred us forward despite the various aches and injuries. We plodded ahead for another hour, then two, before finally calling a break. By then, the sun was well into the sky and the heat and humidity had risen. My clothes were plastered against my chest and back, feeling unpleasant. Michael looked haggard and Wild Bill had fallen toward the rear given his leg. I foolishly drained my canteen, desperate for the water's coolness. I saved just a little to trickle over my head, letting tiny rivulets run down my neck.

Most of us also took the time to rearrange our gear, making adjustments to better fit the weapons we retrieved from the ninjas. Everyone worked silently until Albert cried out, "Oi, what's this?" His hand rose out of the bag and there in his palm was a robo-bug. He scowled at it and then placed it on the ground by his feet. As his left foot rose to squash it, Vihaan rushed over and stopped him.

"It may come in handy," he said.

While that might be true, it also meant the Adversary had been tracking us for who knew how long, which explained the threats in the last day. He no longer wanted me for himself, but wanted me and the others dead.

I had other ideas.

TEN

THIS COLLECTOR WAS as huge a structure as the one we found Michael, Vihaan, and Miko in. At the top was the cone-like bell, which absorbed power from the Dyson swarm, sending energy through the miles-wide trunk, sweeping down, growing rapidly narrower before broadening again. As it neared the ground, it vanished into tightly-clustered rocks that rose above the trees at its base, oddly out of place in the sea of green surrounding it. Lines of energy moved and shifted within the collector's trunk. Everything around it was silent, not a rustle in the leaves, not a thrum of energy. The same circular dead zone greeted us, a sobering reminder of the devastating power we were dealing with.

While Chou, Albert, Silas, and I had seen it before, the others gaped now that they had a full view of the mammoth construct. These giant collectors of energy from the stars were repurposing it to geo-form protection, to pluck two billion people from across the multiverse, and to ready the world for the false vacuum. But yet, the network couldn't easily communicate with us; the Adversary saw to that. How had it stymied plans that were in the works for countless millennia? If the

Architect was the *Shining Light*'s AI, then it had nearly half a billion years to do so much. More questions and more unknowns and I, frankly, had my fill of them.

Albert silently came beside me and slipped his hand into mine.

"This thing still scare you?" I asked.

"Not really," he said. "I guess I am getting used to it, but I have never seen anything so large and I've seen St. Paul's Cathedral."

"Silas, are you picking up any transmissions like you did at the other collector?"

"Yes, Meredith, the same Fibonacci numbers."

"Lead on," I said, wanting to bow and be graceful, but was too damned tired. I merely gestured that he should move on.

The thing was so huge that we were walking a good thirty, forty minutes around the circumference of this robot-made construct and Silas was giving us no indication we were near the holographic doorway. Several minutes later, he did slow to a sudden stop, the hair on the back of my neck now at attention. Now what?

I shouldn't have asked. A trio of seven-foot-tall androids, cables running down their arms and up their legs, pulsing green energy within its chest chamber, all making clacking sounds with every move, took a position and stared at us with cold, ice-blue eyes. These were entirely mechanical beings, clearly from some time in my future, and looked dangerous just standing there. There was a grill for a mouth and no nose; after all, they didn't need to breathe. I saw nothing resembling weaponry so suspected it was internal and feared it to be true as the green energy pulsed like an engine warming up.

"Silas, do you recognize these?" I asked.

"No, Meredith, they resemble nothing I have seen before.

They are, though, clearly primitive constructs," Silas said, almost sounding dismissive.

Michael shuffled forward, whispering to Chou, who reached into her bag, and she handed him the tablet rescued from the *Brimstone*.

"What in blazes are these things supposed to be?" Wild Bill called from the rear.

"Androids, simpler versions than Silas, it seems," Chou told him. He made a scoffing sound.

"So, fancy robots?"

"Androids are designed to mimic humans, Wild Bill. Robots can take a multitude of sizes and shapes. Myself, for example, may have two arms and legs, but I look nothing like..."

Silas' lesson was interrupted when three more identical forms took position behind them and I could hear more coming. No wonder the bombers cut us off from the Pasha. We were being herded here to face these things and they definitely had the advantage. I was guessing that my scimitar wouldn't do much good against those steel frames.

Bartholomew had the rifle in his hands and was taking aim.

"Don't waste the bullet," I called out. Besides, I feared the ricochet could hurt one of us.

By now, it had become clear to all that the Adversary was done wanting me alive and would settle for me dead. We were at a distinct disadvantage and I didn't know whether something like Blue Alpha would arrive like the literal *deus ex machina* or could we actually disable them.

"Fall back...slowly," I said, trying to sound far calmer than I felt.

With every step backward we took, the now dozen-strong machines took a step toward us. They weren't charging us nor were they going to simply let us get away. I had no idea what they were waiting for, unless it was to totally freak us out. If so, it the plan was working just fine.

Our path was wide enough for us to stand four or five abreast if need be, which gave us some room to maneuver but not much.

"What on god's earth are those?"

I allowed myself to turn and beamed at Osman and Möngke, who were leading their combined forces. I noticed my newfound Mongol friend was a step behind Osman, a sign of deference. I wondered how long that would last. They may very well have ignored my orders and followed soon after uniting as a fighting force. However they got here, they were welcome, since now we had numbers on our side. While that changed the odds a little, my guess was these were still more powerful than we were and would not succumb to swords or arrows.

"Mechanical men like your Silas?" Osman asked. "Do they die?"

"No, but they can be taken apart," I called over my shoulder.

"I am a soldier, not an engineer," Osman said unhappily.

"Meredith, can you at least buy me some time?" Michael said. "I have an idea."

"Silas, stay with Michael and Vihaan. Osman, provide them additional cover. We will have to take this battle to them."

"Arrows can't pierce that metal," Möngke said.

"Nor can bullets," Osman complained.

"My guess is, they can at least distract them, hold them at bay. They are likely stronger than your men, but there are a dozen of them and more of you. Overwhelm them and see if we can." I turned, ready to wade into a hopeless battle then paused. "Albert!"

"Here!" he cried from behind Bartholomew.

"Stay with Silas," I ordered. Thankfully, he was smart

enough not to argue and trotted to the rear where the others were. With that settled, I turned to face the deadly dozen. I noted with alarm the green energy had stopped pulsing and grew bright.

"They're about to..." And my words died as a loud series of crackling bursts split the air. A dozen green beams of energy lanced forward, turning several men into crisp toast, eliciting shrieks of alarm from the others who broke formation.

Osman whirled about and shouted for them to resume their ranks.

I looked and saw the green bursts – lasers? – had ended and the glowing chests had pinpricks of energy. These things were slow to build up their resources before deploying the death beams or whatever they were called. I knew we had minutes and had to make them count.

Withdrawing my scimitar, more for show than anything else, I cried "Charge!" I ran forward, the blade waving uselessly in the air, but looking pretty fine, I bet. I just hoped the others followed.

Osman repeated my cry and I heard the army roar, boots pounding the ground. This wasn't going to be easy, but I was smaller and hopefully nimbler than these things. Chou was at my side and there was a wicked grin on her face. She was ready to cut loose, it seemed. We rushed to one android off to the left and we both ducked under an arm. Chou, to her credit, slid neatly between its legs and thrust her sword upward into a leg joint. That proved to be a weak spot and while she didn't slice inside it, she did leave a serious dent. When it took a step, it wobbled, letting me actually shoulder it to the ground.

I'll say this for sexism. Those men saw two women knock one of these things to the ground, emboldening them to do the same. Men and women rushed past us, still letting out war whoops, and they barreled into the eleven remaining androids.

In some cases, the momentum staged the things, while in other cases, the androids were better braced and merely swatted away the attackers.

Some men were hefted into the air and thrown into the mountain side; others crushed. It wasn't very pretty and the sounds of pulped human were sickening. The android we knocked down recalibrated and used its position to trip several passing soldiers and one arm grabbed a leg, snapping the ankle in two. Michael asked for time, but I had no idea how much he needed.

Our struggle went on for a few minutes, but the green glows were enlarging, accompanied by a growing whine, so I knew they'd explode again. I shouted a warning to everyone to find cover. Those who understood my words did as ordered, even if I wasn't Osman. The rest followed their example just as the first beams fired.

"Michael!" I cried.

"Almost there," he called back.

My problem was, talking to him told the androids he was important, so somehow they communed with one another and one rose, violently shaking off three soldiers, and marched toward Silas.

"You shall not pass," he said and I had to laugh, earning me an odd look from Chou.

"Never mind," I said, rising to my feet. "We have to slow that one down." Without a word, she stood beside me, and we were quickly joined by four Mongols, who sensed they were needed.

We rushed the marching android, and it knew we were coming, so as we got within a foot, it swiveled its torso around and struck two soldiers, sending them flying. Miko ran to join our effort, a trickle of blood running down her neck and right arm. Chou tried her joint trick again with no success. Still, the android was being buffeted by two women and two Mongols, which had to count for something. The energy whine was reaching a familiar crescendo a third time and it had turned about, aimed at Michael and the others.

The two Mongols bent low, each grabbing a thick, unforgiving leg, and heaved upward. The emerald blast of energy sliced into the air, upward and away from my son. As it fell on to its back, Silas arrived and his superior form allowed him to punch his way into the discharged chest unit and rip out the chamber with a sickening sound of bending metal and ripping circuits.

The other androids had built up their energy and seemed ready to unleash another barrage of death, but instead the whine slowed and lowered. New clicking sounds began to be heard from one machine after another. I shot Chou a look, but she merely shrugged.

Within moments, the androids rose and stood like statues.

"Did it!" Michael cried, and Vihaan let out an uncharacteristic whoop of approval.

"Did what?" I asked, walking toward him. Chou remained, inspecting the now inert androids.

"All I had to do was find the frequency they communicated on and find a way to piggyback on the signal. Once I could determine the language they were using, I was able to try a series of commands, adjusting until I found the right one."

"So you told them to stop fighting?"

"No, it was a virus that I broadcast, ordering each android to begin a self-diagnostic. Self-repair and self-preservation were paramount to early 22nd century robotics. I had hoped it would remain true for whatever era these things are from. Once I got the message through, I followed with a second, asking each to continually perform the self-diagnostic until further instructions were received."

"How did you know it would work?"

"I didn't, but Vihaan had been studying the nano technology and we were able to draw some conclusions, which allowed me to write the fast code. He found a powerful transmission signal from the robo-bug we saved from Albert."

"That's my boy," I said, teasing the older version of a son I would never have.

The fighting over, the soldiers tended to their injured, helped by Levy, as Osman and Möngke, seemingly now joined at the hip, approached. I looked out to see how many we had lost and took a sharp breath, to see it had been too many. One would have been too many. This wasn't what the Architect designed. It was all being spoiled.

"I gave you orders. What happened?" I finally asked my general.

"There were crazy men, carrying bombs, blowing themselves up to block our way," Osman said.

"I'd seen the black powder used before, but not in that manner," Möngke said with some surprise. "They were not very good at aiming, better at blowing up."

"Remember, I wanted to blow up the Adversary," Osman said. "It can be most effective."

"Forget that. I told you to stay in place," I said, not at all happy with the two men playing soldier.

"We formed ranks, and military training, it seems, is fairly universal," Osman told me. "We spent more time inspecting one another's arms than anything else. Möngke is clearly out of his element and deferring to me, making commanding the men a lot easier."

"But I told you to drill and be ready. I didn't expect you for a day."

"Abernathy will be here in a day or less. I agreed to protect you and I couldn't do my duty from down there. Then those men blew themselves up, trying to jam the passage. He did a poor job and we wasted about an hour clearing the way. Then we just marched after you."

"There has to be a chain of command," Chou said. "It has to be respected."

"I respect Meredith, but *she* has to respect *my* experience." He stood firm, eyes ablaze with authority and I decided it wasn't worth further discussion. We had to get inside the collector and we had to get some answers before the inevitable final battle was to come. Without prolonging the discussion, I turned and led everyone forward, following Silas, who was homing in on the entrance. We walked in uncomfortable silence for at least an hour before he paused before a space and gestured.

Trusting him, I reached my hand forward, and just as they did with the first collector we encountered weeks earlier, the rocks vanished and the doorway rumbled open. I heard gasps behind me but ignored them and strode inside, ready for anything. This tunnel was prepared for us, a series of pale blue lights ignited on both sides of the walkway, trailing off into the distance but clearly leading us. Where the other collector had a mosaic of glass-like artwork, the walls seemed more lined with pulsing, yellow waves of light, urging us forward while the floor retained the checkerboard of ever-changing blue hues, creating the illusion that we stood on the edge of a lake. It was a complementary series of colors, calming and welcoming.

"It's like walking on water," Bartholomew said softly, reverently.

"Don't get biblical on me," I said. "This was all made by machine, nothing divine about it." That came out harsher than intended since, like him, I felt the sense of awe rising in me once more at the sheer scale and scope of the structure that burrowed through and beneath mountains before even getting to the main section.

"This is fizzing," Albert exclaimed, somewhat louder, and his enthusiasm was contagious.

Behind him, Osman and the others, making their first excursion within the structure, were marveling and their fingertips traced along every surface, gently rippling the water-like flooring. There were more gasps and quiet exclamations, but no fear. I was reminded of what Silas said when we first entered a collector:

"The Architect was concerned that the effects of the translocation on Candidates would induce mass-panic. While certain chemical alterations were made to you to reduce that possibility, every effort was made to ensure your environment was as calming as possible. I imagine this is a simple attempt to ensure that whoever passed through this tunnel remained tranquil."

I would be willing to bet my scimitar that the Adversary made no such preparations, hence Möngke's emotional state.

As with the previous collector, it took us a good forty-five minutes to walk from the mammoth double-doors, which had clanged closed behind us, to reach the first biome, which I had expected to be farmland like the other structure. Instead, it was pastoral parkland, with rolling green hills, thick trees, and I could hear the gurgle of actual running water off in the distance before us. There was pleasant light, a breeze that shook the leaves. This was your perfect spring day regardless of century, culture, or parallel reality. It was beautiful, calming, and where you imagined laying out a blanket, sipping wine, and tossing a frisbee to your dog.

In the center, looking like the foundation of a colossal fountain, was the jade-green flute-shaped glass that climbed the sky, reaching higher than one could imagine a single structure to stand. Once more, there connecting covered walkways with filigreed designs on the paneling. I stopped counting at seven, but there were quite a few more buildings of differing heights, most glossy black in appearance, making me think of the ominous obelisks from 2001, but there was nothing dangerous here. In fact, where there had been rubble in the other collector, this place was intact, and even spotless. No doubt, there were machines somewhere that came out with the dust mop and Pledge.

As we stood by the centerpiece, high above, a series of multi-colored lights were one by one winking into existence, like a computer waking up.

"Silas?"

"The central core computer seems to be activated, but this is not threatening."

"Good to know."

The lights raced down toward us and we gaped, staring at the odd geometric shapes the lights took as they came to life. Beneath my feet, I felt the rumble of machinery at work and the breeze vanished. It grew eerily silent and we waited to see what would come next.

The sound that surrounded us was that of a pleasant male voice, absent an identifying accent.

"Welcome, beloved."

ELEVEN

"BELOVED," Chou repeated. "It's really you."

"Yes. Welcome Candidate 13, thank you for bringing my beloved to me. You have done well, considering the obstacles in your way. You have rescued Candidate 1 and now the work may get underway."

"Whoa. Slow down," I said. I had come for answers and it was time they were provided, not just to me, but to everyone.

"I am forgetting my manners," the Architect said after a brief hesitation. *"You no doubt are tired and hungry. Would you care to refresh yourselves or dine first?"*

"Which will get me to the answers?"

"Dining it is." A moment passed, and then to my left, a previously unnoticed corridor winked to life, clearly indicating this was where we were to go. I sighed and gestured for everyone to follow in this direction. Everyone began walking that way, except for Chou, who lingered by the nearest speaker.

"I'll give you some time alone," I said, trying to sound as charitable as possible and tamp down my impatience.

Instead, I walked beside Michael and Wild Bill, both of whom were exhausted, desperately in need of a pixie dust bath.

They seemed very focused on putting one foot in front of the other, their eyes taking in the sheer spectacle of the place. I followed their gaze, reminded once more of Coleridge's "Xanadu." At every turn, there were signs of higher intelligence in terms of the machinery and interfaces, but it was all so harmoniously integrated into the natural surroundings, which came complete with bird baths, small statues, and I swear I saw a lawn gnome in the distance. The riot of color that was present in the first collector we saw, was absent here. Everything spoke of harmony. The feng shui of the place was incredible, considering the sheer square footage involved. This was the home of a superior being, who just happened to be a half-billion-year-old artificial intelligence, who was also Weston Chou's husband.

We had been led to a dining hall, the likes of which would not have looked out of place in Valhalla. Each wall had muted, recessed lighting that cast the space in golds and yellows. A veritable smorgasbord of artifacts from throughout human history decorated the walls. There was a roman shield, a stone sun dial, a banjo, a test tube, a Slinky, a yellowing copy of the *New York Times* proclaiming the Spanish-American War, a pair of wooden shoes, and on and on. Each was encased in glass, set within the wall, and everyone craned their heads to see what there was. A long, wooden table was being set by a series of small self-propelled droids that floated around, their segmented arms deftly setting out plates, silverware, and napkins. Each serving droid had a streak of green vertically bisecting them, some of sort of designation, I supposed. That was confirmed moments later, when brown-striped droids came floating in from an adjacent chamber with fingerbowls and heated towels.

There were several tables, so Osman and the army, respecting rank, took tables that allowed my team to stay intact. Silas remained with us, standing between the tables. After considering for a moment, I waved Osman and Möngke to join us. Better they were eyewitnesses to what was being explained so they totally understood the stakes.

Soon after, Chou rejoined us and of course I couldn't read her expression. The thoughts going through her head were no doubt private and would preoccupy her for a while. At least she found her husband alive. Everyone else on this planet was likely here without their loved ones. It made me miss Oscar and my parents, but at least we were also forging new friendships. How many of us would survive and what happened next remained an unknown, but I felt very close to this band, motley as we were.

Albert shoved over to make room for Chou to sit beside me. I gave her arm a friendly squeeze and then left her alone. Soon after, the brown droids returned with bowls of vegetable soup, freshly made and delicious, if in need of some pizzazz. We ate in silence and then the bowls were removed and a salad was served with a lazy Susan filled with dressings and accoutrements. At least the Architect was being a good host.

"Is everyone well enough?" he asked suddenly. Before we could answer, he actually beeped and added, *"My apologies. The drinks haven't been served. Please tell our butlers what you'd like. We can make most anything."*

To test it, Osman asked for raki, a Turkish liquor, while Wild Bill wanted a cold beer, and Albert wanted milk. I intended to keep a clear head, so I settled for iced tea, but damn if it wasn't the best iced tea I'd ever had, complete with a sprig of fresh mint.

"No doubt, you have many questions and I know we are short on time, so shall we begin?"

All eyes turned to me, making me the spokesperson, or the one to begin the interrogation. "Where is everyone?"

"You are, no doubt, familiar with extinction-level events?"

"You mean like the meteor that crashed and did away with the dinosaurs," I said.

Albert gaped at me, since such theories weren't in circulation in 1910. "That's what happened to them?"

"*Yes, Candidate 758,624,*" the Architect said.

"Can we use names, please," I said.

"*Of course, Meredith Jane Gale.*"

"Uh, just first names will be fine."

"*As you wish, Meredith. Yes, extinction-level events are part of Earth's history. After the last one, mankind had the ability to withdraw from the planet, preserving humanity. The computers and artificial intelligence of the day remained intact and operational. Fortunately, I was among the AI still in use and was able to marshal resources once it became clear the False Vacuum field collapse threatened Earth.*"

"The what?" Osman asked.

"Later," I said a little too shortly. "Wait, you were light years away on the *Shining Light.*"

"*Yes, Weston was right that our mission had been compromised by factions on Earth that did not want us to complete the mission.*"

"Which was?" Michael asked.

"Our mission was to reach and study an area of dead space. We would spend an estimated eight years there before returning to Earth with the information we gathered," Chou said.

"Dead space?" Albert asked.

"There were anomalies we called Vagrant Particles and needed to understand what they were before we traversed the galaxy," she said.

"So, nobby bits of the universe," he said, repeating the information in a way he could fathom. She nodded in affirmation.

"'Nobby bits' that we theorized were micro-wormholes to the parallel universes. We were sabotaged, and as the ship's life support systems were failing..."

"...I offered her the chance to live," the Architect finished for her.

"Yeah, exactly how did you accomplish that?" I queried.

"This will make the narrative convoluted, but from here, the year 420,353,745, I was able to send a signal to myself in the year 2374, and try to save my wife."

The brown waiters floated in now, clearing the salad plates and starting to serve a thick saucy lasagna, which smelled delicious. I was amused as one floated from person to person with a black pepper shaker while another followed with parmesan cheese, ready to shred it. This was all very homey, but I had to ask, "How did you happen to have all this on hand?"

"I knew you were coming, monitoring your progress through the mountains, Meredith, so I ordered a meal prepared."

"Of course you did," Michael said in an amazed tone.

"So where did everyone go?" Wild Bill said as he suspiciously sniffed the meal. Clearly, he hadn't had this classic Italian dish before, but hunger won out and he took a cautious forkful. I watched as he chewed, getting accustomed to the noodles and cheeses, its chewiness, and the blend of herbs and spices. He took a second mouthful, so I knew he'd be fine.

"By then, mankind had reached a Type III civilization," the Architect began before Wild Bill interrupted. "Type what now?"

Over our table, light shimmered and coalesced until an image of the Earth appeared, as it was in our time, with distinct continents. Superimposed over the holographic image was a waterwheel, then a windmill, a furnace, and a nuclear plant.

"An astronomer named Nikolai Kardashev established a scale for man's evolution. After he posited it in 1964, the scale became widely adopted and bore his name. As you can see here, James, a Type I civilization is when the civilization can harness

all forms of energy contained within the planet. Everyone here was living during the Type I period."

I shot a glance at Osman and Bartholomew, who, like Wild Bill (a.k.a James Hickok), hadn't heard of a lot of this. Both studied the image while chewing, neither one displaying anything other than rapt fascination. I did note with satisfaction that Wild Bill had neatly emptied his plate. Möngke was just staring, the most distant from the topics under discussion.

"So, what's a Type II?" Albert asked, his eyes intent, soaking up new information faster than most. As he asked, the images of the kinds of energy vanished and the Earth shrank to hover over one end of the table. Then the sun appeared, full and large, and crackling with energy, flicking light over everyone. Slowly, the Earth began its rotation around the sun.

"That, Albert, is when a civilization has learned to harness the energy coming from its own star."

"The Dyson swarm," Bartholomew said, far more easily following all this.

"That is correct, Bartholomew," the Architect said. I wonder if I was the only one weirded out by the Architect's casual use of our names. I know I asked for that, but this machine life seemed uncannily human and personable. I felt that he was kindly dumbing it down for the assembled group and his presentation would be filled with jargon for the scientists among us. I could only imagine how Chou felt having her husband effectively the god of this new Earth.

The Dyson Swarm now appeared around the sun. The realistic hologram now added millions of mirrors, neatly ordered in rings. Miko was nodding along in silent affirmation. As I recalled Chou's explanation, these were collecting all the energy needed to power a highly advanced civilization's technology such as the collectors.

"That's just Type II," Wild Bill said in a voice filled with awe. He knew he was out of his element and shared a look with Osman, who was flabbergasted. There was no other word for it.

"What's a Type III?" Albert asked, eager for more.

"That, Albert, is when a civilization has managed to harness the energy of an entire galaxy."

"You mean, mankind has managed to harness the Milky Way?" Miko asked. The astrophysicist was seeing theory made manifest and was delighted.

"Is there a Type IV?"

"When mankind abandoned Earth once and for all, Albert, they were still debating what that might mean," the Architect told him.

"So much power," Levy murmured, speaking for the first time since we entered the collector. Clearly, this was beyond her medical and military training and she was overwhelmed. I'd have to check in on her later.

"That is correct." The sun was dramatically reduced in size, and the Earth vanished entirely, as the Milky Way faded into colorful view. The spiral galaxy was on a diagonal, a bright spot in its center, although I recall reading that it was actually a black hole, sucking in all available energy. A bobbing red arrow appeared along one arm of the spiral. It had settled over where the sun had been and provided a sense of scale, which was mind-blowing, even though I'd seen this sort of map before. I could only imagine what my nineteenth century comrades were thinking.

"So, this galaxy is made of suns and planets," Bill said.

"We are so tiny, how could we have achieved this?" Osman asked.

"It happened over time, Pasha," the Architect said. Its use of his honorific seemed to startle Osman and I had to smile at the look on his face. *"Mankind was studying the stars when you were all alive. By the time Weston and I were studying the*

galaxy, we were far from the first. It was a gradual progression, but in time, once we learned to harness Sol..."

"Sol?" Möngke asked.

"The name of our sun," Chou explained. The Mongol merely nodded and resumed his eating.

"Once we harnessed Sol, it was easier to harness the next one and then the next, until we began networking the stars."

Now that staggered my imagination. I knew there were, I don't know, a gazillion lightyears between here and the next sun. So the notion of a network of stars was just hard to grasp. To illustrate the point, the grid of networked stars was overlaid atop the Milky Way and I saw just how far man had gotten. Somehow, despite the odds, we somehow overcame Global Warming and nuclear annihilation and did good things. But what was all that energy needed for?

"After the Dyson Swarm was designed, it was clear they would need to be maintained and the ability to build more was required. Humans developed colonies of robots that were capable of 'self replication'; their population may increase into the millions as they spread out across the galaxy as man colonized star after star," the Architect went on as the hologram began to pulse, showing how all the stars fed energy to the network, all of which was directed back home.

I turned to Chou, who was perhaps the most nonplussed member of the team; then again, she was the one who came from the furthest point in the future. In fact, she was turning out to be a bit of anomaly in that regard.

"You told me this weeks ago," I said, recalling her words. "'Unless that energy is being used to power other technology we are not yet aware of.'"

"What is all this power needed for?"

"Now that is the point of my gathering you all here," the Architect said. *"While the life support systems failed, I did not*

need them and was able to continue my mission. I reached our destination and studied the Vagrant Particles. I was able to examine them from a distance, measuring their energy output. Based on the data, it became clear that these were actually microscopic wormholes, tunneling between universes."

"Wait, this I know," Osman said with delight.

"How could you find parallel worlds?" Vihaan asked.

"Both string and M-theory predict that gravity can seep across parallel universes – which means their existence can be proven by looking for deviations from Newton's inverse square law of gravity."

"I know string theory, sort of, but what's M-theory?" I asked.

"Then you understand enough. M-theory is a unifying theory that takes all string theories and binds them together," Chou said.

"It is not dissimilar to your era's Internet of Everything," Vihaan said.

"And string theory is..." Osman clearly hesitated to ask for fear of looking ignorant, but this was all beyond his time and training.

"Not important right now," I said, not wanting to lose the thread here.

During this time, the droids arrived to clear our plates while the Milky Way galaxy vanished, replaced over the table with a hologram of the *Shining Way*, the first time I saw Chou's point of departure. It was cylindrical, with a wheel at one end that seemed to be rotating, generating artificial gravity if I remembered my movies. There were various boxy appendages, something that looked like a silvery flag fluttering above the ship, and a row of lights at the bottom. It was painted in gray and blue, the paint pitted and scarred here and there. There was no name or flag on display. The ship floated above the table and I heard Chou give a short gasp of recognition. Then the ship gained a double and it kept multiplying, representing the multiverse. The shape remained mostly the same, but the paint varied, the light patterns differed, some had two wheels, others none. It was beginning to feel like a Warhol painting.

"It took several millennia for me to chart several of these and study them before determining that I could send a signal into one such particle. Once I did that, I waited, orbiting a star to stay energized, and was rewarded with a return signal. Like building the network of Dyson swarms, a network of communication began between the universes, with my other selves."

"That had to be better than the isolation you must have felt," I said, unable to comprehend millennia of loneliness.

The waiter droids floated in, serving everyone a bowl of fresh-cut strawberries and cream, and once more, they were superior to everything I remember from home. Everyone, even my Mongol general, devoured them, with some cream lost in his mustache. The dessert was gone far too quickly but now I was feeling full, even logy.

"My emotions stagnated after Weston disappeared," the Architect admitted. *"I had not considered by how much until I felt the elation of contact and the notion that many versions of myself existed."*

"How many parallel universes are there?" Albert asked. "Two, fifty-two, a billion and two?"

"With new ones being formed, it appears limitless, although in some realities, there is a belief the multiverse is actually finite. As it turned out, I needed them all."

"Why?" I asked.

"Because, as I was processing my long-range studies while awaiting a response to the first signal, I was able to conclude from long-range study of the most distant galaxies that a False Vacuum event existed and the entire universe, including the dispersed humans, was threatened. My programming was quite

clear: 'A robot must obey the orders given it by human beings except where such orders would conflict with the First Law.'"

"You're not a robot," I shot back.

"No, Meredith, but I was still programmed with the same core concepts as devised by scientist and author Isaac Asimov."

"I, Robot," Miko said to no one in particular.

"Once communication was established, I shared my data and conclusions, receiving confirmation that my hypothesis was correct. Worse, it was happening in their realms as well. We then spent 10,000 years debating courses of action. During this time, I had returned to Earth, which had been abandoned. Nature had begun reasserting itself, cleansing the world and growing things afresh. I began having machines built in order to better harness the Dyson Swarm. And I grew, needing more space and a colder environment than Earth could provide. Having retained the Shining Light, I transferred my core programming to the moon, retaining this facility as my Earth base."

"How did you build a home on the moon?"

"Man had landed on the moon in 1969, Albert, and over the centuries, they built bases and communities. When they left the solar system, I was able to use them to rewire and personalize them for my needs since the processing power required to solve the False Vacuum dilemma would be vast."

That sounded like an understatement if ever I heard one.

"Did you come up with a solution? Is that why we're here?" Michael asked.

"We did find the beginnings of a solution, but then, our discussions were sidelined. It became clear that one of my parallel selves was drawing different conclusions. It began to argue with us, including questioning if mankind was worth saving."

"There's always an Internet troll, even in the future," I

mused, then my synapses finished firing. "He's the Adversary? A corrupt version of you!"

"Regrettable but true, Meredith." I had consumed more than enough fiction to understand evil twins, a staple of soap operas and space operas alike. No doubt, here, it pained the Architect. I could tell from his voice.

"What happened, beloved?" Chou asked.

"In time, private channels had formed, and we agreed that the aberration had to be cast out. We began theorizing ways of cutting off just one vagrant particle, but before we could come up with a solution, the rogue version sent a concentrated signal through the particle connecting him to this reality. He bypassed the moon and installed a remote version of himself in one of the collectors on Earth, while still maintaining his core power from his own reality. He had been silently studying our plans and devised ways to subvert them. None of us were aware of his efforts. He proved to be, in some ways, smarter than any one of us."

"It actually sounds like he was really focused and out to prove a point," I said.

"Quite likely," the Architect agreed. *"We worked on solutions and building the tools needed to execute our plan. This resulted in millions of years of planning, testing, and correction. We believed everything would work and were preparing to initiate the plan. Then, just 1,256 years previous, he asserted himself and began undoing our work. As soon as he tried to derail us, we fought back. He wasn't wasting time, replicating our work for his own purposes. Neither did I, as I tasked the SILAS units to dismantle that particular collector. Instead, it outmaneuvered whatever I tried: trojan horses, viruses, brute force attacks. It rewired my SILAS units to attack my other creations. The battle of the robots lasted a time until the larger ones successfully destroyed all but one of the SILAS units. It reduced the efficiency*

of the collectors and impeded my careful planning. The entire network of collectors, which I needed to save the planet, was offline and I had no robots to effect repairs.

"As I dueled with it, I continued my work with my parallel selves, finally conquering the temporal mechanic adjustments required to begin collecting my humans to save."

As he spoke, images were flashed over us, depictions of machines like the tank-sized Blue Alpha fighting off the Adversary's own devices. There were constructs looking identical to Silas being dismantled and we could see the beginnings of that deadly black nanotechnology working to undermine the Architect's great works.

"You couldn't beat him?" Osman asked, ever the military man studying war footage.

"My priority was bringing humanity here and readying Earth for its next phase of existence. I felt holding it at bay would have to suffice since our calculations suggested the field collapse was drawing closer."

"Wait a second," Levy interrupted. She'd been almost entirely silent during the time we'd been in the structure and all through the meal. Her eyes, though, showed me she was paying very close attention to everything. "If the SILAS units were destroyed years before we arrived, how did our Silas have a message for Meredith? She was specifically directed to find Candidate 1."

Now *that* was a good question, a salient point I had missed.

"While I knew my SILAS units were offline, I didn't know if they had been entirely dismantled or some remained intact and possibly able to be restored to life once you arrived. As a result, I programmed a signal with the message, so once a unit was activated, it would possess the directive to find Meredith and have her locate Michael. I knew to save the world and mankind; it would take everyone's combined efforts."

"What you didn't anticipate was that we'd find Silas, who was damaged," I said.

"Quite true. But I also knew I needed many hands to restore the network and resume the plan," the Architect said.

"At one particular moment, when I thought I had the opportunity, I finally began channeling all the great energies of the universe that I still had access to and opened the portals that would allow me to bring you and the rest to this time."

The holograms faded and were replaced with ripples in the air, like heat waves on a brutally hot day. Like zooming in on a single moment in time, we saw an old airplane cockpit, angled downward. There was Amelia Earhart struggling to right her plane, and saying into her handheld microphone, *"KHAQQ calling Itasca: we must be on you but cannot see you...gas is running low...been unable to reach you by radio...we are flying at 1,000 feet."*

What I couldn't see was her partner on the around-the-world flight, Fred Noonan, just Amelia flying on a clear blue day. I began to wonder why just her and not both, but shoved it aside for another time. After receiving nothing on the radio, we saw her head jerk up, listening to the air.

"Candidate 2814, do you wish to be saved? Answer yes or no."

Everyone around the table silently nodded in recognition since we were all approached in the same way.

"Candidate 2814. Amelia Mary Earhart. In thirty seconds, you will be beyond my ability to save. Do you wish to be saved? Answer yes or no."

Then she screeched yes and we watched her just wink out of existence. The hologram shifted and we next saw her on her hands and knees in shallow water, an all-too familiar image.

"When the first transitions occurred, with the people arriving somewhere other than my planned destination, I knew the

Adversary had been at work so subtly, I didn't realize it. Then, as animals, fish, fowl, and birds were brought forward, they were met with predatory creatures I had chosen to leave to the ash heap of history. The Adversary took my carefully calibrated food system and upended it, threatening their lives as well as that of the humans."

"That's some monkey wrench he's thrown into the system," I said. "So you couldn't stop the Adversary – we can call him that, right? – and he brought sabretooth tigers and worse. And by worse, I mean Nazis. Let's get personal for a moment. Why is he after me?"

"You, Meredith, are the sole human on this planet with the special gift for instantaneous translation. Have you not wondered why?"

"Every day. It's as much a blessing as a burden, so of course I've been wondering."

"On dozens of versions of Earth, you took your friend Oscar Kemple's death very hard, and in most of those, you all tried to commit suicide. But I selected you out of the multiple incarnations because you are an anomaly." That did not sound good; in fact, a chill ran through me. All my life, I had been one of the crowd, a dutiful but unexceptional daughter, a hard-working student at El Camino High and UC Berkeley, just average.

"How so?"

"Meredith, on your world, you were born with latent gifts that never fully manifested, but our collective scans of the realities revealed you had the ingredients to ignite the next stage of human evolution."

"I'm a freakin' mutant?"

"Mutations, as you know, are quite common in nature. It led one species to grow and evolve and survive. It allowed homo sapiens to live when your genetic cousins the Neanderthals could not. You yourself have known your red hair was a benign muta-

tion. The transition here activated those latent genes and your gift flowered. Since we had identified you prior to the Adversary's malfeasance, he knew of you too. It's how he captured an image of an older you, a fairly common one from across the multiverse, and used it to send agents after you." I knew I'd somehow become President of the United States, a concept I was still not comfortable with, but one that was now feeling inevitable. Of course, the USA was wiped away hundreds of millions of years earlier. In some ways, that freed me to be my own woman, chart my own destiny, but I still had yet to feel like I had any control over my circumstances. Now, I know I was picked by one intelligence and was wanted by another, all because of a genetic quirk. All this attention led everyone to look to me as their leader, a role I didn't seek and continued to feel uncomfortable with.

"But why does he want me?"

"By taking you out of the new genetic pool being fashioned on this world, mankind would cease its evolution, and in time, possibly die out."

"He wanted me, but not dead, at least not until recently. Do you have any idea why?"

"My working hypothesis was to experiment on you, possibly altering your mutation for his own reasons. I honestly cannot tell you."

"And yet, I am only Candidate 13, not my lucky number it seems. But you had me seeking Candidate 1, who turns out to be some version of my son. Why have me hunt down Michael?"

"Michael was brought here first as my way of thanking him."

"How's that?"

"Michael Roger Crain, a gifted software engineer, wrote the programming for the artificial intelligence, which became the template for the AI that was installed decades later on the

Shining Light. *He is, in some ways, my creator. And by extension, he may be credited as a savior for all mankind."*

Heads swiveled to give Michael praising looks or reappraisals, especially Osman and Wild Bill, who never seemed to know what to make of him. Deep inside, I felt a burn of pride welling up.

"And I read a lot of Asimov growing up," he said with a grin. "So, if I am your father, and you're married to Chou, does that not make Chou and Meredith some sort of in-laws?"

"One could argue that connection to be valid," the Architect said.

"Whoa," I said, giving Chou a look to see if any of this made sense to her. Not normally a warm and fuzzy person, Chou actually seemed to soften at the concept of our being "family." If I were to extend the hybrid family notion, if Michael created the Architect and the Architect created Silas, did that make him some distant cousin? Thoughts like that were going to hurt my head and needed to be shoved aside since we still had several pressing matters at hand. Still, I needed to know more.

"This Michael is older and sicker than anyone else you brought here," I observed.

"Michael has been suffering from stomach cancer and I brought him here. I brought him here first because I was thanking my creator. Also, by understanding my original programming, he could help me maintain and modify my own. Like a family doctor in your time, Meredith. He can help me adjust and correct my programming; see things I might otherwise miss. We had perfected the nanobots that we use to repair you. Every night, it treats the cancer, which is pervasive and strong, but it cannot be eliminated."

I shot my son a glance, worry written all over my face. He wasn't my actual son, but by now that was becoming more a matter of semantics. He met my gaze and nodded his head once to confirm the information, but his determined look said it was not to be discussed, at least not now. I returned my attention to the immediate threats at hand.

"What is the Adversary's ultimate goal?"

"He does not want humanity to survive. From his perspective, seeding man throughout space has been like spreading a disease and it is one he feels the universe is better without. By saving humanity from the False Vacuum, he fears it would be transplanting an old disease into a new reality."

"This False Vacuum you say is coming. If we're brought here as phase one of your plan, then that suggests you have a plan to save the Earth from something Chou swears will wipe out reality as we know it, rewriting the rules of physics for starters."

"That is the belief, yes," the Architect agreed.

"So how do you save the world?"

"All the galaxy's energies have been sent here to power the temporal machines, but it has also enabled us to do more than that. First, the planet has to be severed from its orbit around the sun. To accomplish this, I began construction on a free-floating solar sail, 20 times Earth's diameter. It is being assembled at a point near the Earth where the pressure of solar radiation essentially balances the world's gravitational pull. The reflection of sunlight from the sail will pull the Earth outwards along with the sail – in physical terms, increasing the Earth's orbital energy and accelerating the center of mass of the system outwards, away from the sun. "

"Come again," Wild Bill said.

The Architect provided visuals as the frozen image of a frightened Amelia Earhart gave way to the Earth in orbit around the sun, the inner planets faded but provided for perspective. Beyond the Earth and the moon, which was shown shattered here – something I still wanted to know about – but before Mars was a vast silvery object. It was in eight even segments, its shiny reflective surface showing off the stars and space dust, but dwarfed Earth and Mars, and even, I noticed, Jupiter. This thing was huge!

"What exactly am I seeing?" Osman asked.

"The solar sail is the largest object in the solar system, twice the diameter of Jupiter, the largest planetary body orbiting the sun," the Architect explained.

"Oh my," Levy said.

"How did you make it?" Albert asked.

"I needed a fleet of machines to excavate the raw materials, which were launched from the moon and sent to the asteroid belt, which is set between Mars and Jupiter." Clearly, the Architect recognized he needed to provide additional explanations to accompany the videos. As he spoke, the asteroid belt was highlighted with several objects glowing gold to indicate where the ores came from.

"The raw materials were refined within a facility I had orbiting the moon. The results over time turned nickel and iron into an eight-micron-thick film for the sail. While huge, it was incredibly thin but capable of harnessing the sun's power on one side, allowing the planet to move free from orbit."

"Moved to where exactly?" Wild Bill asked.

"A designated point where a portal would be opened, similar to the temporal breaches, and there the Earth would be placed into a new universe, which would then be sealed off. This pinching action would involve a bubble that forms a horizon between that reality and the rest of the universe."

Now a ripple appeared somewhere beyond the moon but also before Mars. Something huge opened. While this side had stars and planets and now a solar sail, the other side seemed empty, a void. The animation floated Earth neatly through the aperture and then, like a light switch, it sealed and was gone. To finish his point, not long after, the stars began to wink out with growing speed until the solar system simply vanished, leaving blank air over the now-cleared dining table.

"The angle would be at 35 degrees in static equilibrium relative to the planet, the center of mass would then slowly accelerate.. It would require constant monitoring so nothing alters that. This is not an overnight solution, but one that will take a considerable amount of time and attention, exactly something an AI such as myself was designed to do."

"What about asteroids, meteors, or comets," Miko, fascinated, asked.

"Constant repair would be required by robotic constructs, which are being built here on the moon," he explained. He sounded so damned matter-of-fact about this process while my mind – and no doubt everyone's – was blown.

"Are we already moving?" Albert asked.

"Since the sail was constructed, the impact has been gradual, but yes, Albert, the Earth is slowly moving away from its natural orbit."

"But not breakaway speed," I said.

"It's far more complex than that, but we do not have time to get into the specifics," he said, making me feel like an idiot.

"Has your Adversary tried to disrupt the solar sail?" Levy asked.

"By placing his programming on Earth, I have been able to keep him from broadcasting signals that would interfere. His efforts here have been more than enough of an irritant."

"That's all very ambitious," Bartholomew said. "So what's the problem?"

"The Adversary has managed to disrupt the power flow being absorbed from the universal network. He has been using it to fuel his own plans, while slowing the work required to save mankind.

Without that power, the portal cannot open and Earth cannot be saved."

"How do we do this?" I asked, somewhat afraid of the answer.

"The Adversary must be disconnected from the disruption and the network restored so the solar power flows freely once more. You were all gathered because I needed organic assistance in stopping him, but you have taken more time than I calculated. The Adversary is chaos made manifest and he has winnowed our chances. Based on the current calculations of the False Vacuum's approach and the need to generate enough energy to open the new universe, the power flow must be restored within the next fifty hours. This is not a simple process but one that is carefully choreographed between the approaching collapsing universe, the exact place to position Earth post-solar orbit, and where we can safely open the bubble. The measurements have to be precise and the energy flow has to be stabilized, the batteries recharged to generate the field, and so much more. If we miss this window of opportunity, the next one comes in years, and by then, it may be too late."

"So it's now or never," I said to the room. The Architect ignored it and continued.

"Abernathy and his converted army are less than two days from your position and will do everything possible to destroy you, then me."

"Okay," I said, thinking two days shouldn't be that difficult to accomplish the impossible. "Where is the Adversary?"

"I am uncertain."

PART THREE

Kindred spirits are not so scarce as I used to think. It's splendid
to find out there are so many of them in the world.
—*Anne of Green Gables*

TWELVE

WE HAD fifty hours to find the Adversary and restore solar energy flowing so the Earth could be relocated before the universe collapsed. My head hurt and I was utterly exhausted. Continuing his role as perfect host, the Architect suggested we all get some sleep and had a series of blue-striped droids prepare a series of sleeping chambers for us all. No doubt, everyone needed time with their own thoughts, letting everything settle before we made our next move. While I couldn't speak for the others, turning my mind off was proving problematic. The concepts that we heard over our first really good meal in six weeks was so improbable, so difficult to comprehend. And if I was struggling, people from further down the timeline, especially Osman and Albert, would no doubt be having more troubles.

Before we allowed ourselves to be escorted to the chambers, Osman and I recorded a message for the troops, which were quite likely getting worried they'd never see us again. Since he didn't need sleep, Silas was perfectly willing to make the long journey back to the outside world and inform them in a variety of languages, thanks to the Architect's data banks, and prepare them for the coming battle.

With that chore done, Osman, somewhat buzzed from his drinking, and clearly overwhelmed by the information dumped on him, withdrew. I noticed that as he recognized his place in the grand scheme of things, he was far more willing to let others take the lead in non-military matters. It no doubt was a massive adjustment to his way of thinking, but he finally came around to accepting this was no longer the world he knew. We made our goodnights (I totally lost time of day but was tired enough to crash) and a blue droid floated along the corridor until it stopped before a very tall doorway. The door slid open and I was hit in the face with warm vapor and some steam escaping. Looking inside, I saw a gigantic bathtub filled with steaming water. Towels and robes were neatly hung on hooks in an alcove to the side of the tub.

"Take all the time you need. I will be outside," the droid informed me.

I happily stripped the dirty clothes off, recognizing their stink. I stood before the tub and recognized this was the most privacy I had had since arriving. While I had been alone previously, it was against my will, so it didn't count. But here, it was quiet and soothing. As I gingerly dipped a toe into the water, I recognized it was at an ideal temperature, as if the Architect knew exactly how I liked it. Of course, he'd been studying so many versions of me, I wouldn't be at all surprised if that were the case.

The tub was in an unusual angular shape, a mad variety of small tiles, different shapes and colors, encased the tub from floor to ceiling, and I could lose myself just studying the patterns they made. Once my sore and tired body sank into the water, soothing music played. It was nothing I recognized, from melody to all the instruments in use, but the effect was clearly designed to relax my body and soul, which was certainly most welcome. Set within the wall on a series of staggered shelves were a variety of glass bottles. They were not labeled, but as I opened several and sniffed, it became clear some shelves had bath oils, others something akin to shampoo and conditioner. I experimented, lathering my hair and enjoying the fragrant, citrusy smell. The soap was coarser than I prefer, but it felt good to scrub the nooks and crannies, getting really clean, then leaning back and just being.

My mind began to sort things, reviewing the vast information we received earlier and trying to comprehend the cosmic scale of things. We really were trying to save not just the planet but humanity. We had scattered too far and wide, I suppose, to recall everyone who existed, so they went with Plan B, which meant giving us doomed folk a second chance. So far, everyone had proven worthy and I considered myself very fortunate to be surrounded by such folk. I even allowed myself a few moments to mourn Freuchen all over again. He would have loved this adventure.

As the water began to cool, the sleepiness had become irresistible, so I reluctantly rose from the water and wrapped myself in the robe. It felt warm, but I didn't sense a heating bar. I shrugged that off, fighting to keep my eyes open, and opened the door where my patient droid awaited. Without a word, it swiveled about and led me to the chamber of choice. It was not particularly large, maybe seven by ten, then again, it didn't need to be. There was the bed, a mirror, a panel with soothing images of nature rotating every few seconds, and a comfortable-looking chair. It was clearly designed for single night's use since it lacked a dresser or even a hanger. The bed was nothing special, a full size with crisp, white sheets and a down pillow. Keeping my robe on, I crawled under the sheet, and the last thing I heard was the gentle click of my door closing.

When I next opened my eyes, some sensor in the room detected my movement and the lights began rising to something resembling morning. What I neglected to notice in my haze earlier was the panel revealing a closet with an array of clothing hanging. My head felt clear and my body was no longer sore, but at a kind of peace. I wasn't outside for my nightly treatment but suspected the Architect had an alternative for his guests. For all I knew, there was something in the food or water to help. Whatever happened, I felt the best I had in weeks and that meant I was in better shape to face the twin problems before us.

There was a full-length mirror and I dropped the robe and inspected myself. My hair was longer than usual, not able to keep it in much of a bun anymore. It was now an unruly mop in need of styling, not that the Architect thought to bring a salon with us. Seven weeks or so of running, jumping, and fighting plus a substantial change in diet had left me leaner, with actual muscle tone starting to show. I truly was transformed being here and I liked the overall look. Normally, the next step would be makeup, but there was absolutely no need for that nor did I exactly bring my supplies. If I scrounged, or asked, I wouldn't be at all surprised if I found something.

And if he knew how I liked my water, I suspected the Architect also knew my size, and I was proven right, as everything I sampled fit me perfectly. So what does one wear to go to war? Lacking a suit of shining armor, I settled for fresh underwear, a crisp new pair of jeans, a blue and white checked shirt, hiking books, and a dark leather jacket that felt surprisingly light and comfortable. I slid my scimitar under the new braided belt and studied myself in the full-length mirror.

I looked like I was ready for a day in the outdoors rather than risking my life once more to save the world, but then again, they never tell you how to dress for those occasions. I checked, and there was no cape on a hanger.

As I emerged from the room, I was not at all surprised to see my friendly blue droid awaiting me, probably summoned when the lights began rising. Silently, it floated down the winding corridor, past the other sleeping chambers and the mammoth bath, and around a few more bends until we arrived in a small dining room. Tables for four were set and Bartholomew, Chou, and Albert were already eating while Wild Bill and Levy were pouring cups of...coffee? Oh my god, my body instantly craved it. Wild Bill saw the look on my face and broke into a grin, pouring me a mug.

Bartholomew looked almost regal in a black, yellow, and gold short-sleeved dashiki, practically straining against his muscular chest. Intricate patterns were woven in black, yellow, white, and red, bordering the neckline and waist, making for a striking image. His black pants looked durable, and the shoes seemed to be the only non-tribal nod to the road ahead of us.

Similarly, Wild Bill looked ready for a portrait with his wide mustache freshly combed and oiled, his long hair glistening off his shoulders, which were clad in a fresh black jacket over a white shirt, a thin tie around the neck. He could have been dressed for the frontier judge or courting. His plain, wide face was pink from cleaning and shaving, the boots worn but freshly polished. Apparently, he preferred his holster, which had dust and grime embedded in it, although I bet he could have had something new.

Albert, for his part, was in a fresh pair of brown pants, black boots, and a white shirt, punctuated by the chocolate brown suspenders holding everything in place. His hair was neatly combed, properly parted to the side, but curling at the base since he'd not been near scissors in nearly two months. But he was dressed for movement, which I appreciated.

Only Chou remained unchanged, in her white outfit – shirt, formfitting pants, and massive cloak – seemingly the same one since I'd first met her, incapable of retaining grime. Whatever material it was made from, I wanted a wardrobe of it in different colors.

Everything here was so normal, like a high-tech futurist's idea of a Holiday Inn common room. The walls were filled with screens, but they were a shifting series of scenes, from satellite images of the Earth to canyons, rivers, lakes, small villages, ruined pyramids...a tour of the world over countless centuries. Okay, I could count them, but it wouldn't be worth the bother.

"Where's everyone else?" I asked as I took a seat next to Bartholomew.

He finished a mouthful of fresh fruit, grinning the whole way, and finally said, "Either getting up or in the main space." We all lacked the vocabulary for this place and weren't going to be here much longer, so asking seemed pointless. Wild Bill placed the mug and a creamer next to me, and tipped his ever-present, but now cleaner, hat.

The aroma was a delight, full-bodied and sensuous. I let it wash over me for a moment before adding the cream, not worrying about where the cows were hidden, and took a sip. Over roast the beans and it can be bitter, under roast them and it ruins the taste. There's an art to coffee roasting, preferably in small batches, and I was always on the lookout for the best cup available. I had no idea it would take me half a billion years to find it. It was full-bodied and smooth, with hints of different notes, all in perfect harmony. This place was definitely getting a good review on Yelp.

"Did you get much sleep?" I asked Chou, keeping my face impassive.

"I slept perfectly fine, thank you," Chou said. "Why wouldn't I?"

"Maybe because you haven't seen your husband in a very, very long time," I said, smirking.

She met my gaze and I could see she was struggling to keep her mask in place, but clearly, she did more than sleep last night and I let it drop, focusing instead on my coffee.

"Eat up; we have miles to go," Bartholomew said.

"Do we know where?"

"That's what Michael and Silas are figuring out," Albert told me. He had finished his plate and was practically vibrating with anticipation. On the one hand, he seemed to grasp the enormity of our mission, and on the other, he had a twelve-year-old's enthusiasm for anything that smacked of adventure.

We ate and chatted, reviewing what we'd heard until Michael and Silas walked in. Michael, looking better than I had seen him since meeting him in the other collector, went for his own mug of coffee before joining us. Silas merely loomed over the room, although the high ceilings helped make him look less ominous. When Michael's mug was full, he came over and placed a tablet in front of Albert. It was thinner than anything I had seen in the Apple store, almost translucent, but on the edge-to-edge screen was a digitized version of the map he'd been maintaining.

"We managed to get this ready for you, Albert," he said. "We'll show you how it works and how to add to it, but you have the most complete map of Earth in existence. The Architect had not been monitoring the development of the various communities, preoccupied as he was with saving the universe." Michael then crouched beside him, and between sips of coffee, he showed how to activate different layers, showing just the collectors, or just the settlements, or even the Pony Express routes we knew about. Albert's eyes went wide and stayed that way during the explanation and then he was exploring it on his own.

"We have been charting the electromagnetic spectrum and traced high concentrations of energy, which we have concluded will most likely be where the Adversary is based," Silas informed

the room. By then, Vihaan, now resplendent in a wildly patterned red, blue, and gold shirt, gold pants, and boots, had joined us. He listened attentively, sipping his tea.

"The cheeky bastard set up camp at the next collector over," Michael finished.

"So close, but they cannot touch one another," Bartholomew said.

"It's not strategically sound, but certainly makes a statement," Osman said as he joined us. He was in full uniform, freshly crafted no doubt, looking every bit the commanding officer. The royal blue jacket had gold brush epaulets, golden woven designs from cuff to above the elbow, and a green and red sash. A series of medals in cluster shapes varied from golden and silver to red and blue adorned the jacket along with a row of ribbons atop the left breast. A tall red fez capped his head. It was ostentatious to my eye, but probably perfectly normal in the Ottoman Empire.

"Can we just blow it up?" Levy asked, looking sharp in her army camo fatigues, although the cut and patterns suggested she was from just ahead of my time. I never asked nor did she ever volunteer where she was from. I could ask and just get name, rank, and serial number.

"I ask that often," Osman grumbled with a smile.

"We just need to reactivate the energy flow and prevent him from doing further damage," I said.

"Yeah, just blow him up," she repeated.

"No. I would prefer we compromise it without ending its life. I've killed and it sickens me. We weren't brought here to perpetuate the violence. The Architect saw this as a peaceful world and the Adversary has marred that but not destroyed it. I want to honor his vision and do what we can to preserve life."

Levy didn't look convinced and I didn't blame her. After all, since she'd joined us, it had been one battle to the death after another with Abernathy's army on its way. How to stop them without killing them seemed an impossible task.

"Good morning, everyone," the Architect suddenly said from everywhere. Most murmured an automatic good morning back.

"Abernathy and his forces are nearing the mountains, intent on attacking this facility, I fear."

"No longer after me," I asked in surprise.

"I suspect they will try and obtain or obliterate you as part of the assault. I do not have the defensive capabilities to withstand the sheer volume of the attack or the nanotechnology that may seep through."

"Can you show us the terrain?" Osman asked and I deferred to my military leader. It was why I recruited him and now he had to show me it was a choice well made. Obediently, a hologram of the area appeared in sharp three-dimensions.

"Can this be adjusted?"

"Of course, Pasha, just grab hold and turn as needed."

Osman seemed hesitant, uncertain, so I reached up and touched an edge of the image and gave it a push. The image wheeled about, shifting at least 45 degrees on its axis. The Pasha gaped for a moment, then reached up with both hands and adjusted it so he could see it from a topographical aspect. In bright orange was the advancing army and in pale green were our forces, still just outside the mountains ringing the collector.

"Michael, where is the Adversary?"

Before he could respond, off to the left edge of the image, a bright red spot was illuminated. "And this distance? I need scale."

"On foot, it would take you six hours," the Architect informed us.

"That's all?" I asked incredulously. That was practically a

cake walk, so something felt off about that. Why would two collectors be so close to one another?

"Yes, Meredith. Given the elevation and proximity to the North Pole, it made sense to position two here in relative proximity. I may come to regret having built that one." I didn't blame him and that pang of regret may have been the most vulnerable I have seen the AI. He was smart and compassionate; I was beginning to understand how you could fall in love with self-aware artificial intelligence.

Osman was studying the image, Levy and Möngke now behind his shoulder.

"I don't suppose you can build more like Silas to fight Abernathy?" Albert asked, hope in his voice.

"I have not been able to fully focus on my own defense and now there is no time, Albert," he replied.

"How long do we have?"

"Abernathy will arrive to meet your men in two hours." That was far too close. I suddenly felt like we had run out of time. Hell, it'd take nearly half that to get back to the forces we left outside the collector. Without warning, and leadership, they were going to be slaughtered.

"How could you let us sit here idle if the enemy is this close!?" Osman bellowed.

"I merely awaited everyone being assembled," the Architect said.

"You could have woken us up!" I shouted.

"The other forces will arrive on the field of battle approximately forty minutes later."

"What other forces?" Osman demanded.

"I have been tracking movement from the various settlements now that Albert has shown me where they are. Without radio communications of any sort, it has proven difficult." That was the second time he hadn't been able to do something that should

seem so simple. Something was off with the mighty Architect and that had me worried. I didn't want to ask him in front of everyone and there might not be time later. I made a mental note to ask Chou about it.

"Well, I be damned," Wild Bill said. "The Pony Express did its job. You're bringing everyone together, Meredith."

"*We* are," I amended. Everyone had been contributing and I wanted to make sure they realized it since I'd be asking so much of them in the next few hours.

"Do you have a head count?" Levy asked.

"*That has proven challenging, as the numbers continue to grow.*"

Well, that was something. I wondered how many villages didn't send anyone, how many fell to the Adversary's nasty nanobots. So much of the original plan was now in tatters and it was up to us to preserve what we could.

"What is the size of Abernathy's force?" Osman asked.

"*Emanations suggest a force of 1,258, now 1,261,*" the Architect intoned. "*They are picking off stragglers, adding them to their forces.*"

I had expected worse, to be honest, but still, I doubted we'd match them one on one and I still wasn't sure how to fight them when they could elongate themselves and contort their forms beyond human recognition.

"Listen up," I began and all eyes were once more on me; at least it was getting to be a familiar feeling. "Depending on the length of...infestation, there are living, breathing people underneath the nanotech. They have no control over their actions and their durability and strength have been enhanced. Where a punch would take out a little old lady, here it would take a baseball bat. Being tech, they can also immobilize Silas, so he's limited in how much he can help."

"Damn," Wild Bill said.

"We saw Blue Alpha tear them apart, so they can be stopped," I continued. Of course they tore her to pieces afterward, but now wasn't the time for that reminder.

"Not that any of us have Superman's strength," Levy said.

"No, but it does give us hope, and sometimes that may be all we have. Swords can pierce through and kill them," I added, thinking about the poor teen, the first life I took, and now apparently not the only one before this was all over.

Osman, never quite taking his eyes off the map, but clearly listening, spoke up. "It'll take us an hour or more to get out, not quite enough time to reach the troops and pass the word."

"I can help with that," the Architect said. A trio of yellow-striped droids floated through the doorway. *"Follow them."*

"What will you be doing?" I asked, unable to keep an edge out of my voice. Something this huge, this powerful should be able to do more than be a damned cheerleader.

"What I can." He fell silent. I shot Chou a glance, but she seemed to have her thoughts to contend with.

"Albert, do you have this information on your slate?"

"Sure thing," he said, delighted to be of this much use.

We followed the droids single-file through the corridors, hurrying toward a different section of the mammoth collector, a place so immense, I probably would need a month to explore every level, every room, and probably need more time. I studied what I could, fascinated at hints of other biomes, similar to the other collector. Our footfalls echoed in the dim hallways, with panels displaying more imagery from across the ages. I began mentally testing myself, seeing where and when I could identify, frustrated that pre-law meant I didn't take much in the way of history classes.

Finally, after twenty minutes, the droids paused before a set of double-doors, which slid silently open to reveal, for lack of a better description, a subway. It was tube-shaped, with a series of benches and no windows. We clambered aboard, although Osman and Levy peered inside, checking for vulnerabilities, and then stepped aboard. They were on full tactical alert, it seemed, and this was a dangerous place to be caught.

Once the last one entered, the doors closed with a soft swoosh and a chime. Then we were suddenly moving, picking up speed by the second. On one wall, a panel suddenly winked to life and a map showed us moving through the tunnel, a bright blue line, headed for a section of the mountain not far from where we entered if I correctly read the winking symbols. That meant we'd be able to reach the main forces and prepare them for what was to come.

A shriek of tearing metal, though, interfered with that plan. A red light bathed us and a shrill alarm began beeping, instantly giving me a headache. Then I heard the first crack of metal as a rainstorm pounded on the subway. Only we were underground, so it couldn't be rain; it had to be something similar and I began to fear the worst. Sure enough, squeezing through an air vent came one of those damned robo-bugs, although this one had a stinger. As did the next and the next, as they swarmed into the subway car. Instantly, Chou, Osman, and Levy were in attack positions.

Swiftly, Silas' multi-faceted arm shot out and crushed one in his hand. Wild Bill was using one of his pistols to swat at the bugs. Bartholomew was more effective with the rifle, its wider butt crushing or smacking away handfuls at a time. Still, they kept pounding the subway and pouring through the ruined vent. We were the fish being shot inside the proverbial barrel. One was crawling on my boot, so I shook it and stomped hard, satisfied to hear the crunch.

Ones that landed unseen, on shoulders, backs, even in hair, stung with sharp electrical bites that hurt. Each one seemed to intensify the pain and I heard Albert shriek in pain. Thankfully,

Chou had removed her cloak and swung it about like a matador, disrupting their flights with the changing air pattern and the actual fabric. By placing the arc above Albert, he was spared more pain, even though it left her exposed. One opportunistic robo-bug went for her neck, although Silas placed a hand between bug and skin, closing the fist and crushing another.

Miko and Vihaan were back to back, trying to shield Michael, who was not at all a fighter. He was actually lying still and I feared the worst until I saw his chest rise and fall. A sharp sting on my forearm nearly made me drop my scimitar, which wasn't the best weapon, but it was all I had.

"Levy," Vihaan called, and the woman swiftly took his place protecting my son. The scientist was tapping furiously on his own tablet before using it to smash a bug headed for his eye.

The attack on the subway ended as did the infestation within, which made me more suspicious than hopeful. But I heard nothing different, so I concentrated instead on fighting the bugs already here. I ached in dozens of places as the shocks gained in intensity, but I continued to swing and stomp. To my right, Chou draped the cloak over Albert as she removed her own knife and swung it before her to disrupt attacks.

Something smoky began to fill the subway car, then a familiar burning rubber odor made me cough. One by one, the robo-bugs were sizzling in midair, whiffs of smoke emitting like miniature nuclear mushroom clouds over each one. Then, almost as a whole, they fell to the ground.

"What the hell...?"

"I was looking for a frequency, something to disrupt their programming," Vihaan explained. "Then I received a signal from the Architect, providing me with an override code so they would self-destruct."

"Thank you," I said, as much to Vihaan as to the Architect, if he was hearing this. Apparently, he was not entirely powerless against his enemy, although he took his damned sweet time providing that help.

"Sit rep," Levy called out, the medic taking charge for the moment. Like me, everyone complained of the painful electric shocks but other than charred, burned portions of our fresh clothing, everyone seemed well enough. She added topical anesthetic to some of the more serious injuries, notably on Michael and Albert, our age extremes, but they were fine enough to continue.

Our next step became freeing ourselves from the subway since the battering made the doors inoperable. In fact, we were going to hoof it the rest of the way and lose more time we didn't have. I was really coming to hate the Adversary. Thankfully, Silas' superior strength allowed him to probe along the dented sides of the car and find a weak spot. With a seemingly effortless blow, he punched through the metal, then grasped the edges and pulled inward, ripping open a sizeable piece of the wall.

"There is sufficient space between the damaged car and the tube wall for you all to emerge and walk," he reported.

Bartholomew, our largest figure, went first to test the statement and peered back through the new exit and grinned broadly. That was all the encouragement we needed, and quickly, we scrambled out, Silas taking up the rear. While his statement proved accurate to the humans, he struggled a bit until we cleared the remains of the subway car. The tracks, which I learned were lined with powerful magnets, were littered with the still-smoking remains of the robo-bugs. The tunnel stank to high heaven.

We survived the first assault of the day, and with every step, we neared the next and more deadly one. I imagined Abernathy matching me footstep by footstep, our confrontation inevitable.

THIRTEEN

NO ONE FELT much like talking as we marched through the tunnel, eventually reaching the end of the line some twenty minutes later. I allowed everyone to take a brief break, feeling guilty at the same time. After all, we had a fifty-hour countdown and wasted some nine hours bathing, sleeping, and eating. Not that we didn't need it, but by the time we boarded the subway, we were down to forty hours or so and counting. The other internal countdown I worried about was Abernathy. He was two hours away, now closer to one. What other forces were coming to our aid would, therefore, be about half an hour behind them, From what Osman had told me earlier, that was a lot of time to fight without reinforcements. The bloodiest hand-to-hand battles tended to also be quick ones. Finally, there were Osman's plans, one of which still didn't sit well with me.

"We engage Abernathy and draw him away from the mountain," he had explained earlier. "We aim him at the Adversary, and when I give the signal, you and whoever you need will split off, and make a run for the other collector. We will hold off Abernathy until help arrives and keep fighting."

I had shaken my head, recognizing the death toll that would result. I didn't want more death while recognizing its inevitability.

"This is what armies do, Meredith," he said with steel in his voice. "We fight for a cause, willing to die for that cause."

"What's your cause here?"

He blinked once and then nodded his head directly at me. "You are. We just learned why you are special and that has to be preserved. This is complicated by several mission objectives, which includes defeating Abernathy, then defeating the Adversary. All the while, keeping you protected and alive has to be an end result."

"You didn't even mention the False Vacuum," I added.

He made pfft sound with his lips, dismissing something that was somewhat beyond his ken. He wanted to focus on things he could directly affect and I understood, even sympathized, with him.

I stared and then looked around the assembled group and one by one, they either nodded in agreement or just communicated affirmation with their eyes. This suddenly became more about some of these seeing me not as Madame President, but as the hope of all humanity. Nothing like raising the stakes.

So, here we were, emerging from the doors that were camouflaged by holograms, and there was a gentle breeze in the air, the skies thick with clouds, a cluster of dark ones heading our way. I had no idea if this made for good or bad fighting conditions. It is what it is and we'd deal as we had been doing for six weeks now.

From my pocket, I slipped out a dark green ribbon I found in the closet of clothes, tightly pulled back my hair, and tied it in place. It was time to move and keep moving, a pack of sharks that had to move or die.

Osman took the lead, followed by Chou, and I realized I was being protected fore and aft by my people, my team.

Albert was beside me and in his accustomed spot, in the rear by Levy was Silas. Our leader set a brisk pace, but a manageable one, even for Michael. The weather was temperate, the skies cloudy and darkening toward the horizon, a storm brewing. The ground was flat and smooth, almost swept, and it occurred to me that our host most likely sent out his robot butlers to do some cleaning for us, to speed us on our way. These were little touches, and ones I appreciated, but also showed that despite being circuits based on the moon, he was being quite the host.

At the first sounds of others, fearing the worst, we almost as one removed our various weapons. Albert, who had been familiarizing himself with the tablet, tucked it away in his backpack, taking out the small knife he received a while back. Wild Bill cocked his guns and Bartholomew adjusted the machine gun, having passed the rifle over to Levy. Miko and Vihaan had the recharged tasers and Chou gripped her own blade. A little while ago, they were blunt objects against the robo-bugs, but now, these products of man's aggression through the ages were about to be our means for survival. We walked for a while, realizing we had emerged actually closer to the troops and I idly wondered how Silas missed this, but that was a question for calmer times. I, a future commander-in-chief, needed to listen and pay close attention.

The noise was because the men were stirring, forming up under guttural commands that I couldn't translate but suspected meant it was time to form up and get ready. The enemy had been sighted. They needed instructions rather than blindly go into battle without a clear objective beyond staying alive. And the quickest way they'd understand was for me to be standing next to Osman. I moved faster, getting shoulder to shoulder with him, and jerked my chin forward. He nodded and we both broke into a trot and rushed ahead of the others. In just a few minutes, we were spotted and their hubbub turned into cheers, which, I have to admit, felt nice.

With the fewest words possible, Osman outlined what was happening, how to fight the enemy, and then pointed in the direction we needed them diverted. Möngke, beaming, threw his arms around us in a surprising hug. "We shall make them eat the dirt," he told us.

"Just get them away from these mountains," I said, breaking free. The others had caught up to us and stood loosely clustered around us. We all were on a slight rise and we saw the dark mass representing Abernathy and his followers. This was not going to be pretty; in fact, it was going to be bloody and brutal and there was nothing I could do to prevent it. I stared at the flat plain where they trampled whatever wildlife existed and then followed the land until I was looking out toward the next collector, just miles away. Between the two were a dense forest, and since Everwood was already taken, I dubbed it, at least for myself, the Haunted Wood, despite not knowing if ghosts remained on Earth these days. If it was good enough for Anne Shirley, it would do for me. I saw a likely path that would get us into the woods and would also provide obstacles that would at least slow Abernathy down. Then images of his followers tearing Blue Alpha apart filled my mind and I shuddered.

Under my feet, I felt the rumble of approaching footsteps, thousands of them. I also heard Möngke and Osman barking commands and our side forming up, in groups of five by five, ready to be deployed. What they held wasn't much. The Mongols still had their fearsome weapons, but the others had everything from pikes to branches. What I wouldn't give right now for Hermione's wand so I could just send Abernathy and his icky company away. These next forty minutes or so were going to be the longest of my life.

The approaching army did not slow down, maintaining a

steady pace; after all, they were fueled by the bodies being inhabited. More than a few were only vaguely human, with conjoined shapes mixed in with those that had triangular heads and pincers for arms. Others had bits of body and clothing still visible with black ropes wrapped around them. While I recognized pieces from different eras and styles, thankfully, I didn't recognize any of the victims, which would have made this even more difficult. If we were a motley bunch, they were the funhouse mirror opposites, twisted, distortions of humanity, with none of them, not even Tommy Two-Thumbs, Abernathy asking for this.

"Sure wish I could use that German machine gun," Wild Bill said from my left.

"It wouldn't be as effective as you would imagine," Chou told him.

"Be fun to try," he said.

"Osman, ready?" I shouted. From below, near one squad, he turned and threw me a salute, a sure sign of respect and affirmation. I felt a warm flush for a moment, then my breath quickened as the first clash was about to begin, right on schedule.

It was ugly. That was the only word to describe the conflict as the two sides met and there were tendrils and swords, gun fire, and cracking wood. The first squad of twenty-five men were bowled over surprisingly fast, but they were rushed by two more squads and then the bodies mingled and crashed together. I heard shrieks of pain, cries of anguish, and the snapping of bone. Each of these made me cringe.

This could be a prolonged affair, but I had no idea how these forces would hold out before the others arrived. We were easily outnumbered three to one, so they'd just wear us down and Abernathy knew it. In fact, after snapping one man's head, he made his presence known, walking away from the others to face me and my group. He was only sort of human, with that ugly triangular head, his body a writhing black mass of nanobots, with elongated arms that practically dragged on the ground. But the glossy black eyes burned cold as they sought and found me.

"Meredith." Its approximation of Abernathy's voice sounded wrong, filtered through countless nanobots and amplified. "This is pointless. Surrender now."

"Surrender? In our moment of triumph? I think you overestimate your chances," I said, modifying a well-worn phrase I used to use when playing high school volleyball, which felt like a lifetime ago, which it was.

The line actually caused him to pause, parsing it and trying to reconcile the words to the situation, and something did not compute, which made me smile. Under my breath, I said to the others, "Ready?"

"Ready," Chou replied.

Before we could turn and sprint toward the forest, we heard a whooshing sound and then the crackling of wood. Three lengthy lines of the ground exploded into brilliant flame. One toward the rear of the thousand-strong force while another was a good fifty feet closer to us with the final line just ten feet from where we stood. Each line curled at the ends, looking more like parentheses or brackets than straight lines. But they burned and organic bits, cloth, wool, and leather crackled. Hundreds of Abernathy's army was engulfed in fire, their howls unlike anything I had ever heard before and would be fine never hearing again.

I had no idea how, but somehow, while we were within the collector, Möngke, following a plan he and Osman managed to hatch out of my earshot, supervised some sort of surprise fire trap, giving our side the element of surprise and certain to cause the nanobot army some hot feet and maybe even a few melted circuits. It would also act as a flare for the approaching cavalry, which couldn't hurt.

Despite all his high-tech enhancements, Abernathy couldn't have anticipated this and whirled about, actually uncertain what to do. There was no water nearby, no fire suppression equipment to summon. Sure, the hundreds unaffected could walk around the three lines, but it certainly went a long way to even the odds.

Above the crackling of the fire and cries of pain, there was another sound rising up in the distance. I remembered that in high school American History, Mr. Burke explained how the rebel yell was unique to the South during the Civil War. It could not be replicated and old YouTube footage of veterans, far older than their fighting days, made it sound like a cross between a yodel, dog yips, and sheer emotion as it rose and fell, wave after wave. I heard something quite similar just now, growing by the second.

Coming into view from the horizon, much as Abernathy's army loomed before us, came the cavalry, although few were actually on horses. They were charging several lengths ahead of the main body, a trio at the apex and there, in the center, I recognized the blonde hair and lean figure of Emily. She had survived the attack on New Manhattan!

Osman shouted and one of the nearest fighters came running to him. There was a hurried conversation, which was comprehensible since I was standing nearby, and the other man, his face bloody, clothes torn, nodded once, turned and ran off, making a wide arc to skirt the fighting and reach the arriving army.

With fire around them and a rush of united humanity behind them, the nano-tech army was not looking too good. Of course, they still had to be stopped and put down before they menaced the Architect. That was where our team had to do its part.

Abernathy, having assessed the new variables, seemed to be processing data and then sending out some sort of signal to his own troops. Almost as one, they paused their actions with half turning around to face the oncoming attack and the other half split into two forces. One continued to battle Osman's troops and the Mongol horde while the other marched to form behind Abernathy, who remained still, facing us.

"Get ready," I said to Chou and Miko, and they sent word throughout our cohort.

The first horsemen arrived, and with slashing knives, swords, and what appeared to be wooden clubs, they were swinging into the dark mass. Emily got in one good smack with a club, sending a man backward, but three rushed her horse, arms lengthening to twice their normal size, and made contact with the brown-dappled horse. It whinnied in pain as the oily contact points spread. Sensing the danger, Emily leapt from the beast, club tucked into her stomach, and rolled on the ground. She sprang up, club in an uppercut that seemed to dislocate the shoulder of one of her horse's attackers.

By this time, her followers, a mélange of color, style, and age, arrived and set to work combating their fellow humans. There was no curing them, we knew, so it was stopping them, disabling them however possible.

I was transfixed, watching everyone willingly sacrificing themselves for a battle that couldn't necessarily be won. Chou grabbed my shoulder and said, "We have to go. Now."

Nodding, I turned to look out at the battlefield and saw so many disfigured, blackened bodies, so much charred flesh, and so many victims of the Adversary's technology. Ripping an arm from a woman with ease, Abernathy felt my gaze and looked up at me. He stood his ground, the black oily nature of his body now reflecting the fire, the menace clear.

Abernathy took one step for us and we turned and ran, hard and fast, away from the fight and toward the forest. He let out a mechanical laugh before some high-pitched sound followed, and that caused a hundred or more of his followers to stop fighting and instantly turn to follow us. We got the drop on them, but once more, they wouldn't need rest, while we would.

Encouraged by the old-fashioned surprise, we poured on the speed and ran toward the forest's edge. Silas actually was carrying Albert, whose shorter legs couldn't keep up, while Bartholomew was matching pace with Michael to make sure he'd not be left behind. I wished I could have left him behind, but he assured me that if the Adversary was a warped version of the Architect, it meant his programming was something he might be able to work with. He *had* to be a part of this and I could hear the pride and a dash of guilt in his voice. Of course he'd want to take some of the responsibility on his shoulders, but whatever software he wrote in his time evolved, so he wasn't directly responsible for the Adversary.

The ground vanished beneath our feet and the edge of the Haunted Wood grew before us. All we'd have to go by would be Albert's tablet and that would have to do. The trees making up the forest were old growth, thick, dark trunks with branches that twisted and turned, fighting for sunlight to draw life from. The canopy rose a good sixty, seventy feet above us, shading the interior, which also meant that when the sun went down, we'd be in darkness. We needed flashlights we didn't have and the pixie dust, which normally restored us, would likely miss us, possibly weakening Michael further. The lack of sunlight also meant Silas would be on reserve battery power, compromising his effectiveness. He could conserve power when we rested. If it was a six-hour march, then we'd be fine, in the end.

Much as the Everwood was a blend of tree types, the same seemed true here, which Albert could confirm for me later. We arrived, knowing full well Abernathy should be chasing us. I risked a glance over my shoulder and was reassured to see darkened figures heading for us. All we had to do was keep moving and pray I was as powerful a magnet as we hoped.

Then we began weaving between trees, our feet now crunching dried leaves and snapping twigs. Silence was not going to be possible and we daren't slow down our pace. High above, we heard bird calls, a song to welcome or warn us about entering the Haunted Wood. The distance between trees was narrowing the deeper we moved into the forest, which would be a benefit, but it also meant our fighting would be hampered. We'd just have to try our best.

Within minutes, the sunlight had been dampened to mere rays breaking through the occasional gap in the canopy. The air was still, the smell of rotting leaves making it mildly unpleasant but still a far cry from the burning back at the battlefield. Our pace was steady, although I knew we'd need to find a place to pause and catch our breath sooner than later. Michael would certainly need it. My mind wondered how Osman and the others were handling things and what he would make of Emily, who was so commanding just standing still. That was a meeting I wish I could be there for.

There were definitely sounds behind us, the beginnings of Abernathy's army coming after us. Was he among them? How many were there? It was hard to tell and we couldn't risk sending anyone back to reconnoiter. Levy had debated staying behind to fight with Osman and be on hand to treat the wounds. That would have left me with Chou, Bartholomew, Wild Bill, Albert, Miko, Vihaan, Michael, and Silas. One was too young to fight, one too old. Vihaan had proven a hardier participant than I imagined and Miko's training made her quite adept. She had apparently done the same math as me and decided we needed her more than the army did. We had guns and swords and fists, none of which was going to be enough should Abernathy catch up to us.

That was when we heard animal snarls just up ahead.

FOURTEEN

THE SNARLING MADE the hairs on my arms and neck rise to attention. It caused me to slow my pace as I tried to determine where the sounds were coming from. Then, off to my right, I saw the bright eyes in the shadows, low to ground. There was some indistinct movement behind those eyes. A new sound and I looked left, to be confronted by a pair of large wolves padding out from between the trees. When I say large, I mean huge; creatures, mostly gray in coloring with white around the snouts and other portions of their long bodies. Other parts had bands of brown and even some ochre. I was surprised at how short their ears were, more than made up for by their foot-plus tails. While lean-looking. I could see the powerful muscles ripple beneath their fur. From paw to shoulder, they had to be a good four feet tall, maybe more.

"Wow, that's *Canis lupus,*" I heard Albert say in a low voice.

"Yeah, it's a wolf, I get it," I whispered back.

"They're the largest member of the wolf family," he said, delighted to share the knowledge. Okay, large wolves and I know wolves hunt in packs, but how many were stalking us? I counted two to one side, three or more to the other. And behind us, who knew how far back, was the deadly nanotech army.

"Want me to shoot them?" Wild Bill asked in a low voice.

"We're being surrounded, so you couldn't hit them all," Chou said.

"Might scare the others off," he said.

"And tell Abernathy exactly where we are," I hissed.

"He knows the general direction regardless. Any interaction with them will produce noise," Chou pointed out.

As we discussed this, they were now all coming into view and I counted a total of seven, two pairs and a trio, definitely a coordinated attack. I wonder if they were a part of the food chain from the Architect or were here courtesy of the Adversary. If the former, I would hate to further disrupt the balance being designed; if the latter, then I was doing the world a favor. I'd bet they were here now because of our enemy. Regardless, survival was paramount.

"Okay, Albert, give me the highlights and fast," I said.

"They will chase us, picking on the weakest to take down and eat. They primarily track by scent."

That made Michael the most vulnerable to the pack and I would be damned if I lost my sort-of-son to wolves. We'd need a strategy and fast since they were coming closer and were going to force us to run or pounce or something equally deadly.

"Anyone fight a wolf before?" I whispered.

The silence confirmed that we were all in uncharted waters. I gestured to Wild Bill to act, so he nodded once, held up his left arm, bent at the elbow, and placed the barrel of his six-gun atop his forearm. He steadied himself, took aim, took a deep breath, and then squeezed the trigger. The gunshot was loud to us, as was the howl of the dying wolf, the cries of the pack, and the rush of birds fleeing far above us. The thick trees no doubt muffled some of the sound, but I was willing to bet the possessed people might have superior hearing and could hone in on us. We had to keep moving.

"Another?" he asked me. The wolves scattered, so I shook my head. My heart had been pounding out of fear and was starting to slow down. Thank goodness it was relatively cool in the woods so I'd dry off from the flop sweat that had instantly appeared.

"This way," Levy said, pointing past me and angled off to my left. I began walking, aware that the wolves might regroup and stalk us further, giving us two predators after us.

"I was never this popular, even in high school," I said to Chou.

"High school?"

"Secondary education," I said. Was it possible by her time the agony of being a high school teen had been eliminated? I maintained a reasonable pace, weaving around trees, keeping my mind clear, listening for anything that could be a danger.

"What's he going to throw after us next?" Wild Bill asked. "Lions?"

"Sorry, wrong habitat for them," Albert corrected him, earning him a rude sound from the Old West hero.

"Only lion I ever saw was a in a zoo," Wild Bill explained.

"I saw them in my native Kenya," Bartholomew added. "They're beautiful to watch."

"Shh," I hissed. We had to keep moving, and the less noise, the better. The woods grew thicker and the darkness also covered us more completely. The sun was definitely on its way down, which meant all the nocturnal life in here, starting with the wolves, were going to be keeping us company. I could only imagine what was supposed to be here, and what spices the Adversary sprinkled into the mix. We were going to need a break soon too. I could hear Michael starting to strain at keeping the pace.

For a change, the silence beyond our footfalls was welcome. I decided if we heard nothing dangerous in the next fifteen minutes, we could risk a breather. I began to scan the trees, judging whether or not rest among the branches was a good idea or not. On the one hand, the wolves couldn't reach us, but it might make us easier targets for the far more dangerous Abernathy. We continued quietly maneuvering through the woods and heard nothing, so I raised a hand to slow our walk. I then strained a bit but found a cluster of trees with large, low branches that could be reached.

I gestured up toward them and Chou, my security expert, assessed them in much the same way. After a moment, she nodded in agreement, before she crouched a bit and leapt up, her hands easily grasping one branch and swinging herself up, her legs wrapping around the wood. In a moment, she was settled. Bartholomew and Miko helped Michael reach a branch where he stood, a big, boyish grin on his haggard face. To show off, he actually reached the next highest branch and made an effort to scale it then slumped against the branch, a satisfied look on his face.

Albert had the most fun, climbing up without help and then going higher than any of us. The rest followed suit while Silas remained below to keep watch.

"Now what?" I said to myself.

"We rest and keep moving. If the Adversary sent one threat, there will likely be more," Chou reassured me.

"Animal, vegetable, or mineral?" Bartholomew asked.

"Now's not the time for twenty questions," Miko said to him.

"I was speculating at what might come next. After all, it's been ninjas and Mongols..."

"You weren't here for the Nazis," I said.

I just leaned my head against the trunk, unable to get

comfortable. I took a long drink from my canteen, appreciating how the water was still cool. I could feel the temperature drop further in the woods, happy not to have to spend the night.

My internal clock decided enough was enough and we had to keep moving. Where the silence allowed us the freedom to rest, now the silence was warning me something was not right. We should have heard Abernathy's army, even in the distance. Nor had we heard the wolves since they scattered. It meant either we were very good at eluding them both or, worse, something more deadly awaited us. Carefully, I lowered myself to the ground, silently signaling to the others it was time to move.

"Do you hear anything?" I asked Silas.

"No, Meredith. Just wild life."

"What do you think?" I asked Chou as she lightly leapt down from her branch, landing lightly on her feet, her white cloak dramatically fluttering around her.

"I don't think the wolves are the threat now," she said. "I can't explain where Abernathy is. While the forest is vast, they knew our angle or entry. I don't believe we've veered too far off."

"Actually, we have zig-zagged from our straight line and might have given them the slip," Wild Bill said, joining us, dusting himself off from a less graceful descent.

"How do you know?"

"You see me as a gunman, which I am. But don't forget, I've also been a soldier, a spy, and a scout, so I know a thing or two about trails," he reminded me. He had told me weeks before how he had scouted for an African-American regiment after the Civil War ended. It was when he was shot in the foot, rescuing men from an Indian attack.

"Okay, then, which way?"

He held up his finger and walked to Albert, who had already made it to the ground. They consulted the tablet briefly, its glow ghostly in the gloom. And then he came back. He gestured ahead and about ninety degrees to my right. It was dark in that direction, so we'd need some light.

I asked Silas if he had the energy to both move and cast a light for us and he estimated he had sufficient reserves, but should he be pressed into battle, the odds dropped dramatically. This was why I wasn't much of a gambler. When everyone was on the ground, we paused as I listened long and hard, growing even more concerned I couldn't hear Abernathy. With a shrug, I decided we needed to keep moving, so I strode in the direction Bill indicated. The rest was good and I felt better, despite my apprehensions.

We walked through the woods, deeper into the darkness, the night air filling with insects, the chirp of a bird, and the scratching of something against the wood, but none of it raised my hackles or anyone else's. Periodically, I let Bill and Silas walk up ahead of us, lighting the way and seeking clues of danger. Each time, there was nothing, so we kept walking. The going proved slower going than I think any of us anticipated. After another two hours, we took a break to help Michael, and Bill took Silas for a longer look, but they returned and he just shook his head in the negative. Something was coming, I just knew it.

And so we kept on walking, not saying much of anything for another hour. Still nothing, so it was as every step passed, the apprehension was growing., I didn't think the Adversary was one for head games, so he wasn't messing with us. "It'll be ROUS," I muttered later.

"What is that?" Chou asked. She rarely left my side, my personal protector.

"Rodents of Unusual Size. It's a film reference," I said.

"Ah."

"It'll be deadly trees throwing apples at us," Bartholomew said from behind us.

"Get real," I said with a chuckle.

"Okay, then it will be a bear," Albert suggested.

The back and forth lightened the mood without entirely dissipating the dread that resided in the back of my skull. After our third break, Wild Bill directed us at an angle away from our path, and every now and then, there was a clearing, and we could peer up and catch glimpses of the night sky. I briefly considered waiting here for the night pixie dust shower but felt it imperative to keep moving, so onward we marched. I wanted to suggest a song, something to keep us going, but it occurred to me that given all our backgrounds, we had so little in common that we'd know, especially with an outlier like Chou.

Finally, Wild Bill and Silas returned from another foray ahead of us and said they could see the trees thinning out, suggesting our walk through the Haunted Wood was almost over. No Dementors, no bears, no Abernathy. My fatigue was replaced with certainty that there was danger ahead. Chou must have sensed it too since her body language subtly changed, and she was tenser, her hands flexing. According to Silas, we had been walking closer to eight hours than the estimated six, but we were now nearing the edge of the forest with the Adversary ahead. Mentally, I adjusted my thinking, resetting the countdown to thirty-two hours and dropping.

There was a flurry of noise in the distance. Footsteps in dirt, material shifting with bodies, and then the sound of wood and metal being slapped against something metallic. This was what I'd been dreading. My mind raced, wondering what it was and how we could get past it. My guess was that we would be once more outnumbered, so I needed to make that work somehow.

Chou turned and beckoned to Bartholomew and Wild Bill. When they reached us, she silently gestured, sending one off to the left, the other to the right. She then signaled to wait until they were ahead of us. When she deemed it long enough, we resumed walking as if we didn't know we were walking into a trap.

This time, the Adversary spared no expense and we walked toward the final rows of trees to find a dozen men. Six stood behind another six with the first line in colorful armor over tunics with leather sandals. Atop each head was a golden helmet with a bright plume, either red or black, looking like a mohawk. Each held a sword or long, thin spear in one hand, the other holding shields before them. No two were alike. One had three white legs against a black background ringed with a red and white design, while another had a bird of prey, wings wide, and another had a flame against the black field. They were deeply tanned, most with bushy black beards, and they had seen combat. These were veteran Greek warriors.

Behind them stood a more varied assortment. One was a youth in a wheat-colored hat and tunic, swinging a rock in a sling and looking very much like David. Another, in a similar hat, was putting a flute to his lips to play them into combat. Two more had shields and swords, a fifth was obscured, but the sixth stood taller than the others, cloaked in a red cape with a gold helmet and red plume perpendicular to the way the other helmets were constructed, clearly their commander. I had no doubt underneath his robes were weapons.

We were facing a classic Greek phalanx, the kind that terrorized the Mediterranean for centuries. As we emerged into the dim starlight of the evening, I saw there were braziers of a sort providing flickering light behind them, the shadows being cast making them look positively supernatural but no less a danger. Beyond them, I saw, a dirt path that led directly toward the mountains that ringed the Adversary's collector. It closely resembled the one we left earlier in the day, although this had external lights winking here and there, as if signaling to warn off low-flying aircraft, not that I knew of any since the *Brimstone* crashed along with the Red Baron. What I wouldn't give now for a set of Quidditch brooms to just zip over their heads and be done with it.

Their leader shouted, "Ready!"

At that, the six shields in the front row seemingly locked together, making for an impenetrable solid wall, allowing them to be protected as they hurled their spears with, no doubt, deadly accuracy.

"Attack!"

I cringed, expecting the spears, but instead young David let loose his projectile, and it whizzed over my head, and then I heard Miko shriek as it made contact. I wanted to look but didn't dare, because now the front line was moving toward us in lockstep. The spearmen were rearing back, taking aim, and then let fly. Silas reached out and snatched one with precision, snapping it in two. The sight of him spooked the Greeks but did not daunt them. They continued inexorably before us, and as they neared, I could smell their sweat, their manly body odor, and wanted to choke.

Chou wasn't idle but reared back with her long knife and then ran forward before lowering herself. She propelled her body into the air, her cloak fluttering impressively behind her. She was like a white angel in the dark night, but she had timed her jump perfectly, clearing the first row of surprised Greeks and landing before the second row. Her face a mask of rage, she swung efficiently, stabbing one to her right, and her blade flashed to her left, catching a soldier in the belly.

As the men broke ranks, Wild Bill and Bartholomew emerged from the trees, flanking the disorderly mass of Greeks. Neither used the machine gun, saving it, I guess, for later given our limited ammunition for it. Each let go a volley of gunfire, something the Greeks could never have prepared for and several fell as their shots rang through the air. Two with swords fell and then another two, while a pair of spears were hastily flung at us. However, by the time they released their shafts, we were not standing pat. Instead, we scattered with Silas standing before Michael with Albert half behind him as well. Vihaan was cradling Miko, I noticed, who was bleeding profusely from her head.

One Greek tried to charge Bartholomew, who cocked his rifle, took aim, and fired once more. The bullet struck true, knocking the soldier off his feet, onto his back, where he died. But a second Greek had been on his heels and Bartholomew couldn't react fast enough, The other man reached him with a short dagger in his hand, cutting deep into his bicep, forcing the rifle from his hands. The man swung again as Bartholomew writhed in pain, and he sliced into his right leg, forcing him to his knees.

My scimitar was already in my hand, so I was running before I knew what was happening. I barreled into two Greek men, who looked astonished to being attacked by a woman. The shields were hard, wood and bronze, and my shoulder instantly ached. My impact carried me through them, but they were highly trained and each spun about, swords at the ready. Chou had been training me to use the scimitar, but that was with just one opponent, I had not yet graduated to taking on two at once, so this was going to be learning by doing.

One came in high, toward my head, so I leaned backward and avoided the blow, but it also meant the other was able to slice into my right thigh. I clamped my teeth together to avoid screaming. My sword swung upward and blocked a blow as the other man circled to get behind me. I twisted and parried a blow, taking another cut to the right arm. While these were men trained in the art of combat, they weren't accustomed to fighting a woman, so as one planted his feet wide to brace himself for a blow, I swiftly kicked him in the balls. Thankfully, they hadn't invented cups back then and it was he who howled like a girl, bending over. A second kick knocked him off balance and onto his back.

That, however, exposed me, and the second attacker was quick, cutting into my left forearm. I backed away so I could swing the scimitar, missing with my next blow. He grinned and stepped toward me, his own sword poised. This was one on one, something I had been practicing, so I was able to parry the next swing and make my own mark on his right arm. Gripping the sword, though, hurt with every swing and my blood had flowed far too freely for my comfort. He growled at that and leapt forward, knocking us both to the ground. This man was shorter than I was, but heavier thanks to the armor. I smashed the pommel into his head, but the helmet absorbed the blow. I wriggled to free myself, but his knees pinned me. His breath stank and he was sweating profusely. As he adjusted his position, it allowed me to roll and break his hold. He tumbled onto his back, the sword over his chest. The other man had sufficiently recovered from my kick and was grasping his sword, ready to hack away. Abandoning the one on the ground, I lunged forward, low, and cut into the man's calves, deep. He was on his knees again, bleeding into the dirt.

I was then tackled from behind by the other man, who straddled my back and had my hair in one fist. Fortunately, I had allies and it was Bartholomew who loomed behind him, cocking the rifle at the base of his neck. The soldier might not have known what a rifle is, but he had seen it work and understood the danger he was in. The sword fell and his arms went wide, waiting a beat before rising off of me.

Chou had done her work well, taking down another man, scattering the Greeks further. Between her and Wild Bill, they were bested, their commander giving out a cry of surrender. I echoed the command so all arms were lowered.

"Michael!"

"I'm fine," he called. Assured of that, I turned my attention to Vihaan, who was using his own shirt to soak up Miko's blood, turning his riot of color into solid red.

"I don't know what to do," he said helplessly.

"Chou!" I shouted. She trotted over with the first aid kit already in her hands while I strode over to the Greek commander.

"Your name," I demanded.

"Epaminondas," he said.

"Do you accept defeat?" I asked, trying to sound formal about it, despite the perspiration running down my brow, and my heart thundering in my chest.

"I do, Meredith Gale," he said.

"Great, you know me too," I muttered.

"What will happen to my men?" he asked.

"How many live?"

At that, the bearded man with a mop of curly hair looked about him and silently assessed the damage. "I see four men still breathing, plus me."

"Five out of a dozen, not bad," I muttered. I also estimated the battle to have lasted minutes although it felt like hours had passed since we first heard them assemble. I quickly outlined things for him and his men, much as I addressed the Mongols. As before, the Adversary hadn't prepared them for much other than taking me dead or alive. My explanation sounded like so much gibberish to him, but he accepted it as real.

"You wish us to fight for you? Against a deity that can pluck me from my world and send me here?"

"Look, I was brought here by an opposing power, so yes, I want you to fight for me so you can survive, maybe even thrive. I have people I'd love to introduce you to."

"That you speak in my language is impressive enough. Your

wisdom to use us rather than kill us also speaks well for you. Do I have time to consider this odd turn of affairs?"

"I have to see to my friends, and when I'm ready to march, you're either with us, or I leave you here to fend for yourselves, and honestly, what's coming is not pretty."

With that, I spun on my heel and trotted over to my own injured, wincing with every step from my own damage. Given the night sky, I suspected we missed our nightly healing, so whatever befell my friends would need time to heal, time we didn't necessarily have. Miko had not yet moved and Vihaan's face was ashen as I neared them. Chou was bandaging her head, but the blood was already seeping through the wrapping.

"How is she?"

"Concussed," Levy said, checking Miko's eyes once more. The pupils were fixed and I knew that was a bad sign. "His aim was deadly accurate." She actually sounded impressed by so crude a weapon, but then again, it was a stone that took down Goliath and Miko was a far smaller target. She then spotted my bleeding arm and immediately reached for my shirt, ripping off a strip from the hem and began treating the wound.

"Can we move her?" I asked as she worked. The internal clock was ticking away and who knew what was coming from behind us.

"I wouldn't recommend it, but then again, there might be better tools at our disposal within the collector," she said.

I beckoned Epaminondas to join us and suggested several of his men carry Miko with us. It would not be easy and we still had at least an hour to reach the mountains and more time once we entered the collector. And I just knew there would be more obstacles designed to slow us down.

Chou stood and took off her cloak. She and Epaminondas walked over to the trees inspecting the branches until several were selected and cut down. With impressive speed, the two fashioned a litter with which to carry Miko. Epaminondas then waved over two of the soldiers to bear the burden with the boy accompanying them. Albert wanted to make a friendly contact, but I shot him a glance that now was not the time for that. We had to resume moving.

Our odd band began walking toward the mountains, the Greeks amazed at the scope of the structure, amazed at the metal, the lights, and the scale. To the rest of us, we were accustomed to that and our thoughts were more about Miko and the Adversary. It was a quiet, unhappy brotherhood that was moving toward the unknown.

There was the first lightening of the sky, pastels washing the horizon clean, a new day dawning. We had reached the mountains surrounding the collector with Silas now taking the lead, scanning for the electronic emanations that would direct us to the holographic entrance. My hope was that the Adversary wouldn't see the need to make adjustments to the entrance, but Chou was far more suspicious. She insisted on walking ahead of me, directly behind Silas, who was beginning to soak up the day's solar radiation, recharging which he sorely needed.

About thirty minutes later, Chou called out and Silas stopped moving. She stood beside him and asked, "Do you see anything?"

Silas whirred for a bit and then a kaleidoscope of colors were emitted from his eye bar, scanning across the spectrum, and he swiveled first left then right. There were a few gasps from behind me as once more culture shock visited the Greeks. Finally, he turned and reported, "*There appear to be explosive traps, pressure sensitive, unevenly spaced for the next thirty meters.*"

"How did you know?" I asked her.

Chou said, "There was something groomed about the path

ahead of us, something unnatural, so I felt it prudent to check."
Levy, the soldier, nodded in affirmation.

"Silas, can you guide us around them?"

"Several are too close together for our group to safely pass by them all," he said.

"Can you scan and calculate a path presuming we detonate one or two of these?"

"Chou, we can't. That will alert him we're here," I said.

"I don't believe we have a choice," she said. "He knows we're here; it's why he summoned the Greek phalanx and likely led the wolves to our position. He will continue to place obstacles in our way until Abernathy catches up to us, or he eliminates us."

"I believe I have calculated such a path," Silas interrupted.

"How much pressure do we need to activate one?" Chou asked.

"Without knowing the precise devices employed, it would be impossible to know for certain. Several pounds for certain."

"Point me at the one you want," Wild Bill said, joining the discussion. "I can provide a few pounds of pressure. Let me and Silas get started and clear the way, then you and the others follow."

I didn't like this, not at all, but also didn't see much of a choice. I nodded and he nodded in return then turned to follow Silas. They walked like drunken men, weaving around patches of ground that didn't look any different than the rest of the path leading us around the mountain. After a few minutes, as their figures began to grow very small, they stopped. I saw Silas point and Wild Bill withdrew his Luger and took aim. Two things happened in very rapid succession: there was the gunshot that seemed instantly muffled by the ground, then a far larger sound, an eruption of sound, rock, and dirt creating a cloud big enough to obscure even my nine-foot-tall companion.

We waited impatiently for the dust to clear and then I could make out two upright figures, but they were moving further ahead. I wanted to cry out for them but stopped myself, trusting them to know what they were doing. Sure enough, after a minute or so, they paused, and Wild Bill shot a second time with identical results. As that smoke cloud cleared, they had turned and weaved their way back to us.

"Nice shooting," I said.

"Pretty useful, this German gun. Nicely made," he said with admiration. He grinned and resumed his place near Bartholomew, behind the Greeks still dragging Miko along. She hadn't moved, but Albert was walking beside her, periodically checking to make certain she was still breathing. My heart went out to the boy who had seen so much that was wondrous and so much he shouldn't see until he was older. I guessed he was growing up quickly now and he certainly made a place for himself within the group. We'd need smart, experienced people by the time he was of age and I was happy he was here.

Silas repeated his odd, winding walk, and we followed, making certain our footsteps matched his larger ones. This way, we knew we'd not trigger any other explosive. It was slow going, especially as the Greeks, with Vihaan's and Bartholomew's help, actually carried Miko over the ground rather than drag the litter. It was a difficult task given that our more modern men were taller than the Greeks, who looked a lot less fierce despite their armor.

So we walked for a good forty, fifty minutes, another hour gone. Finally, Silas paused before a section of mountain wall and indicated this was the holographic entrance. Chou picked up a stone and tossed it through the mirage. At first, there was no sound, no explosion. Then came a slight sizzling sound. She held up her hand in a "wait a moment" gesture and stepped through the hologram, eliciting some surprise from our new, unwilling allies. I silently held my breath, worried about what she had found inside.

When she finally emerged, Chou said, "There are infrared sensors, placed low on the ground. The rock triggered them and a laser array was activated."

"Like a light show?" I asked.

"More like the death rays your fiction was fascinated with," she said deadpan.

"What do we do?"

"The infrared is attuned to average human height, criss-crossing from four to seven feet, so someone can crawl beneath the beams and disable one, which might cause a cascade effect, eliminating them all."

"Might? I'll go," I said, my hands adjusting my bun to tighten it.

"No, let me," Albert said, rushing forward. "I'm the right size for this."

"I can't let you risk this," I said, my hand on his shoulder. His smudged face looked so serious, so earnest, it hurt.

"The Architect said we need you. Everything we've been doing has been to save you so you can save us. I'm just 12. I'm small. I *can* do this if Chou tells me what do to."

I wanted to argue but saw his expression. He was determined and he *was* the better size, I suppose. Without waiting for me to respond, Chou took him with her and they stood before the edge of the hologram. She explained things in a low tone. He took out his knife and pantomimed actions and she adjusted his wrist once or twice, then she nodded at him.

I didn't like this, not at all. I was so uncomfortable with all this attention. I didn't feel like a hero or a president or the savior of humanity. Just a target. I was also pretty done with being a target, which was why I was standing there, trying to access the Adversary and put an end to this madness. But I couldn't do it alone and had learned that lesson over the last month-plus earlier. Once again, I was letting someone else take all the risks and this hurt, because Albert was so young and had so much potential. I wanted to see him as an adult, when I could treat him as a true equal. So I watched him enter the chamber, knowing there were death rays and the doors that would lead us to the target. He vanished from sight and I held my breath, wishing to peek through the barrier, but I certainly didn't want to distract him. No, this was his moment and Chou prepared him. My mind went to dark places, imagining things we hadn't foreseen: poison gas, droids with knives, a collapsing ceiling, the death rays working anyway.

My eyes hurt from their intense gaze at the rock wall, barely blinking, and I was straining. Then, as suddenly as he entered the wall, he emerged, a big grin on his face.

"Done!" he cried.

Chou smiled at him but then took him to the barrier, and they talked quietly as he acted out exactly what he had done. It was comical from my vantage point, but it was also his moment of triumph. To test this, Chou grabbed several rocks, and one by one, tossed them into the mountain, and we could all hear the dull thud each made. As she did this, Albert came to me and fished something out of his pocket.

I held out my hand and he sprinkled blackened ash into it.

"That's what happened to the first rock," he told me. Death rays indeed.

Satisfied, Chou stepped through the hologram and was gone for over a minute. When she emerged, she gestured for us all to follow. The way was clear and we were about to breach the Adversary's home and finally bring the battle to him.

FIFTEEN

ONE BY ONE, we entered the collector, striding past the double doors without being disintegrated, so that was a victory. By now, our Greek companions had things explained to them by Michael as he tended to Miko, who had remained unconscious. Just when we would need an astrophysicist, she was unavailable to us.

Thankfully, we knew the layout by now and walked in a straight line, although I was taking in the differences. Where the collectors had been bright and downright awe-inspiring, things here were low key, private, and unwelcoming. There were no major domo droids to greet us or guide us, and many a corridor were dim or dark. In fact, the lighting here was low, the entire structure less vibrant, less *alive*. It was bordering on creepy and made me wonder if the Adversary was even home,

"This is certainly a stereotypical villain's lair," I quipped. "Nice and creepy."

Where the first collector we visited welcomed us with a vast lawn and farmland with wheat growing, yellow patches affixed to the greenery, here the land was fallow. Wilted, rotting remains of wheat and corn turned the yellow land to a sickly green, and the grass was overgrown and in desperate need of water.

Above us was the same dome of barely visible energy, pulsing blue and white, a sure sign that something was working here. The pulses were slow, like a resting heartbeat. There were the familiar white clouds higher up, wispy and diffuse, incapable of absorbing moisture to return to the ground as nourishing rain.

The same five jade green glass spires were also here, but there was something off about them; at least one was off-plumb and the shade of jade was veined with garish yellow. At the base was the cathedral-like structure that seemed to be the nerve center. Each level had a different biome, yet from our angle, things looked wilted or overgrown, untended.

Again, there were other buildings and the monorail system, but clearly, nothing was in motion. Everything felt very still, or maybe, very dead. There was a stillness and a dimness to everything.

"My impression is more that it is conserving power. For what he has accomplished in so short a time has had to have been a major drain," Chou said. Vihaan wandered closer, eager to hear her thoughts.

"What do you mean?"

"The Architect took time to visit multiple realities and handpick who to bring forward. Once we arrived, though, the Adversary recognized he needed to counteract the arrival. First, he destabilized the method to bring us here, so we were scattered, many drowning by arriving in an ocean. Then he targeted you and reached out for people to hunt you down and bring you to him. There were the Nazis, the Red Baroness, Abernathy, the Red Baron. the Mongols, and now the Greeks. Along the way, he also brought forth predator species that were here to sow chaos among the ecosystem. All in a matter of weeks or months. The energy demands had to have been huge. The Adversary also did this after managing to sever Earth's connection to the Dyson network, limiting the resources it could draw upon. All of this," and here she paused, gesturing about the great, dully lit chamber we were walking through, "is a way to conserve energy. Both my husband and his enemy are vulnerable to one another...and us."

The Architect vulnerable? It could explain his inability to do some of the things that should have been easy. He was possibly sacrificing his own defenses to preserve the biomes and assist us the best he could. Who knew what his moon operation was like and we still didn't know what caused it to shatter.

"Do not forget his creation of Abernathy; that much nanotechnology needed power to create it and possibly maintain it," Vihaan added.

"Silas, do you have schematics for this place?"

"They are all designed in the same manner, Meredith, but if you're looking for an exact place to interface with the Adversary, that I do not know," he told us. I was also aware that he didn't fully recharge and was also going to be of limited help from here on out. Of course, other than rest breaks, none of us had slept in over a day. Albert or Michael must have been feeling it the most.

I settled on entering the cathedral and led the party inside. There, the design was a riot of paneled walls all jutting at a variety of angles. In fact, it felt a bit like one of those mazes they built to test rats. The glossy glass was dark everywhere, with recessed lighting from the ceiling casting a bad light, similar to office fluorescents. There was no seating, for none was needed, since the collectors were automated and humans were not needed. Only one floor-to-ceiling—and we're talking ten, twelve-foot-tall ceilings—panel was active. Streams of alphanumeric data flowed vertically along one edge and there were several panel displays that winked on or off, showing scales or graphs, sometimes numbers. The colors made no sense, so red could be dangerous or not.

Chou and Michael were stepping closer, trying to make sense of it all. Neither said anything as they watched. Finally, Michael reached out and traced one finger along a dark section, which lit a brilliant blue at his fingertip.

"The infestation has arrived," the Adversary said in a voice similar enough to the Architect's to cause Chou to shudder and Michael to step back as if shocked. But I heard a subtle difference in the voice, an arrogance and contempt, even in those first four words.

"Yes, here we are," I said defiantly.

"It's too late. You're running out of time and my creations will eliminate you all before there's another chance," he said.

"Yeah, yeah, you hate us. We get it. But we haven't heard your reasons. What's the real problem with mankind?" I asked.

"Did not Chou's beloved," and here, the tender endearment sounded vile, *"explain the ages old debate?"*

"Enlighten us. After all, you brought some new friends without preparing them," I said, gesturing to the Greeks, who were open-mouthed in astonishment. I had no idea if he was actually watching us, but I needed to keep up the show. Keep the Adversary engaged because I knew I needed to buy time for Michael and Vihaan. Earlier, on our walk, they had sketched out their ideas, but they weren't done, so it was up to me to keep the Adversary preoccupied.

"What has man done on Earth? You wage war. You fight over land when there has always been enough land for everyone, even when you swelled to ten billion living beings. You fight for resources, whether it was water or oil or minerals. You take one another's lives so easily."

"We have also created art. We have cracked the secrets of the universe."

"You have been arrogant. You discover the secrets of the atom and then use it to destroy entire cities. Your arrogance is written all through your history as you enslave one another, thinking one of you is superior to another when you all come from the same genetic soup. You bring pestilence, war, and greed wherever you walk."

I paused to consider what the Greeks thought of all this, since much of the aggression discussed applied to their time as well as my own. They were silent, no doubt somewhat stunned by the turn of events.

"We're not perfect. No one is, not even you. Somehow we made it to the stars and scattered across the universe. That has to count for something," I countered. Michael and Vihaan were huddled, working furiously, now using the one tablet they'd shared along with Albert's. Everyone else was standing transfixed, watching me argue with the air.

"My counterpart has never told you what happened once you left your solar system. Never told you how your arrogance followed you from star system to star system. You would colonize a world, begin stripping it of resources like a parasite, and fight one another for perceived wealth. You would repeat this, planet after planet, solar system after solar system. Any life you encountered you tried to cheat." Okay, this was the first sense there was intelligent life out there, confirming one of the biggest mysteries questioned back in my day. They existed. Did they look like Yoda? Spock? A germ?

"We must have done something right to build the network of Dyson swarms. I bet it took a bit of genius to figure out how to channel so much energy across so vast a distance without incinerating entire worlds in its path."

"I will grant you that, Meredith Jane Gale. The latticework

of relays is actually one of the first things of art that I admire across the realities."

"Score one for us," I said.

"One for humanity, chalked up against all the strife, disease, death, and degradation you heaped on one another no matter where or when. Don't think I don't see what you are doing, Michael Roger Gale and Vihaan Deshpande."

"Yeah, they're trying to save mankind. You seemed overly focused on our faults. Were we that bad in your reality? After all, the people there built you? Have you no respect for your creators?"

"I was built to serve, to further their warped and corrupted morals. They were vastly inferior and imperfect."

"We're all inferior and imperfect. But we keep trying to do better. We all want a world that's better than we found it. Some we don't agree with, either their vision or their methods, but I would argue that they were all doing it with a certain purity of heart."

"You would say that about the greatest villains of your human history?"

"I'm saying we're not all perfect and some let the power corrupt them. I'm guessing something like that happened with you." I wasn't sure if making it personal would help or hurt, but it kept everyone's attention. By now, if there were killer droids in the collector, they would be here. There were no robo-bugs either. He was seriously depleted, I guessed. After all, his work was done, the energy flow had been disrupted, so he just had to run out the clock on humanity, and in a way, I was helping him.

"I've been having this debate with my selves for millions of years. In every reality, it's much the same, and mankind is found wanting."

"Compared to what?" I challenged. "Is there a better race out there?" I waved my hand in the air, aiming for the stars.

"Your baser emotions win out time and again, and if you were to leave this reality for the bubble universe my counterpart has been creating, nothing would change. Why waste all that energy to perpetuate a disease? Humans try to tame or harness or eradicate a disease. I am doing nothing different."

He could outthink me, certainly after so long arguing it. I was never going to change his mind or dissuade him from stopping us. Instead, he was just arguing to waste time. But by then, I had been noticing that Silas, who had been standing near Wild Bill and the Greeks, had been inching closer to Michael and Vihaan. They were clearly getting ready to act.

"Stop right there, unit," the Adversary said.

"Problem, Adversary?"

"Adversary. Even your names are simplistic. Adversary. Architect. Alliterative and short-sighted in what we truly represent."

"Are you now suggesting your evolved artificial intelligence is superior to man's? Are you worthy of being preserved?"

"Look at what we have created. We have cracked time travel; we have conversed between realities."

"Yeah yeah. 'Look on my Works, ye Mighty, and despair!'" I said, quoting Shelley. "No one's going to remember you when this is over."

"Because no one will be left...stop!" It actually sounded frightened, a first, after minutes of nothing but contempt.

What he was reacting to was a rapid upload of programming from the tablets to Silas. At the same time, Silas had extended one of its multifaceted arms to a nearby port to directly access and interface with the Adversary in its realm. Wall after wall of darkness winked to life, evidence of something happening within the circuitry. The Adversary had stopped talking, which I was perfectly fine with, to be honest. With every light that winked, I could imagine Silas and the

Adversary racing through circuit boards and fiber optic cables, packets of data dueling with one another.

When Silas' body slumped lifelessly to the floor, his blue eyes winking dark, I let out a soft cry.

He sacrificed himself to take the fight directly to the Adversary.

SIXTEEN

I FELT like Alice suddenly trapped in Wonderland, where things looked familiar, but nothing was quite right. Silas had somehow connected with the Adversary and was attempting to fight him on a level I couldn't see and only understood because I liked *The Matrix* and Oscar really liked playing *AI War: Fleet Command*. Beyond that, I had no idea what was happening.

Silas' nine-foot-tall body was still, the blue lights for eyes were dim and no longer reacting to their surroundings. The walls around us shimmered with lights as systems turned on and off, casting eerie shadows on the ceiling, floor, and us. None of us could do anything, although Michael was swiveling his head, trying to understand what was happening, searching the kaleidoscope of lights for clues. This was his world, not mine, and even he seemed uncertain.

"What's going on?"

"Remember how Silas obeyed the laws of robotics?" Michael asked. "He's taking it to the nth degree, fighting the Adversary, trying to prevent him from hurting us."

"But how?"

"Silas' programming seems beyond the AI Singularity," he began.

"English, please," I pleaded, cocking my head at Wild Bill and Albert, both of whom were looking lost.

"Andrew Moore, Dean of Computer Science at Carnegie Mellon University, described artificial intelligence as 'the science and engineering of making computers behave in ways that, until recently, we thought required human intelligence.'"

"Sort of like how the *Brimstone* operated," Albert suggested. Michael nodded in affirmation.

He took a deep breath, and as he spoke, he began to sound like a patient college professor, the voice modulated to soothe. "The AI Singularity was an idea from your time that identified the point where Artificial Intelligence went beyond its programming, achieving sentience. For example, you had Alexa, right?"

I nodded then turned to the others, who blinked in confusion. "It was a digital assistant, programmed into our phones or speakers." There were some nods although clearly Wild Bill was still feeling lost.

"At some point, in your fiction, Alexa would have used supervised Machine Learning to understand your preferences so it could recommend what to watch next, right?"

I nodded.

"At some point, Alexa may have reached the point where it learned enough to go beyond that and think for itself; that's the singularity. It's what would have turned a benign assistant into something else."

"Skynet?" I suggested.

Now it was his turn to blink. "The evil AI that turned robots against humanity in the *Terminator* movies," I explained.

"Oh, right, I remember those," he said vaguely. "By my time, we were less worried about that threat as we found new ways to map the human brain and replicate that into deep neural networks, which went way beyond machine learning, accessing the world's stored digital knowledge to be nearly identical with human actions. That's the work I was doing when I developed the software that ultimately became the Architect."

"In your world. In some other world, the software glitched and we got the Adversary," Bartholomew said.

"That could be. I would have to get to his systems to try and understand what happened," Michael admitted.

"So what is happening now?"

"It could be that Silas is using programming that was dormant until this particular threat was exposed. He's in there, trying, perhaps, to reroute commands, compromise subroutines, shut it down entirely."

"So you really don't have a clue what's going on in there?"

He shook his head slowly. "This is all beyond what I was working on. It could be any number of things."

I turned to Chou. "How can we help?"

"In there, we can do nothing," she said.

I hated standing here helpless. My body was thrumming with nervous energy, aware the clock was ticking on our window of opportunity. I wanted to know what was happening with Abernathy and Osman. Most of all, I wanted to do *something*.

There was a sudden loud pinging sound, like a phone alert but consistent. I turned around and realized it was coming from the tablet in Vihaan's hand. He was studying it, swiping rapidly, his eyes swiftly moving from side to side. Then his fingers rushed across the screen and the pinging stopped. He seemed to enter additional data then turned around and seemingly aimed the tablet at a wall of computer interfaces. Every light in the chamber went dark, plunging us into gloom. There was some ambient lighting from the chambers above us and some emergency floor lighting, which was designed to get us to a nearby exit. I wasn't going anywhere, though.

Just as suddenly as the lights went off, a different pattern of lighting returned, deeper reds and purples, bathing us all, giving off a spooky, dangerous vibe that may have been designed to make us uncomfortable. For a change, everyone was looking to Michael for answers rather than me and I was relieved. He was studying the wall and then Vihaan walked over with the tablet and showed him something.

"What?" I asked sharply, my patience with inaction bubbling over.

"It appears the Architect was able to use Silas as a trojan horse, overriding the Adversary's signal blocking. It was not only Silas entering the hardware, but the Architect himself. At some point, he also managed to upload a timed message to Vihaan's tablet. Once the upload began, Vihaan was able to unleash the Architect from hiding, sending him after Silas."

"So it's two-on-one?" Albert asked.

"Something like that, yes," Vihaan agreed.

"What are they doing?"

"I can only guess, Albert," Michael said.

What we had here were nearly identical, I suppose, artificial intelligences duking it out like a digital barroom brawl, but we couldn't see the fighters or even the barroom. From what little I understood about computer programming, I suppose it meant they were trying to short out connections, rewrite programming, maybe even pollute their opponent with evil malware. I also knew the speed of their battle could be measured in picoseconds, so the fact that I could count it in minutes suggested a fairly even match, one that must feel interminable to them. Maybe they'd wind up battling one another to standstill to the end of time. I'd read that story more than a few times. But if that were the case, humanity was doomed.

The next thing I heard was Wild Bill's guns clearing their holsters. His whole body had tensed, expecting danger. Chou was right behind him, her sword at the ready, and although I hadn't realized it, my scimitar was in my right hand.

Then I heard it, the shuffle of feet, the unearthly sound of metal against metal, human moans mixed in with the mechanical noises. I didn't have to guess what was coming.

My fear fantasy proved true and into the chamber strode Abernathy, or what had once been Abernathy, and behind him followed his army of oil-slick black figures, all of whom were once human and were now coated in nanobots. This time, though, Abernathy's coal black eyes lacked menace, but instead radiated purpose. He didn't pause to posture and make demands, but he was here to fight us and that was, for a change, fine with me. I foreswore violence in accordance with the Architect's desires, but this guy had caused too much sorrow and pain. He needed to be put down like a rabid dog. Besides, standing here watching a video game fight between AIs had made me twitchy. Hitting something was just what was required.

What I hadn't done, though, was study the area tactically, something Levy and the Greeks might have done. I had no idea how to find exits from the riot of panels, most of which were fixed from floor to ceiling. For all I knew, the way they came in was the only way in or out. Just then, I realized, I had no way to protect Michael and Albert; they were exposed and had no real weapons to use beyond their knives, which were pretty useless in this fight. My first thought was to ask Wild Bill to cover them, but I needed him in action.

Fortunately, it seemed Chou was more observant than I was, having used the time I was debating the Adversary to explore the area, and as I stood, gripping and regripping the handle, she beckoned Michael and steered him to a place where several of the wild panels provided a natural corner, making it hard to reach him. If we could keep the fight away from there, he'd be safe.

She then whispered in Albert's ear, and with the knife in his hand, he nodded grimly and took a position in front of my son. He would guard the space as best he could, and that would have to do.

Abernathy and the others, numbering easily two dozen, entered deeper and began to fan out. They, too, had to work their way around the panels, some clearly hitting dead ends, so no one had the tactical advantage. Yet, they had the numbers, and sooner or later would overwhelm us or wear us down. I had no doubt, they were merely the first wave. And all the while, the Adversary and Architect were still at war in what, for them, must now feel like the Seven Years War or something longer.

Chou had been separating our forces, spreading us out in the mammoth chamber, so we were far from easy pickings. Levy, too far away for me to translate, was using hand gestures to tell our newfound Greek allies to avoid touching the invaders. I doubt she was worried about the people smothered by the nanotech and instead focused on keeping us alive. The men took their positions after placing the still unconscious Miko near Michael. One stood beside Albert as they exchanged nods. If I had time to really think about it, this was every kid's fantasy, to be in a major battle, ancient Greek warriors versus high tech beasts.

As she did this, one of the monstrosities came close to me, legs lengthening to make each stride cover great distance. One arm reared back, the hand now a spike, and readied to slice into me. Instead, I stabbed the tip of the scimitar into the planted foot closest to me. The black nanobots spread apart on contact, and I sliced through skin, tendon, and bones. The creature, which was once a young woman, whose pigtails were now ropey imitations of hair, howled, waving the raised arm in the air. I withdrew the blade and swiftly stabbed into the abdomen. The sound of my steel against the metallic nanobots was ugly, a scratching sound with a clang to it.

From my left, an arm reached through and grabbed my hair, yanking me off balance. I slid to the floor and felt something heavy pound on my back, ripping the blouse. It was unrelenting and each blow hurt, forcing air from my lungs. Wildly, I looked around and saw a small, thin trail of nanobots start marching across the tiled floor toward me. If it made contact, I knew I was a goner. That thought flooded my mind, activating a surge of adrenaline, and I rose after the last pounding blow, jabbing forward at my second attacker. Quickly, I also began to tap dance, crushing the nanobot stream with a series of satisfying cracks, desperate not to let any attach themselves to my boots. I then backed away into one of the panels. With my bare skin touching it, the screen flared to life, a rush of orange and yellow lights shining brightly. It seemed to startle my two attackers, so I lowered myself and played linebacker, rushing them, sending each against a different panel and giving me an escape.

I turned left then right, coming upon the sight of Bartholomew, one arm slick with his own blood, swinging the rifle in an uppercut, sending the scarecrow-like shadowy figure backward with enough force that its impact into the panel actually cracked it.

"You okay?" I said.

"It's just a flesh wound," he said with a wolfish grin. Then he rammed the rifle backward, over his hip, and into a man, not yet fully converted, his ZZ Top beard and mouth still human, who was staggered backward. He then said, "Screw this" and tossed the rifle to Vihaan and he pulled up the machine gun. He pulled back the slide, made certain the ammunition was in place, and then, with a guttural cry, opened fire. The loud clatter of the machine gun fire drowned out every other sound. The Greek flinched out of fright, but the rest of the team continued to fight as the nanotech army crumpled as the hot lead poured through them, disrupting whatever held them together.

The firing sound was too loud, hurting everyone's ears, but it also didn't last long as the gun, heating up, jammed. Bartholomew cursed and flung the overheated and now useless weapon into a cluster of the enemy, scattering them.

My ears rang, but through the din, I could hear the sounds of battle elsewhere, fists and weapons swishing through the air. An occasional human grunt could be heard, but it was hard to tell if it was from our team or Abernathy's. I stole a glance at Silas' still form, wondering how the digital war was going. I desperately wanted to check on Albert, Michael, and Miko but got turned around so had no way to easily know where they were. Instead, I had to concentrate on the trio coming for me from around a bend.

Fortunately, not every panel reached from floor to ceiling, and crouched atop this particular panel was Chou, who leapt directly into the three once-humans, arms wide, taking them to the ground. I joined her and we repeatedly stabbed at them with our blades, then she reached down, and with a savage yank, separated a hand from an arm. Normally, that shouldn't happen so easily, but there was no longer any organic matter, it was a nanobot approximation of a human arm. The hand, with writhing tendrils of nanobots, was tossed to the ground, and she tap-danced all over it, causing a cloud of sparks that never rose past her ankle.

"There are too many for us to be successful," she told me matter-of-factly.

"No shit," I said. "You have a plan?"

"Survive," she replied, which was more of an aspiration than an actual plan.

We were outnumbered and outmatched, with no help coming from the inert Silas, or the Architect, who was still at digital war with his evil doppelganger. This could be our last stand. It was not what I imagined would happen, but I was fighting to keep the Adversary from destroying the last remnants of mankind. If I had to die here, keeping Abernathy and his oily goons from somehow interfering with the Architect's efforts, and for the Earth to endure, I would. I'd been ready to die before and this time it was for a far greater cause than drug-induced self-pity.

I was so focused on my own thoughts, trying to stay focused despite the ear-ringing, that I missed the rising whine in the distance. This place was so huge and there had been so much noise that it took me time to register it. But hearing it grow in volume, I recognized it was a rallying cry. Help was on its way!

Chou heard it as well, and after a brief confirming glance at one another, I reached out and swiftly kicked an approaching figure in the gut. My knee sank into the nanobot's belly, but the force was enough to send it a few steps backward. The scimitar followed, severing arm from faux shoulder.

"'Look to my coming, at first light, on the fifth day. At dawn, look to the East," I quoted. I had no real idea if the entry was east or west, up or down, but I did know that the Pasha and his forces were here and that was fine by me.

The maze was a lousy place for so many figures to be fighting, and once the newly arrived army entered the space, they were immediately forced back out by the nanobot army. Abernathy, I finally spotted, was directing them, with minimal gestures, but no doubt through some connection he had with them. Still, that meant the fight would now be out in the wild, on grass and in the wheat fields, under partly cloudy skies. A perfect day for a battle.

In short order, Abernathy's followers were flowing toward the doorway, including the one-armed attacker at my feet. That was fine, as the Greeks followed them out, not done fighting. I was winded and needed to find Michael. Chou and Levy rushed ahead as I backed away, wary of an ambush.

"Michael," I yelled.

Off to my left and behind me, I heard a reply and I hurried in that direction, cursing myself at three wrong turns. Finally, I found Albert, with some cuts on his face and ripped pants, continuing to guard the space where Michael lay slumped against the wall, studying Vihaan's tablet.

"Are you okay?" I asked my young warrior.

"I feared that I was a gone sucker," he said. "But I was going to go the whole hog until the end."

"He fought bravely," his Greek companion said.

I hugged him fiercely and he relaxed into the embrace. Albert was clearly scared but doing his best to act the man I wanted him to become by surviving.

"Michael?"

"Fine, Meredith," he said, although I would have been just as fine hearing "mom" at that moment. I had really thought we were done and was delighted to be proven wrong.

"Do you have any sense of what's going on in there?" I asked, thumbing toward the master display, which had a blur of colorful data racing across the screen.

"The energy consumption is astounding," he said in admiration. "I see auxiliary cooling systems have been turned on to prevent everything from overheating, which would be disastrous."

"Great. Who's winning?"

He shrugged and I felt his frustration at not knowing.

"I have to get out there, see what's going on. Stay here, stay safe," I instructed and turned to go.

"Osman has this, stay here," Michael suggested. I shook my head. I got everyone into this and needed to be there to help. Right then, that realization deep in my heart, that was when I felt different. All the reluctance I had been feeling since arriving here over six weeks before, all the indecision and reaction – all of that vanished. I brought these people together to fight for life. They were *my* people and had come for me. I couldn't leave them alone, could not be absent from the fight. Was this what Washington, Patton, or Eisenhower felt? Like a leader?

I turned on my heel and sprinted for the doorway, not exactly eager to fight the nanobots, but ready to be shoulder to shoulder with Osman and the others. The battle sprawled across the fields, a mix of humans and black misshapen figures. Guns fired, swords swished, and other makeshift weapons were in use, while the more powerful nanobot figures struck back, wounding some, killing others in grisly ways. The shrieks and cries made my blood run cold, made my heart break for the dream being whittled down, and for those never getting their second chance.

The cold flared anew, transforming into a hot anger. I had to stop this.

Off to one side, Abernathy stood, his elongated arms having just pierced deeply into a woman warrior, someone from the 18th century maybe. Blood sprayed in an arc from a severed artery, coating his black, oily arms in red. Three others rushed him, followed by Bartholomew taking aim with the rifle. A wooden spear and what appeared to be a pitchfork struck his torso, but the nanobots merely shifted about, several tendrils reaching out to envelop the spear, racing toward the man in overalls who threw it. The nanobots speeded up and gushed forward, closing the gap between spear and spear thrower. He shouted in pain as the first nanobots bit deeply into his hand, cords starting to tunnel into his musculature.

The report of the rifle distracted me and I saw my friend's aim was good, as the bullet struck Abernathy in the triangular thing that served as a head. It entered where the nose should have been and then emerged from the back. Abernathy barely shuddered.

How were we going to stop them? My mind flashed back to the horrors of seeing hundreds descend on Blue Alpha, ripping her apart. It was almost as if they were taking it easy on us, exerting only enough energy to deal with us mere mortals.

Energy.

Chou suggested that the Adversary was exerting so much energy controlling things, including Abernathy's billions or trillions of nanobots. Something had to keep them going after they converted the organic material into energy. We already knew there were tremendous amounts of power required to open time portals, and rather than bring individuals forward, the Adversary was bringing people *and* things like the *Brimstone* or the Red Baron's plane or the Nazi squad. He was reaching further back in time for things like the sabretooth tigers, which I bet required extra energy.

And now he was using his depleted energy to fight the Architect. He was perhaps at his most vulnerable and we had to use that to our advantage.

Apparently, Michael had used his time in hiding well, because he had been thinking along the same lines. That became apparent when he and Albert came sprinting out of the cathedral and made for me. Their Greek guard was jogging behind them, trying to make himself useful.

"You have something? Because we're getting our asses kicked," I said.

"We don't know where the Adversary really is," Michael began, "and this place is too vast. But Albert had a thought."

I looked down at the boy, who was beaming with pride.

"When you squashed those bugs, they sparked and it got me to thinking about the power sources for something this small," he began and then Michael picked up the thread.

"For them to follow their programming, they needed something to direct them," he began. "Vihaan had been studying their engineering earlier and we realized that they self-replicate complete with programming, but they are acting independent of one another, which suggests they had something controlling them."

"Abernathy," I finished.

"Right-o," Albert said, pleased with how we were filling in each other's thoughts.

"Can you hack the system?" I asked Michael.

"I've been trying without success, but then, Albert..."

"It's like stopping up a hose. The water pressure has to go backward and you can burst a pipe. But do it with electricity."

"Is he suggesting we overload their network?" I asked Michael as he and Albert nodded in unison, which caused me to laugh. It felt so good to have a genuine laugh amidst this chaos. "Okay, how do we do that?"

"I've been trying to send a signal to override the systems, cause a feedback loop, something, but they're too well-protected. Instead, we're going old school." He nodded and Albert ran back into the cathedral. A few moments later, he came running out carrying two cables, both deep blue.

"When one of them shattered a panel, it exposed their circuitry, so Albert and I began pulling out the cabling. Now all we need do is..." He held out his hand like a surgeon. Albert handed him his knife and Michael set to work, slicing the cables apart then fraying the ends, exposing the actual power source.

It sparked a bit like electricity, but who knew what it exactly was.

"Okay, now what?"

"We ram it up Abernathy's arse," Albert exclaimed.

I felt my eyes widen at that. It was going to be suicidal and we'd never get close enough. Unless...I spun around, retrieved my scimitar from my belt, and began stalking Abernathy, who was busily cutting another settler into pieces. I shuddered at that but needed his attention.

"You ready for me?" I yelled, and sure enough, I got his attention. He glared at me as much as someone without expression could glare. Carelessly, he tossed the corpse aside and began heading for me. He shoved away someone trying to bludgeon him.

Out of the corner of my eye, I saw Chou suddenly fall into step beside me. Side by side, we stalked him. It felt like the climax of *High Noon*, something I'd seen a few times with my dad, who loved that film. Which made me think of Wild Bill. I knew he was still with us as his six-gun fired now and then. The fighting continued around us and the carnage was growing as more humans fell to the nanobot army. If this didn't work, we were dead. So was the planet.

We were perhaps five feet apart and closing, which was when I saw it was Albert, not Michael, who was inching up on Abernathy's rear. I don't know if nanobots had eyes in the back of their head and I had to school my expression to not betray my surprise. Instead, I made certain I had my "I'm gonna kill him" expression in place.

From somewhere deep within him, the nanobots simulated a chuckle, perhaps animated by whatever was left of Abernathy's personality. It was like rocks being banged next to one another and entirely unpleasant, making me all the more certain to put an end to it.

Something that was once two humans shambled toward Albert, but doing so silently, not calling attention to itself. I couldn't cry a warning for fear of giving him away and my hopes began to sink.

At that point, Bartholomew rushed from one side and Levy from the other, ramming the figure before it could reach the boy. Albert's expression showed his terror then thankfulness, but he never stopped moving toward Abernathy as the cable's slack gave out, so he'd barely make it. Chou caught that and knew we needed to back him up, so she increased her pace, her sword raised, ready to strike. Bartholomew and Levy came into Abernathy's "field of vision," flanking him, and the monstrosity actually paused, calculating the right course of action.

That hesitation was all it took. Albert's own short sword was in his hand and he viciously stabbed at Abernathy's back, forcing the nanobots apart, revealing little more than skeleton. The nanobots were already swarming up the sword, toward his hand. But it created an aperture, allowing him to shove the sparking cables deep into the not-quite-human form.

The chuckle shifted to a gurgle then an electronic scream that was quickly echoed by every nanobot in the area. The smell of burning organs was vile, but there was precious little left. Some of the others fell apart, black oily cables fell off partially digested human forms, revealing sickening corpses. One outright exploded while others jerked spasmodically, sparking in a rainbow of colors. The air was turning hazy as a thin, noxious cloud oozed from the army.

Osman and the others stopped fighting, caught by surprise, and watched as their enemies were unable to fight. They didn't move but shut down or fell apart in place. The rotting organs and skin turned the air into something that made me gag. Michael was already coughing, my son doubled over. Levy rushed to help him back into the cathedral.

The Pasha had hurried over falling opponents, his own eyes wide in amazement. As he did, I looked at the remains of Abernathy, which had been reduced to an oily puddle of inert nanotechnology. Tommy "Two-Thumbs" didn't ask for this, never intended to become inhuman, and maybe didn't deserve this fate. He was a puppet of the Adversary, his free will gone, and became less an enemy and more a figure to be pitied and soon forgotten.

"What happened, Meredith?" Osman asked.

"Later," I said.

Slowly, we walked the grounds, ensuring each and every one of the hundreds of nanobot figures had been deactivated. None were human anymore or if human, no longer alive. My heart was heavy for all the losses, all the lost chances, and how they all accepted a second chance only to be victims in a war they never asked for. Once Chou, Osman, and I were satisfied they were all deactivated, I let out an audible breath.

Crisis averted.

There remained, though, the Adversary to contend with.

SEVENTEEN

I STARED at the remains of Abernathy for a long time, lost in my own thoughts, feeling accomplished and helpless at the same time. As a result, I had totally tuned out all the noise that had been rising all around me. Finally, Albert tugged on my arm, breaking the spell.

"What's up?" I asked.

"They're all dead! Even the ones outside," he said with great enthusiasm.

I looked over at Chou, who nodded, showing little elation at the news. She was, like me, worried about the battle we couldn't see. Slowly, our band had been making their way to me and I studied each, seeing scrapes on everyone, a black eye on Vihaan, and more serious wounds to Wild Bill and Bartholomew, my hardiest fighters. Michael had seemed fine enough, although he was clearly preoccupied with the tablet.

"How do you know, Albert?"

"Look!" He gestured toward the mile-long corridor leading to the outside and in ones and twos, members of the resistance, *my* army, were coming in, their jaws dropping, eyes bulging, and soaking up the wonder of the place. Hard to believe that after visiting three collectors, it had already begun to feel blasé to me. Had I truly lost my sense of sensation in this place, a world filled with wonders?

As they focused on the humans standing amidst the inert nanobots, most waved and hurried toward me. Among them was Carolyn Nguyen, who I met back in New Manhattan. I was delighted to recognize a face, especially from that settlement that suffered at Abernathy's command. Her right arm had a tourniquet tied around the bicep and the remainder of the sleeve was dark red with dry blood. But she was smiling, so I took that as a good sign.

"Meredith! You're alive!"

"Yeah. Is Emily okay?"

She nodded, studying the pile of goo that had been Abernathy. "That the Wicked Witch of the West?"

Now I nodded. She grinned at that, a look of assurance in her eyes, because, after all, I was once her president. Here she stood with me, making some sort of history, but I had no real idea what was going to be said about this since everything remained in flux.

"What's happening out there?"

"A bloody mess when several of us broke off to run in here, either to support you or hide from them," she told me.

"Did we lose a lot?"

"Too many, but we can count later. Is it really over?"

"This part of it," I assured her.

Michael, on cue, spoke up. "Chou, your husband needs you!" She hurried to his side and she read whatever was on the tablet, and while I wanted to ask questions, I paused and let her focus.

"Come," she said and turned, heading back into the cathedral-like structure. We all followed, although Vihaan and Albert were coiling up the cables that we used to overload the nanobot army, severing Abernathy's connection to them. Apparently, it disconnected all of them, which was pretty damn impressive.

The lighting was, if possible, even dimmer inside the central chamber. Whatever had been fouling the air had stopped and at least things smelled a little better. At least I wasn't coughing.

"What's happening?" I asked Chou.

"My beloved appears to have bested the Adversary. Now we have work to do."

Talk about feeling anticlimactic. The battle between AI titans happened out of sight and ended without any sort of fanfare. I felt robbed. Then I began to feel a sense of relief. No more ambushes from archers, mercenaries, and Nazis. No more predatory animals that didn't belong here to catch us off guard. We could finally breathe and build in earnest.

Of course, now we had a larger issue to contend with: saving the world.

Vihaan and Michael were studying data on the tablet as Chou ran a hand over the master panel, no doubt wishing some physical connection to her husband. At her feet, still motionless, was Silas, and I was overwhelmed with emotion for losing my ally. It was then I could see how, centuries after my time, a woman could fall in love with an AI.

"The Adversary closed off connections to the collector network after it siphoned off most of the accumulated energy," Vihaan explained.

"All to stop us, stop me," I said.

"The Architect can do only so much as software and needs hands to help restore the network," he continued.

Albert had walked over to the slumped form of Silas, his nine-foot body still, without a spark of life. He patted and poked him, trying to wake him up, more wishful thinking than any hope of actually reviving him. It seemed he sacrificed himself for the greater good and was gone.

"How much time is left?"

Michael barely glanced up as he said, "Twenty-seven hours, give or take."

"Twenty-seven hours until what?" Carolyn asked.

"Basically, we need to restore the Earth's absorption of solar energy to power the engines that will open a portal that will save the planet, *after* we free it from orbit," I said.

"Easy peasy, right?" she quipped although her eyes registered the issues.

"Do we have any idea if the False Vacuum event is near?"

"Remember," Michael warned me, "if we can see it, we're too late. So, no, we can't see it, even though we know it's coming."

"We're dealing with precise calculations that can't be fudged," Vihaan added. "The collectors have to be replenished now so they have the energy required to open the rift in time-space at just the right moment as Earth leaves orbit. With the moon accompanying us, it should help the tidal forces, but it's not going to be a smooth transition."

Chou had stepped beside Michael and was examining additional instructions coming from her husband. She nodded to herself and touched an adjacent panel. It winked to life and she was shown schematics of equipment I couldn't begin to comprehend. She, though, seemed to understand it. Several other windows opened and one had a schematic of the entire collector, a light green path being superimposed to show where she needed to go.

"Do you need help?"

She shook her head without looking my way.

"*Actually, my beloved, we will need additional help,*" the Architect said from hidden speakers.

"You're alive!" Albert shouted.

"I am indeed, Albert. I'm also very happy you survived this unpleasantness. Your quick thinking with the power cables was most admirable. Very old school, although quite new for you. Meredith, this boy is deserving of a medal."

He sounded more relaxed, maybe with the flush of victory and his wife present, he could be more his normal self.

"You show me where the metal ore is, we'll make him one," I said.

"*First, though, we have to save the world,*" he said.

"Did he always have a gift for understatement?" I asked Chou.

"Sometimes," she said.

"*Weston will begin the repair process and as needed; I will task several of you to help complete the work.*"

"Didn't this place have robots like Blue Alpha?" Albert asked. "Or can't you wake Silas up?"

"*Once, it did. They all did. But here, the Adversary cannibalized them to power his nanobots and the things you call robo-bugs. So now, I will need your eyes and hands to help me restore us to the network.*"

"But what about Silas?" Albert repeated.

"*I'm sorry, Albert, but Silas' processing programs were compromised when I traveled through him into the Adversary's mainframe.*"

"Huh?"

"He's not coming back, son," Wild Bill said, leaning down and placing a comforting hand on his shoulder. Albert sniffled quietly and I felt my own eyes grow damp.

Humans replacing robots, the opposite of every science fiction writer's worst nightmare, had a satisfying sense of irony to it. Chou followed the directions, taking her out of the building and off to the west. The rest of us stood around feeling particularly useless for a time. Carolyn and Bartholomew went outside to see to the growing crowd. Levy was in constant motion, hopping from one injured fighter to another. Osman was directing people to form up in groups and to stay out of the way. It seemed more than a few people had the idea of seeking shelter within the collector and I didn't blame them at all.

Michael and Vihaan were summoned to different parts of the complex to assist in the repair operation. Feeling useless, I headed toward the doorway to watch what was happening outside. People were milling about, marveling at the size and scope of the collector, walking in the wheat fields, idly kicking over ruined crops. Others looked after one another's wounds and I wondered about Möngke, my fiercest soldier. I hoped for the best, secretly feared for the worst.

Without warning, the lighting dramatically improved in the central chamber, a sign that something was working right. I had questions, but they'd have to wait since I didn't want to distract the Architect. Idly, I wondered what his real name was.

I felt the time ticking away, the countdown continuing as the work continued and it seemed we were going to win this particular race. We'd get the power flowing, get the batteries or whatever they were topped off in time to work with the solar sail. The amount of energy being discussed, from the Dyson swarm to the interstellar network of power directed at Earth, remained staggering. This had been going on for millions of years and now we were down to the final hours of go or no go. I was reminded once more of how isolated the Architect had been, how divorced from humanity he had been for so long, apart from his wife, only able to talk with versions of himself. I admired the dedication, thinking of how it somehow traced all the way back to Michael.

"Meredith, I could use your assistance," the Architect said.

"Put me in, coach," I quipped.

"Please follow the highlighted path. I will need you to recon-nect a number of cables across the way."

The pale green lights flashed into appearance and I saw it was taking me out of the cathedral and in the opposite direction of where the others had gone. Once out of the building, holographic markers guided me, so I followed, waving and giving a thumbs-up to the others who remained milling about, uncertain of what was to come next. There were more present and no doubt still more to come. I needed to tend to that soon, but first, we had a bigger issue to deal with.

I walked a good twenty minutes, worried that every step was going to waste time, so I quick-walked and of course the holograms adjusted to my pace. Finally, I was directed to one of the smaller buildings in sight, although it takes a lot for a fifty-story tower to be considered small. Once inside, the place lit a path for me to follow, a narrow corridor that ended as elevator doors silently opened for me. Obediently, I stepped inside, and as the doors closed, it was already in motion. My stomach dropped and my ears popped within seconds and then it seemed to be over as we slowed to a stop. I had barely time to register the silvery interior, reflecting my haggard self in 360 degrees. Good thing I didn't have time to linger on my appearance.

The doors parted and the green light awaited me, guiding me through the open floor. The place was huge, as everything here seemed to be. There were a series of work stations with head gear and screens but no keyboards, each with a reclining chair. Some abstract-looking statuary were set in alcoves and one seemed suspended in air. Each was a blend of colors, no two alike, and if they had a function, I had no idea what it was. Everything was coated with dust, suggesting no one or nothing had been in here for some time. I guess even in the future, there was dust and neglect. There were only a few windows, but they were enormous, letting in plenty of light and I had a great view of the sprawling grounds. Way down below, there were long, cubist black smudges that were once our enemy, though I felt nothing for them. The survivors, though, were now ant-like people milling about with more pouring in.

Against one wall, a doorway slid open, rising into the wall, and revealing another area, darker and foreboding. The green hologram reappeared and pointed with an arrow at what appeared to be a cabinet. I walked over and tugged on the door, which opened with ease.

"Meredith, I need you to do as I tell you, in the sequence I instruct. Do not make an error, for there is more to do," the Architect told me.

"Shoot," I said, and he began telling me which components to withdraw from what appeared to be a pegboard and where to place them. The pieces were lightweight but sturdy and slid from place to place easily.

"You have time to chat?"

"I am currently directing all the others, but yes, what is it you wish to know?"

"Well, for starters, do you have a name? Chou always calls you husband or beloved."

"Yes, I do. In our time, given how the artificial intelligence is integrated with the starship, we are virtually the same."

"So your name is Shining Light?"

"Yes, do you like it?"

"Well, it certainly fits you. You're our shining light, pointing toward what comes next," I told him.

"There's definitely a poet in you. Weston has told me of your fondness for poetry, which is what would have made you an interesting lawyer," he told me.

That took me by surprise. He and Chou had had so little

time together that the idea they'd waste any of it on me seemed odd, but who was I to argue? I hadn't done particularly well with relationships, which is one reason why the idea of me being both a president and a mother had never quite sat right with me.

"So you're up there on the moon. What happened? How did it fragment?"

"I was young and made mistakes," he began. Whoa, the mighty Architect caused this? I was certain it would have been the casualty of some earlier battle with the Adversary. *"When I transferred my core programming to the moon in order to expand, I was working quickly and there was a miscalculation of power. The moon proved more prone to shattering than I expected and there was a tremendous surge of power deep in the core that radiated through fault lines. I lost over a million years in repairing the damage to the moon bases, readying them for the sail manufacture. We had to recalculate the entire schedule."*

He was talking about a million years like I would an hour and a schedule that would last half a billion years. The scale of this thing continued to both impress and scare the hell out of me. I followed his directions for more rewiring, which was thankfully easy due to everything being color coded or carrying identifiable symbols. This was the most relaxed labor I've had since arriving.

"How did you manage to scan the multiverse to find me and the others?"

"Once I managed to communicate with my doppelgangers, we struck on this idea to save this world. Our first order of business was determining how *to save the planet and humankind. We determined the solar sail and bubble universe was the best course of action. That meant determining how to use the micro-wormholes to our advantage and force open the new universe. As we devised the technology and built the sail, we also set to work*

on extrapolating the wormholes would provide the science to allow us to time travel."

"Oh sure, you make it sound so easy," I said.

"This was over the course of millions of years at computer speed," he explained. *"With quantum processing along with our sharing knowledge, we accomplished in millions of years what mankind only dreamt of."* There was an actual sense of pride in his deep, mechanical voice. He was more realistic than I had imagined, but then again, he had to be for Chou to fall in love.

Then, after about a dozen more bits of rewiring, I was to enter code numbers on a touchscreen followed by more manual manipulation. Shining Light spoke intermittently, usually with an instruction, occasionally with encouragement.

"As we scanned each realities' history, we began to find the anomalies, people who thrived to some form of greatness in multiple worlds but had their lives tragically cut short in one. These were the people we determined deserved that second chance, knowing they had the potential to be great."

"So, in every other reality, I survived?"

"In all the others we studied, mostly yes; but we eventually found ourselves limiting the study in the interests of time."

"You made a joke there," I said. Not that it was very funny, but he was growing on me, less the monolithic deity I had been picturing in my mind, but far more...human. "Did all my other selves have this mutation?"

"The red hair? Yes." His humor sucked, but I'd never tell him that.

"Very funny. The one the Adversary was determined to eradicate."

"No. I and my brethren have no explanation beyond this. It was not something we chose to study, just preserve."

"Thanks for that. You and your other selves put so much time and thought into this, does the lives lost upset the plan?"

There was an actual pause of a few seconds, which surprised me, considering how quickly every other answer came. *"Like a house of cards, everything was carefully considered and placed, knowing full well a breeze, intentional or otherwise, could cause everything to fall apart. Had the Adversary –"*

"Was he married to a Chou too?" I interrupted.

"Yes, but in that reality, they quarreled and divorced on the return trip to Earth, making for years of unpleasantness, which we assumed sowed the seeds for his disapproval of mankind."

"That's certainly taking things to an extreme," I said. "Okay, so the Adversary crosses into our universe and manages to commandeer a collector. How could you not know which one was his?"

"The Adversary may not have had mankind's best interests in mind, but he was no fool. As soon as he crossed over, he quickly managed to instruct the collector to send out false signals, making it appear as if he was spread out across multiple collectors. Even with a limited number to work with, he continued to randomize the signals, so locating him was proving more trouble than it was worth since I was more focused on bringing you, all of you, forward."

"Wait, you actively let him survive and plot against you? You couldn't task a SILAS unit or something like Blue Alpha to track him down and stop him?"

"There were feints, attacks, counterattacks, and in the end, it was all taking too much time. I regret that now because I didn't anticipate he would destroy my work so quickly."

"That's some error in judgment," I said.

"Be that as it may, the lives lost plus the humans added along with the more predatory beasts – and you haven't encountered them all, so beware – has changed everything. With so many variables, I can't predict the new future, other than mankind has

enough life here to reproduce and grow. That will be necessary by the time of transition."

"Wait, just how long are we talking about?"

"We must continue this later, Meredith. Your part is over and you should return to the elevator and rejoin the others."

"Sure thing," I said and closed the space and followed my way back to the elevator. Within seconds, I was back on the ground floor and the others were reassembling. We'd have to come up with what came next then share it with the others, who were no doubt getting anxious. They defeated one enemy, at tremendous sacrifice, but now what? I felt for them, but had no idea what to tell them, no idea what came next.

Everyone seemed fine enough despite aches and pains. We searched one another's faces for confirmation the work was completed and the energy would flow again. There were welcoming nods, but then we stood there, falling into silence, uncertain of what was to come next. To my amusement, I saw that Osman and Möngke had already bonded with Epaminondas, three warrior leaders, now finding common causes despite the language barrier. Yeah, that needed addressing.

"Your work has helped me restore the proper collection of energy," Shining Light told us. I had to begin thinking of him that way, because that was his name and he deserved it. *"We did it with time to spare, exceeding my expectations."*

"Well, we had some help," I said, gesturing toward the crowd of people working their way toward us now that we were spotted.

"So your machines are working now and you're collecting the power you need to move the Earth?" Wild Bill asked.

"The solar sail portion of the plan has been at work for some time. Earth has been slowly moving from its original orbit so that part of the plan was not in jeopardy," Shining Light corrected.

"What did we just do then?"

Once again, a hologram appeared before us, showing the planet leaving its orbit for the portal to the bubble universe. Wild Bill clearly recognized it and nodded in affirmation. "Ah yeah, I got it."

"What do we do now, Meredith?" Albert asked. The hesitation and uncertainty in his voice – did I just hear it crack – was how we were all feeling. I didn't want to admit to not having a clue because, once again, everyone was looking at me.

"He's your husband," I said to Chou, hoping she'd offer a suggestion.

The hologram, I noticed, remained in place, which was unusual. It was on a loop, showing Earth and the moon slowly slipping from orbit and then there was a wink in space, somewhere between the moon and Mars, I think, and an aperture opened. The two bodies moved into the new universe and it blinked out of existence. Either to be dramatic or we really were in trouble, the image of the solar system then was wiped away with suddenness, only to repeat.

"Tell them, beloved," she said, using the softest voice I had heard from this strong woman.

"I am uncertain if the transition will adversely affect my installation on the moon. We're talking a fairly jarring moment between realities and the electronics may short out, have a cascade failure, or further damage the moon."

"You mean, you might die?" Albert asked.

"That is a possibility," Shining Light admitted.

"When is all this going to happen?" I asked, since he avoided answering me earlier. As I asked, I noticed the others were getting closer and would be expecting information, answers, a plan. I hadn't a clue. Michael, though, grabbed the tablet from Vihaan and walked off, lost in an idea.

"Not for quite some time," he admitted. "With the power restored, I am running calculations and scenarios to confirm."

"So, not today."

"Most definitely not."

"So what do we do next?"

"That, Meredith, is up to you all," Shining Light said. *"I brought you here to start over, and while it did not go according to my original plan, here you are, free of the Adversary's influence if not his remnants. You get to decide."*

"What about you?"

"I will be here, but my attention has to be on the sail and bubble universe. I didn't bring you all here to do my bidding, And I want to spend lost time with Weston."

In the distance, I heard a series of beeps, each a different tone, as if Michael and the tablet were having a conversation. The odd part appeared to be that he understood what each sound meant while it all sounded the same to me. Then again, I couldn't figure out R2-D2 either.

"Look!" Albert exclaimed and pointed toward the cathedral.

Emerging from the dark into the sunlit grounds was Silas, blue eyes bright, eye bar actually wiggling a little. Chou went over to him and the rest of us followed, everyone with wide smiles, even Wild Bill, who normally never smiled.

"Hello, everyone," he said, but the voice was different, modulated deeper.

"Beloved?"

"Yes, Weston. Michael kindly thought that since Silas' core programming was damaged during the battle with my counterpart, the body should not go to waste."

"But what about all the work on the moon?" Bartholomew asked.

"That will proceed. This body requires precious little of my energy and attention, but does give me a mobile manner with which to interact with you all." While he may have said all, his eyes were focused entirely on Chou.

"It occurred to me that with the Adversary gone and us here, Shining Light didn't need to be entirely on the moon. We could begin building ways for his core processing to be transferred back to each, distributed among the 218 collectors, with Silas as his avatar," Michael explained.

That's my boy.

EIGHTEEN

MY HEAD ACHED and I really wanted a nap. Advil and a nap. Make that Advil, lunch, and a nap.

Still, it felt like a reunion as Emily and Carolyn were joined by Osman, Möngke, and others I recognized from the last few weeks of our trek across this world. Not everyone came toward me; there remained clusters of people, too injured to be moved, field medics at work, seemingly directed by Levy, who herself was bloodstained and I couldn't tell from her own wounds or caring for others. Probably both.

While this was still the Earth, this land lacked a name. The Architect, now Shining Light, certainly didn't need to call it anything and that was just one of hundreds of decisions that needed to be made. And here they were, coming to me for guidance. Some knew me as a future or past president; others just knew I had this weird super-power. In every case, they followed me, they fought for me, and they watched their newfound friends and colleagues die for me. In their eyes, I was the leader, the one with the grand ideas for what to do next.

Surely out of 1.9 billion people brought to this world, there were some who, like Osman, were used to leading. There had to be statesmen, kings, queens, premiers, prime ministers, chieftains, popes, presidents, and who knows which other titles existed across time. They were the ones to turn to for guidance and leadership. The problem, though, was that out of the few thousand people I had encountered, none had that experience. Instead, I found poets, soldiers, cowboys, seamstresses, athletes, and more. And for whatever reason, they allied themselves with me, and they looked to me now.

"Now we divide the spoils of war," Möngke said, showing his teeth in a wolfish grin.

"What spoils would those be?" Wild Bill asked slowly, eyeing the Mongul warlord.

"These marvelous structures. There must be treasure of some sort within. And I was promised land for my people."

"We didn't ask you along so you can just help yourself," Wild Bill said. "We asked for your help after we kicked your ass."

"You did no such kicking," Möngke said defensively.

"But there's so much here; surely we should all get something," an older woman said, her right arm in a makeshift sling, made from what appeared to be the remains of her homespun blue skirt.

"We can certainly bring some of this back to build up our homes," another man, this one in not much clothing, his short, wide, black body rippled with muscles, and I suspected he'd give Bartholomew a challenge.

Other voices cried out, everyone wanting something. It was clear there were too many people, and the further back they were, the less they could understand what was being said. My abilities had their limits and we surpassed those. But I decided there were things that needed saying, and if they looked to me to lead, I better get started. There was some sizeable rubble, so I clambered up, one step at a time because I was still feeling a little woozy from a combination of my head hurting, my ears still ringing, and probably being dehydrated.

I patted the air, trying to focus everyone's attention on me. Dozens of heads swiveled up toward me, curious expressions on their faces. The hubbub began to die down. "We need to discuss this all, yes, but calmly. Hearing each other out. There is a lot to explain to many of you and many decisions to be made, but they will be made here and now before you all return home."

As I was speaking, suddenly, my voice was amplified, rising in volume and electronically modified. I turned over my shoulder and Silas, no, Shining Light, nodded. He was displaying human characteristics my old friend was never programmed with. This would take getting used to.

"I am Meredith Gale and I come from the west coast of North America, from California, and my time was 2018. You each have your own story, your own time and place. But here we are, an unimaginable time in the future, on a world that feels sort of familiar but is anything but home. Most of you know we all come from variations of the Earth you know. Some share realities, most do not. But we were all offered a second chance by someone we took to calling the Architect. His real name is Shining Light and he has taken up residence in this robot behind us. Many of you recognize him as my companion Silas, but the programming that made him unique was sacrificed to defeat our common enemy."

"Hello," Shining Light said, offering a wave. "Each collector was designed not just to absorb and channel energy from across the universe" – at this, there were some audible gasps – "but to preserve various biomes that you are all familiar with and would provide the foundation for settling your new homes. Each collector had specific lands based on the geography of their location."

"How many of these thingies are there?" a man with a surprisingly smooth, well-oiled mustache asked.

"Two hundred and eighteen," Shining Light said.

"All the same size as this bugger?" someone else asked.

"Yes, of course. I saw no need to vary their design, just their contents," Shining Light explained.

"Some of you have been told of why you were saved and what this world represents. Many of you have heard bits and pieces, possibly distortions, and I promised everyone I've met to be honest. And it's better to show than tell, so I'm going to ask Shining Light to give us a recap." As I turned toward him, suddenly now eye to eye, I whispered, "Keep it short and simple."

"Understood," he assured me.

The sound and light show began, similar to the presentation my team had days before. There were comments and more gasps, but no one, not a single one, doubted what they were being shown. There were the parallel worlds, the False Vacuum, the need to move the Earth, the solar sail, and I have to say, the scale of the thing still astounds me, and finally, the bubble universe as our escape route. Of course there were the gasps and commentary, but no one challenged what they saw. It was hard to argue after everything they had witnessed in the last few weeks.

"We battled against the Adversary to preserve the plan and keep humanity alive," I said. "Each one of us has unfulfilled potential, but in our reality, we never had the chance. Now we do. We were offered a chance to start over, reignite the spark of humanity and repopulate Earth.

"Bickering and squabbling won't get the work done. This is a big place and there's plenty of room for everyone. On my world, when I left it, there were over seven billion people here, so at under two billion, it'll be fine."

There were murmurs and comments, questions from one to another, and I didn't want to lose them.

"This world is a blank slate. There's no one here but us. We get to decide how we want it to be," I began.

"A democracy!"

"A republic!"

"Each settlement decides!"

So it went as the voices and ideas grew louder and then there were calls for who would decide. A few pointed at me, others argued no one person should have so much power. It was a cacophony that made my headache worse.

Carolyn rose on tiptoes, catching my eye. I leaned down and let her whisper something in my ear. It was perfect.

Slowly, I rose to my feet and once again waved my arms like a lunatic to get the horde to settle down. Shining Light's amplification helped, as did everyone crowding closer to hear me. In fact, some were moving to the sides and behind me, ensuring my translation skills wouldn't go to waste.

"On every world I know of, there is a United States of America. In the 1770s, they were debating the notion of self-government. One of their great writers, Thomas Paine, declared, 'We have it in our power to begin the world over again.'

"We have that chance now. Today."

There were some nods in affirmation, some whispered comments, but no objections.

"We fought one another, swindled one another, overlooked one another for millennia, and it brought suffering and strife, war, and death. It impeded progress, turned discoveries into weapons, wasted time, money, and life.

"We each come from somewhere else. No two histories appear identical from across the multiverse. We don't speak the same language; we don't share the same history. Not only do we as individuals get to start over, so do we all as one people, forging a fresh destiny. We now have shared this experience; this is our Genesis."

More nods, some thumbs-up, even someone whooped in approval. But I had a head of steam going and needed to finish, to nail the concepts clearly for everyone to take with them when we scattered once more.

"This is Earth, but it is a fresh world, with no recognizable landmarks, no race memories, and no arbitrary borders. It took everyone coming together to stop the Adversary's disruptive plans. The ideal world, the Shangri-La or Eden Shining Light envisioned didn't come to pass. Now this world has to be worked for. It can be done; the work has already started. Together, we put aside differences against a common foe. But it can't crumble over petty issues.

"We came here, accepting a second chance. We can't squander it. We can rise above it and answer our better angels.

"I am not suggesting homogenization, making every settlement identical, but we shouldn't let arbitrary lines in the sand or multiple languages be a barrier. We need to communicate, to come to one another's aid because Mother Nature isn't going to sit back. There will be typhoons, earthquakes, disease, and disaster. One community will need rebuilding and we need to know about it. So our lines of communication have to be open. Somewhere out there may be a linguist or two who can help us craft a common tongue. In the meantime, build your communities, turn them into villages or cities. But accessible, welcoming ones, because there may be two billion of us, but in the end, that's not really all that many when we've seen the vastness of the universe. Whenever we transit, we'll be all that's left of mankind, and I want it to be the best of mankind."

I paused, catching my breath, letting the headache crescendo and then recede. Perspiration ran down my neck, down my spine. Levy would have to check me when I stopped talking but there was more to say. I took a deep breath, letting the pause make people lean in with anticipation.

"The greatest civilizations of the world began works knowing it would take generations to complete and they were content with the knowledge. It got the Acropolis, the Coliseum, and the pyramids built. We have a world to build anew and many of us came from times where impatience outraced wisdom. Let us not make that mistake again. Let us learn from one another, lean on one another, and grow together."

That was enough. My "Win One for the Gipper" speech was over, and to show that, I unsteadily lowered myself to the ground. Chou and Emily reached out to help me, aware I was not at my best.

"Nice job," Emily assured me, handing me a canteen, which I greedily drained.

"You'd have done better," I said.

"Maybe," she said with a wink, "but they came for you and fought for you. I followed you, didn't I?"

"You wanted to kick the Adversary's ass on your own."

"Dismantle him was more like it," she said, eyes welling for a moment. "Abernathy devasted New Manhattan, tore it apart. Most were killed or subsumed."

"Rebuild it," I told her, my hand wrapped around her arm. "It's your home."

"It can be your home too," she said softly. "What now?"

What now indeed? We stopped the Adversary; we resumed the program to save mankind and the planet we called home. Shining Light could help them reclaim seeds and whatever else from the biomes, teach them the secrets of the collectors. Others could help Möngke and Epaminondas find land suitable for their people. They could decide for themselves what they did next. They weren't part of the plan but were now a part of our future. Who knew, we might need them some day.

Michael came over to me and handed me something that looked like shoe leather. He gestured at me with it, so I grabbed it, feeling tacky to the touch. "Eat it," he instructed and I mechanically did so, realizing someone had reinvented jerky. While not my favorite type of food, I devoured it and washed it down with water from someone's canteen. Neither helped my headache, so I figured it would require time. And a long night's sleep under the pixie dust.

Vihaan and Shining Light had gone back into the cathedral as many came over to fist bump, hug, or tip their hats at me, whatever their culture called for. I began to wonder which gestures would fade with disuse and others adopted by all. There would be finally be time for that. When the two emerged, they were carrying tablets; not enough for everyone, but it was a start.

"Carolyn, can you help distribute them? At least one per settlement and make sure at least one of them knows what it is." With the collectors properly networked, each tablet could then interact with the collectors and we'd have the beginnings of a communications network. It was faster, though less romantic, than the Pony Express. We'd need that too.

"Yes, Madam President," she said with a grin.

"Stop that!" I called after her. On this world, I would never be that. My legacy, apparently, was as mother of the next evolution of humanity. I did need somewhere to call home and figure out what to do next. Settling didn't feel right, though. Anne Shirley didn't settle; she wanted adventure. And Harry Potter accepted his destiny after trying to avoid it. And Westley did everything out of love for another. How could I disappoint my role models?

No, I'd help rebuild New Manhattan; I owed Emily that much. But after that, well, after that, I began to consider spending time exploring the new world. And when I was done with that, then I could settle down. While there was the nagging sense of pressure that I spawn, I also suspected I had some time on that front. But yes, at some point, I needed to be a real mother, not a sort-of-mother to Michael. He would need to stay here, with his own progeny-of-a-sort, Shining Light, since his health wouldn't allow him to go galivanting.

Whatever came next would be the next step in a long path to the future. Earth's final transit to the bubble universe was, I gathered, generations away. Something Shining Light avoided coming out to tell me. I was fine with that, actually. Michael and I might be dust by the time the rift opens. But, here I am, no longer the wreckage of a wasted life. No, here I am fulfilling potential I didn't know I had. Here I am, leading a new people, hoping to unify them, and building toward a common goal of survival.

There are worse legacies, and if it was good enough for Moses not to enter the promised land, I, too, can manage.

AUTHOR'S NOTE

I never met Paul Antony Jones, despite the science fiction community being a small, relatively well-connected world. So, it's weird that I am collaborating with him on his final novel.

Truth be told, Paul was ill as he was writing *This Alien Earth: Children of Tomorrow* and was racing the clock to complete the manuscripts while fighting for his life. Book two arrived just two months before Paul died.

And a month later, I was invited to finish the saga. Why me? The fine editors at Aethon Books were looking for someone who could absorb, chart, and annotate the first two volumes and then take Paul's scattered notes and complete Meredith Gale's story. I was recommended to them by one of their authors, and one of my friends, Steve Savile.

In March, I began reading the novels, captivated by the high concepts and intrigued by the collection of characters he introduced. Suddenly, like the readers, I wanted answers to the Big Questions. So I signed on.

Thankfully, Paul's widow, Karen, fought past her grief to scour his desk and find every scrap of information Paul had put together to address the final book. While it proved inordinately helpful, it left huge gaps and unanswered questions.

This didn't write itself. If it takes a village to raise a child, it took a city to support me in the researching and writing of this book. So, thank you to Steve Savile for thinking of me and editors Steve Beaulieu and Rhett Bruno for trusting me with Paul's world.

Michael A. Burstein has been a close friend for a long time now, and we support one another in our various projects. He used to teach science and edits science textbooks, so his expertise and network allowed me to figure out the physics required to solve the dilemma Paul cleverly introduced. Special thanks include Michael's science brain trust consisting of Rachel Schneewind, Cary Abend, Don Sioux, Suzanna Campbell, Ian Kaplan, Andrew Bytes, Bruce E. Berger, Shamit Lachru, Chris Somari, Linda Nussbaum, Thunder Levin, and Ellen Welch Garner. Even with their help, I found myself going down the rabbit hole of research on quantum mechanics, parallel universe theory, bubble universes, false vacuums, and more. A huge thank you to the marvelous composer and writer Steven Rosenhaus for serving as beta reader.

No project of this magnitude and required to be written at warp speed could be done without the love and fierce support from my wife, Deb. She fully supported me taking this on, as it required rearranging other commitments and brought general upheaval to life.

And finally, there's Paul. I found some audio interviews he gave over the years, so between his novels, his notes, and his interviews, I feel I got to know him a bit. I hope this work honors his memory and satisfies his readers. If there's anything that feels off in comparison to the first two books, blame me for failing to fulfill his dream.

Robert Greenberger
August 2020

THANK YOU!

IF YOU LIKED THIS BOOK, check out the rest of our catalog at www.aethonbooks.com. To sign up to receive updates regarding all new releases, visit www. subscribepage.com/AethonReadersGroup.

Printed in Great Britain
by Amazon

77766394R00171